# DARKENED SOUL

# Darkened Soul

CECILIA AGETUN

Darkened Soul (Freya's Legacy, book 3)
Published by Cecilia Agetun
www.ceciliaagetun.com

ISBN: 978-1-7396488-6-2 (ebook)
ISBN: 978-1-7396488-7-9 (paperback)
ISBN: 978-1-7396488-8-6 (hardcover)

Book design:
Brittany Evans, https://bedesigns.ca/

Editor:
John Gunningham
Catherine Dunn, https://catherinedunn.co.uk/

To Claes Agetun

I hope you're finally at peace

# ACKNOWLEDGEMENTS

First and foremost, I'd like to thank the readers for believing in me and following me through this writing journey.

A special thanks to Trena. Despite everything you've been going through, your light shines strong, and your strength is an inspiration to everyone. Our friendship is invaluable to me, I just wish you didn't live on the other side of the pond.

I'd like to thank Samantha for always taking the time to provide constructive criticism, and for not being afraid to tell me when things aren't working, it means a lot to me.

I'd also like to thank Chrissey, Branan, Randy, Brooke, April, Sophia, Daniel, Mia, Linda, Gabbie, and everyone else that provided feedback on how to make the story better.

A special thanks to John, not only do you point out what isn't working from a developmental point of view- but you're always happy to brainstorm how to fix it.

I'd like to thank Cathrine for making sure my writing is as error free as possible.

A massive thanks to Lewis for drawing the sword and making it look awesome, and thanks to Brittany for making another amazing cover.

Last but not least I'd like to thank my partner David for his love and support.

# Darkened Soul

# NICK

## Cassie's Birthday

My leg shook under the table as I scanned the room from the corner of the restaurant, where we were seated. The low music was drowned out by the clacking of plates, along with loud conversations and laughter. Everything appeared normal. *Human.*

Cassie giggled, ketchup smeared across her cheek. Lily leaned over to wipe her sticky hands and face before settling back down beside me. 'See. This was just what she needed. A chance to experience a normal human birthday.'

'I guess you're right,' I said, watching Cassie, 'but it's still risky.'

Lily let out a breath. 'You've been like this since she was born. It's been a year and nothing has happened. Relax.

You're being overprotective. How is she going to learn about the world if she's not allowed to be part of it?'

I placed my arm around her shoulders and leaned towards her. 'I'd rather you ere safe.'

'What's the point of being safe if you're not allowed to live? You know how much I hated being stuck in my realm. I couldn't wait to finally grow up and get my powers so I could leave that place.'

I shrugged. 'I know, but I still don't feel like I deserve this life.'

Lily squeezed my hand and gazed into my eyes. 'There's so much light and goodness in your heart. You shouldn't let your demon side dictate what you think you deserve.'

'You're the light that keeps it in check,' I said as I pulled her closer and kissed her temple.

Ever since I'd found out I was part demon, I'd never believed I deserved happiness, yet I'd been blessed with our lovely family. It felt like a dream come true, and ever since Cassie was born, I was constantly looking over my shoulder. I knew I was being paranoid. I'd been with my beautiful wife for forty years and nothing had happened. But the darkness inside me had put people I cared about in danger before.

I scanned the crowded restaurant again for anything amiss, but nothing stood out. Despite that, I couldn't shake the gnawing worry from my mind.

The server approached, wearing a silly balloon hat of multiple colours and carrying a small chocolate cake with a single candle. Cassie's face lit up and her smile widened. Her excitement warmed my heart, and I was glad Lily had persuaded me to go out to celebrate.

The server placed the cake and the balloon hat on the table. Cassie's eyes sparkled with curiosity as she reached for the balloon hat, but Lily moved it away from her. 'We can play with the hat when we get home.'

The light in Cassie's eyes faded, and my heart sank. I took the balloon hat from Lily's hands and gave her a pleading look. 'It's her birthday. What my girl wants, my girl gets. And that goes for the both of you. Besides, what harm will it do if she plays with it now?'

Lily poked my ribs. 'Always a big softy. She can have it on her head while she eats her cake, but if she tries putting it in her mouth, you have to take it off her.'

'Deal,' I said with a smile. I reached over to Cassie and held the hat over her head. 'I will put the hat on your head, but it needs to stay there.'

Cassie clapped her hands, and when I placed the hat on her head, she started laughing. My heart swelled with joy as the beautiful sound reached my ears. It was the best sound I had ever heard in my entire life. She was such a cute baby, with long dark eyelashes and ice-blue eyes like mine. However, her petite nose and smile were a mirror of Lily's. The love I had for them made my chest ache sometimes. There was nothing I would not do for them.

We finished the celebration and headed towards the exit.

'I told you you'd enjoy it,' Lily said with a playful smirk as she pushed Cassie's buggy through the door I held open for them.

It had been a lovely sunny September day when we'd arrived at the restaurant, but now the grey clouds were looming closer. There was a change in the air that caused the hair on my arms to stand up. I turned to Lily as the door closed behind us. 'How about we teleport home?'

She gave me a stern look. I held my hands up. 'I know. No magical abilities unless we have to. But there's something in the air that makes me uneasy.'

Lily scanned the area. 'I can't sense anything sinister. Maybe it's just the pressure in the air that's playing tricks on you.'

I let out a sigh and tried to relax. 'Maybe you're right.'

'You know I'm right. It's the middle of the day, and I was looking forward to taking Cassie to the park. I want to see if the nemesias have started blooming yet. Besides, humans are out and about, and we fit right in.'

What she really meant was that to the humans we looked like a couple in their mid-twenties out with their baby. No one would be able to tell I was sixty years old and my beautiful wife was four times as old as me.

She held her hand out for me as she continued walking. 'Come on, I promise we'll take the short way through the park home.'

I hesitated. I knew, logically, I was being paranoid. But a deep sense of unease had settled within the pit of my stomach and refused to budge. A being of light falling in love with a demon like me was unheard of, so who could blame me? Not that I was evil. My human mother had made sure of that, showering me with love at every opportunity she got, and that was something I had passed on to my wife and beautiful baby girl. This was as close to perfect as it could get.

'Nick? Are you coming?'

I looked up. Lily was standing by the road, ready to cross. I caught up with her. 'Sorry. I was thinking about my mother and how I wish she was still around to meet Cassie.'

Lily smiled. 'She's around. You just can't see her. She's very special. Even after forty years, she still remembers her human life. We have her blessing, and she would have loved to hold Cassie.'

A longing ached in my heart. My mother had been my light, my everything, before Lily came into my life. Without her, my life would have been very different.

'Can you tell her I miss her?'

'She knows.'

We strolled along the paved path, where large trees lined the side of the road. On the other side of the path was a massive field and several flowerbeds dotted with colourful flowers. I wouldn't be able to name most of them, though I was sure Lily could. The path we were walking on split into several smaller ones snaking around the field. The odd jogger passed us, and the sound of kids playing could be heard in the distance, but overall it was a quiet afternoon.

The sun peeked out between the clouds and cast shadows through the trees. A cool breeze danced around us, carrying the scent of the jasmine bushes nearby. I was pushing the buggy while Lily carried Cassie.

'Look at these beautiful hydrangeas. We should plant some in our garden,' Lily said, standing next to a bush with Cassie on her hip to get a closer look at the cluster of white flowers she was admiring.

'If we plant all the flowers you find beautiful, we won't have any space in the garden.'

She smiled, grazing the flowers with her fingertips. 'Maybe we should get a bigger garden? Hydrangeas come in several colours.'

I rolled my eyes in amusement.

'I'm not saying we should move. You know I love the house just as much as you do. But we don't need all that grass by the front porch.'

I chuckled. 'Is that so?'

She flashed me a grin. 'Yeah.'

'I can get it sorted for you when we get back. What flowers would you like?'

'I'll have to think about it.' She pushed Cassie higher on her hip and strolled back towards me. 'But you are not conjuring them. I want real flowers, not some hybrid because you weren't sure how they were supposed to look.' She looked at me with a serious face, but the smile on her lips betrayed her.

'The sunflowers looked fine to me,' I said with a smirk.

Lily snorted. 'You made them into a bush.'

She put Cassie back in the buggy and we continued our walk, which included a few more interruptions to admire some marigolds, roses and blooming nemesia.

The wind picked up, taking on a chilly edge as it blew through the trees. The sky had darkened further, like it was preparing for a massive downpour. There were no humans around anymore, but that wasn't unusual at the edge of the park. A shadow crossed the path in front of me and sent a chill down my spine. I studied the area around us and peered through the trees, my senses on high alert.

'What's wrong?' Lily asked, a crease appearing on her forehead.

'I'm not sure. It feels like we're being watched.'

She placed a hand on my shoulder. 'I'm sure it's just your mind playing tricks.'

Cassie fussed in the buggy, and Lily quickened her steps, continuing down the path again. 'Come on, we should get her home before we all get soaked.'

I caught up with Lily, who had stopped by the road we needed to cross to reach our house.

Our brick terraced house with bay windows came into view, and I let out a breath of relief. The front garden had yet to experience Lily's obsession with flowers, but the back garden looked more like a jungle, with patches of grass in between various flowerbeds. But whatever made Lily happy. She could spend hours out there.

'Don't you think the hydrangeas would look great in the front garden?' Lily smiled at me as we crossed the road and stepped onto the green in front of the houses where our neighbour's kids normally played football. 'Maybe we can even get some petunias and hang some baskets ...'

I stopped listening to Lily as dark, sharp-edged shadows slithered around the area, cutting us off from our path. My heart pounded in my chest. Why were they here? I hadn't seen another demon since before I met Lily. I wrapped my arm around her, bringing my lips close to her ear. 'Take Cassie and teleport to the house now.'

She looked at me, her worried expression mirroring mine. She followed my gaze, tracking the abnormal shadows around us that had yet to take corporeal form.

Lily nodded. Without saying a word, she picked Cassie up from the buggy. She looked at me with wide eyes. 'I can't teleport.'

Cassie started crying. The shadows were becoming more solid, circling us. Knowing that we were running out of time, I placed my hands on Lily and Cassie and tried teleporting us to the house, but to no avail. 'It's not working for me either. Something must be blocking it.'

A demon materialised from tendrils of shadows. At first it was just a dark humanoid shape, but it transformed into a muscular male in his twenties. To anyone nearby, he would have looked human, but I could feel the sinister being behind the glamour. He took a step forward and flashed an evil grin, displaying his jagged teeth. His eyes burned with wickedness. 'Did you think we didn't come prepared?'

The adrenaline pumped around my body. 'Prepared for what?' I asked as I scanned the area.

He sneered. 'To fight you. The mighty descendent of Surtr. Your house can't save you. We made sure you wouldn't be able to teleport to it.'

What had they done to it? Would it still be safe inside? I sent out my senses and checked the protective layers surrounding the house, but they hadn't been breached. I pushed Lily and Cassie to the opposite side of the path from where the demon was standing and sent a telepathic message to Lily. *I'll distract him and you run to the house. The protective layers are still working, so you should be safe once you're inside.*

Lily bundled Cassie safely in her arms.

The demon made a face of disgust. 'You really are a disgrace. How that being doesn't make you nauseated is beyond me.'

Hate burned through me. 'Watch your mouth. That being is my wife, and you'd be long gone before you even think of laying a finger on either of them.' I conjured my blue fire in my hands. *Now!* I yelled into Lily's mind as I threw my fire at the demon, killing him before he even had a chance to scream in pain. His body turned to ash, but before the ash had hit the ground, three more demons materialised from the shadows.

I summoned my sword. Between that and my fire, I should have the upper hand.

Lily ran towards the house. Her path looked clear. As long as I could keep the demons' attention on me, she should be able to get inside and be safe.

I threw my fire at one demon and lunged at the other with my sword before homing in on the last one. I thought it would be the last of it when a flapping sound caught my attention. A dozen big dark-winged creatures were making their way across the sky, not even bothering to use their glamour.

I didn't have time to study them further, as a blade whistled through the air. I ducked, and it sliced the buggy Cassie had been lying in moments earlier.

I threw my fire at the demon, but he dodged the flame, hissing as he advanced. With one decisive sweep of my blade, his head was no longer attached to his body. I thought I'd finally caught a break, but as I tried to see if Lily had made it to the house, more demons appeared from the shadows nearby, blocking my view. I sighed and moved around them, picking them off one by one.

A piercing scream from Lily stopped my heart. I spun towards the house, my eyes instantly locking on a demon that had appeared on our front porch, blocking Lily from the door. His human form was taller than most but badly glamoured, with black shadows swirling on his skin and glowing red eyes. Shadowy tendrils gathered in his hand, creating a dagger. He lunged forward, stabbing the knife deep into Lily's side as she twisted to protect Cassie.

'No!' A scream clawed its way up my throat as thunder roared above. Anger and hatred tore through me, waking an inferno in the depths of my mind that had been asleep all my life. My body shook from the pressure. When I couldn't take it any longer, I cried out and fire exploded from me. All the remaining demons disintegrated in flames, including the winged creatures. I stared at the aftermath. Only burning embers and ash remained of the demons, while everything else appeared untouched.

Lily let out a gasp, and I dropped my sword and rushed to her side. Ash fell from the sky as I reached her and caught her and Cassie before she buckled. She cradled a screaming Cassie while blood gushed from her side.

'Lily,' I cried as I bent down and brushed some blond hair away from her face. She looked around, her golden eyes struggling to focus. 'I'm right here, baby,' I said. My eyes blurred as I took in the extent of her injury. I tried to put pressure on her wound, but she became distressed.

'Cassie – where's Cassie?' The panic in her voice was unsettling.

'You're holding her,' I responded in a calm voice, even though I was anything but. I carefully removed a screaming, crying Cassie from Lily's iron grip. She was covered in blood and had a nasty cut on her arm.

'She's bleeding. Let me see.' Lily tried to sit up and reached for Cassie. I placed her by Lily's side. 'Mummy's going to make you feel better,' she whispered to Cassie as she placed her hand over the wound. A brightness escaped her hand, and Cassie stopped crying. When Lily removed her hand, Cassie's arm had healed.

How I wished she could heal herself the same way.

I conjured some gauze. My hand trembled as I pressed it against Lily's wound. The blood kept seeping through. There was so much blood and I couldn't stop it. It covered the ground, slowly dripping down the steps. Desperation clawed at my chest, and I placed Lily's head in my lap, making sure Cassie was next to her. I tried to remain strong in front of them, but tears fell down my cheeks. Each ragged breath tore me apart from the inside. Despite my best efforts at putting pressure on the wound, it became abundantly clear that Lily would not survive this.

'I'm sorry,' Lily murmured. I looked down at her, wiping my tears away with the back of my hand.

'It's okay. It's ... it's not your fault. Everything will be fine. You just need to rest.' My voice broke as I tried to comfort her.

Lily slowly lifted her hand to stroke Cassie's face. 'My beautiful baby girl. Dad will take great care of you.' She looked up at me with watery eyes. 'Promise me Cassie will be safe.'

'I promise. But you'll be fine. We'll make sure she's safe together.'

'Together,' she said, squeezing my hand and offering me a weak smile. Her breathing hitched, and a shudder ran through her as she let out a gasp. Her grip loosened, and her body relaxed. Her eyes stared vacantly ahead.

My world crashed down and my heart broke into a thousand pieces. I gathered her in my arms, hugging her close. 'No, no, no,' I sobbed over and over again, swaying back and forth on the spot. This could not be happening. I couldn't lose her. The world around me blurred and faded away. It felt like time had stopped, along with my heart.

What was I going to do now? Why had they killed my light?

# NICK
## The Vendari

The sky opened and rain poured down, but still I didn't move. I continued to cradle Lily's lifeless body in my arms. I knew her soul wasn't with her body anymore, but I couldn't leave her. I couldn't accept that she was gone. A massive hole deep within myself swallowed everything up, voided me of all feelings and caused me to become numb. I didn't know how to live without her. She was my light, but now there was only darkness.

Cassie's cry brought me back to reality. She was still sitting next to me, but the rain had soaked through her blood-covered clothes. If I didn't get her inside and into dry clothes soon, she would become ill.

With my thoughts and heart still with Lily, I slowly released her from my arms and conjured a blanket to place over her body before pushing myself off the ground. My muscles were fatigued, and every movement was exhausting.

After I'd brought Cassie inside, dried her off, changed her clothes and put her in the cot, I went back out into the rain. I needed to move Lily's body before the humans saw her. I picked her up and brought her to the sofa. Her face had lost all its natural glow.

I collapsed on the floor, not sure what to do with myself. I put my face in my hands. Lily loved the human world and its customs. She would want to be buried in the human world, but how could I sort that out without the authorities starting an investigation into her stab wound? I leaned my head back, closed my eyes and took a deep breath.

As I thought about what to do, a humming noise that turned into a purr got me to open my eyes. A big grey cat was rubbing against Lily's body and headbutting her. I jumped up, ready to blast it with my fire.

An elderly woman with white hair appeared in the room. 'I would not do that if I were you.' She stared at the flame in my hand.

I extinguished it and turned to her. 'Freya?' I blinked a few times to make sure I was actually seeing her. 'Is the cat with you?'

'He is,' she said as she looked over at me. Her blue eyes held compassion, and she gave me a warm smile. 'I am sorry for your loss. Lily was a lovely soul.'

'I failed her,' I said with a painful lump in my throat. 'She died because of me – because I was too slow to save her.' My vision blurred as tears welled up in my eyes.

'Nonsense. You gave her a perfect life. You made her feel alive. You allowed her to experience the beauty of the human world.'

I scoffed. 'What good did that do?'

She came over and squeezed my shoulder. 'It did more good than you will ever know. Now let me take her body. I will make sure she gets the burial she wanted.'

I let out a deep breath as a tear fell down my cheek. 'I don't know if I can go on without her. She was my everything. She kept me on the right path after my mother died.'

'Then what more fitting way to honour her life than to bury her next to your mother?'

I looked up at her in surprise. 'You can do that?'

'Of course I can.'

I clasped her hands. 'Thank you.'

'You do not need to thank me.'

Cassie started crying in the cot next to us. Freya went over and picked her up. 'If you need some time to grieve, I am happy to look after Cassie.'

The thought of losing both Lily and Cassie on the same day caused a hollow feeling in my stomach. 'No. She's the only part of Lily I have left.'

'Whatever you need.' It wasn't long before Cassie was asleep in Freya's arms, and she placed her back in the cot. 'If you change your mind, you know where to find me.' A bright light developed in the room and a moment later, Freya, the cat and Lily's body were gone.

I sat on the sofa, staring at the lit fireplace as the emptiness inside me grew bigger. It became harder to breathe as the reality slowly sank in. I had lost my light, and my family had been destroyed. Every time I closed my eyes, I relived the horror. In an attempt to drown out the sorrow, I conjured a bottle of whisky and downed it in one go.

Cassie's crying woke me up where I had collapsed on the sofa. The cry echoed inside me like a pain I couldn't soothe. As I got up, an empty bottle of whisky fell to the floor.

I ignored it as I made my way over to the cot and picked Cassie up, bouncing her up and down in my arms like Lily used to do. It used to make her stop crying immediately, but it wasn't working. I checked her nappy and changed it even though it hadn't been soiled. How long had it been since Cassie had been fed? I wasn't sure, but I conjured some baby formula. As I did so, I could feel Lily's disapproving gaze, the one she always gave me every time I conjured something. She made everything from scratch, even though she didn't need to. She used to say that because we lived in the human world, we should try to live like humans and minimise our magic usage. I used to humour her, but she wasn't here anymore, and I didn't have the energy to sort anything else out. I held the bottle up to Cassie, but she refused to feed.

'Cassie. Please stop crying.' I took a deep breath and held the bottle to her lips again, but she squealed and writhed in my arms, refusing to settle. Then I remembered Lily had completely transitioned her to solid food a few weeks ago. I went over to the fridge and got out a jar of fruit puree Lily had prepared. Sitting Cassie down, I got a spoon and attempted to feed her, but she sealed her lips, refusing to eat it.

I started singing a bedtime song Lily used to sing. Cassie looked up at me with her big blue eyes and offered me a quiet smile. Her features burned my eyes and made my knees weak. Her smile mirrored her mother's, causing my already shattered heart to crumble into more pieces. Why had we not just stayed home?

Resentment built up in my heart. I closed my eyes and tightened my jaw, horrified by my own feelings that bubbled up from the depths of my being, telling me my daughter was responsible for Lily's death. Had we not gone out to celebrate her birthday, Lily might still be alive. But in my heart, I knew it wasn't true. It wasn't Cassie's fault. It was mine. I hadn't been able to protect the woman I loved. I clutched Cassie to my chest, unable to look at her as guilt overtook me. 'I'm so sorry. I know it's not your fault,' I whispered to Cassie as I rocked her back and forth.

The little energy I had left escaped my body. Tears streamed down my face as I thought of my beautiful wife and the perfect family we'd had.

Desperate for some relief, I placed Cassie in a playpen and made my way back to the sofa. Every step was excruciating, like someone had turned my body into lead. I slumped down on the sofa, conjured another bottle of whisky and took a large swig, hoping it would numb my pain. Some spilled on my shirt, but I couldn't be bothered to change. Cassie started crying, but I didn't have it in me to get up again. Instead, I downed the bottle so I could drown out the sound of Cassie's crying, drown out the sorrow that lay heavily inside me.

I closed my eyes and took a deep breath. The moments before Lily's death played on repeat in front of me. I should have protected her. I should have kept her by my side instead of making her run to the house. I should have been there for her when she needed me, just like she had been there for me when my mother died. My thoughts went to the memory of when I first laid eyes on Lily.

I was twenty and had arrived home from my work as an accountant, ready to tell my mum about the day like I'd done since I was a small child. But in those days she was usually too out of it to even realise I was there. She was bed bound and in awful shape. The cancer had taken over her body, and there was nothing more the doctors could do except keep her comfortable. It broke my heart seeing my mother like that. Some days I wished I could just take all the pain away, whereas other days I was begging her not to leave me.

As I stepped inside, I noticed something was different. There was a floral fragrance in the air. Had Fatima, our neighbour, brought some flowers over? It wouldn't be the first time. Ever since my mother had fallen ill, Fatima had started bringing food and other things over and helping around the house.

I took my shoes and coat off and stepped into the living room to check on my mother. At her bedside, a young woman in a white dress with long blond hair sat in a chair and held my mother's hand, whispering to her. At first I thought she might be a nurse, but light radiated from her, making her skin glow. She reminded me of an angel, like the ones my mother collected on the mantelpiece. One thing was certain, she definitely wasn't human. I reached out with my powers, checking the wards around the house. They were supposed to let me know if someone supernatural entered the house and be impenetrable to anyone that had not been invited in. It was a precaution from when my powers had still been maturing and beings had been after me. Even though I hadn't had any encounters in the last couple of years, I still kept it up and restrengthened it regularly, just in case, especially considering how vulnerable my mother was. So who was this woman? Friend or foe?

I summoned my blue fire into my hands as I marched towards her, the reassuring heat crackling at my fingertips. 'What are you, and why are you here?'

She turned, her hair swirling around her face as she looked up at me with wide eyes. 'Y-you can see me?'

I rolled my eyes. 'Of course I can see you. What are you doing to my mother?'

Her warm golden eyes locked with mine and her soul pulled me forward before her gaze went to the fire in my hand. 'I'm not going to hurt her.'

Despite her reassurance, my eyes remained on her. I tried to read her mind, but there were no direct thoughts, just a sense of happiness, warmth and goodness. It caused a soothing lightness in my chest that told me she wasn't a threat. I extinguished the fire in my hand. 'What are you?'

She gave me a smile that tugged at my heart. 'I'm a Vendari.'

I raised an expectant eyebrow, waiting for her to elaborate, but she didn't. 'What's a Vendari?'

She took a deep breath. 'It's a bit hard to explain. But I will try.' She placed her hands in her lap. 'I'm what you would call a guardian angel. We protect beings who have been touched by darkness. We give them our light to help them fight the hold the darkness has over them.'

'Darkness as in demons?'

'Yes, though it doesn't have to be.'

I tilted my head to study her. 'Why are you here now? She was touched by darkness a long time ago,' I said as I moved another chair over and sat down next to her.

I wasn't sure I wanted to know the answer, because in a way I was darkness, born of my human mother after something happened between her and my biological demon father. My father couldn't leave his realm, so whatever had made it possible couldn't be good. I'd never asked how it happened. I didn't want to remind my mother of the horrors she must have been through.

As far as I was concerned, my father was Neil Pearce, my mother's husband, a human war hero who had died in action. It wasn't until after my seventeenth birthday, when I befriended Jax in school, that I learned he wasn't my real father.

The woman placed a hand on my mother. 'I've always been around. Edith has been my charge since before you were born. But as her relationship with Neil grew and as you came into the picture, she needed me less and less. She learned to create her own light. You two were her light.'

'I don't understand. How can we be her light?'

'Every human has some amount of light inside them. It's hope, faith, happiness, but it can be tainted by darkness – evil forces, depression, hate, jealousy. If a being has been touched by darkness, the Vendari helps to provide light so they can fight against it. But you and her husband gave her joy and happiness, and from there she created enough light on her own to fight the darkness that had taken hold of her. And despite her own battle with darkness, she made it her life's mission to give light to others.'

She brushed some hair away from my mother's face before she continued. 'A few weeks back, I noticed something was different, so I came to check on her. I found her in this bed and realised she was soon to leave this world. I've been with her ever since, so I'm not sure why you can see me now.'

I frowned. 'So you've been around my entire life?'

'In a way. I've been monitoring her light through the good and bad times. Offering my light when she needed it.'

An awkward silence developed. I cleared my throat, searching for something to say. 'What's your name?'

'Lily.' She gave me a shy smile that lit up her face. 'And you're Nicklause.'

'Nick,' I corrected her. Nicklause was what my mother called me. My body relaxed. Lily was obviously telling the truth. 'Can you help her?'

'Not in the way you want. I can take away the pain and heal her soul, but I can't heal her human body. What she has is not caused by darkness. It's a human disease, and for that there is no magical cure.'

'She's only forty-five years old. It shouldn't be her time yet.'

I rose in my seat, but she put her hand on me, stopping me from getting up. 'I know you love your mother very much, but there's nothing that can be done. A life cannot be spared without consequences. It's a life for a life.'

'Then take mine,' I pleaded.

She looked at me with sorrowful eyes. 'Your mother would never forgive me. She sacrificed a lot to give you the best life possible. If you do this, you would condemn not just your life but hers as well.'

I took a ragged breath. 'I can't just let her die.'

She put her hand on my mother's fragile one. 'You won't. Her soul will transform and she will become a guardian angel. Even though she was touched by darkness, she never let it consume her. The fact she had you is proof of that. She never really needed me. Her light calls out to help others, and that's what she will continue to do.'

'So she's not going to die?'

Lily's warm golden eyes locked onto mine. They were full of compassion and sorrow. 'You misunderstand me. When her soul leaves this body, she will in all human senses be dead, but her soul will live on. She will become what we call a Vendari Mannvera, a guardian angel by choice. People are not born guardian angels but instead become one due to the light and compassion in their heart.'

'So she will become like you?'

'No. I've always been a Vendari. I have my own corporeal body, though I often choose to only appear to my charges. And when I die, my soul will be reincarnated and reborn. Her becoming a Vendari Mannvera means she won't be able to appear in a corporeal form, and her soul will no longer be reincarnated. Instead her soul will travel and give light to others that need it to fight the darkness.'

There was a moment of silence as I reached over and brushed some hair out of my mother's face. Due to the amount of pain medication she was on, it was impossible to tell if she was aware of anything around her, but her facial expression seemed softer, more relaxed, when I was around.

'You're lucky,' Lily said in a calm, quiet voice.

I scoffed. 'How am I lucky?'

'Your mother's love and belief in you is what has kept you on the right path – the path of light. She's the reason you've been able to control the demon inside yourself.'

'I don't understand.'

'The faith your mother had in you and your need to protect her and the things you love meant your father could not persuade you to leave your human life behind. This faith, and your conviction to protect others, is what caused your flame to turn blue. It's what sets you apart from Surtr's other children and their orange flame.'

I was startled out of my memory-induced dream as the fire alarm went off. Cassie was sitting in front of the hearth, her favourite stuffed cat in the fireplace, being devoured by the flames. How had she escaped the playpen? Had I forgotten to close it?

She reached into the fire with her hands, but before the flames touched her, I conjured some water above the hearth and put them out. As I rushed to her side to pick her up and make sure she was okay, she moved towards her stuffed cat. I conjured a new stuffed cat for her, but she refused it, pointing towards the one in the fireplace. 'Meow meow.'

'This is also meow meow,' I said as I tried to give her the new stuffed cat again.

She started crying, pointing toward the fireplace again. 'Meow meow.'

I rocked Cassie and tried to get her to stop crying, but it wasn't working. In the end I gave up and got the ruined stuffed cat from the fire. 'Here's your meow meow.'

Cassie grabbed hold of the stuffed cat and hugged it to her chest. Black droplets of soot-infused water ran down her dress, but at least she wasn't crying anymore.

# NICK

## CASSIE

Restlessness churned within me as my days repeated in a loop. I sleepwalked through them while drowning my sorrow in liquor at night. It was the only way I knew how to stop the horrible, vivid flashes of my beautiful angel lying motionless on the ground. The days melted into each other. I wasn't sleeping, and I hardly had any energy to make sure Cassie had everything she needed. The house became a mess while the world receded further and further away from me, dark and distant. It was like I was stuck inside my grief, unable to pull myself up from the depths of the sea. The house used to be filled with love and laughter. Lily had a knack for making everyone around her happy, and nothing was too much trouble. I missed those days like a night sky misses the stars. But I knew I would never have them back.

Cassie cried a lot, and even though I tried, I didn't know how to console her. As much as I loved Cassie, I didn't have the energy to cope with it all. The old me was buried deep within, below all the grief that made me numb. Her resemblance to Lily caused me debilitating heartache; even breathing felt like a chore. The only thing keeping me rooted in reality was the promise I'd made to Lily to keep Cassie safe.

About a week had passed since the funeral, and this was the first time I had visited Lily's grave. I hadn't had it in me to visit before. Seeing the grave made everything final.

I sat on the grass with Cassie in my arms, overlooking the two graves of the women who had meant the world to me. I was trying to stay strong for Cassie, but silent tears made their way down my face and fell to the ground.

The wind caressed me, carrying with it the smell of my mother's perfume. Was she watching over me? I looked around, searching for my mother, but the place was deserted. I let out a breath, recalling the day I lost my mother. Had Lily not been by my side, I wasn't sure how things would have ended. She'd become my new light – the reason I kept on fighting and didn't give in to the impulses of my demon half.

Cassie stood up and took a few steps towards Lily's grave. She held her hand out in the air before she tumbled over in the grass. My chest constricted. It was the first steps she had ever taken by herself and Lily wasn't around to see them. I let out a sigh of longing as Cassie pointed behind me with a smile. I turned around and scanned the tree line where the forest started, thinking she might have seen a rabbit or a deer, but instead I detected a slight shimmer in the air. A bright light appeared around the shimmer and revealed a middle-aged couple.

Even though I had only seen them once before, I remembered them. Lily's parents. When Lily and I got together, they gave her an ultimatum: me or them. I never expected her to turn her back on her people, but she did. And I had been grateful for that every day.

With a set jaw, I bowed my head in respect. They ignored me and wandered over to the grave, placing a large bouquet of white lilies by the headstone. 'Our beautiful flower. If you hadn't fallen for that demon, you would still be alive.'

Their words cut into my heart, but I couldn't say anything. They were right. I was the reason she had died.

I cleared my throat, trying to think of something to say. 'Do you want to say hi to your granddaughter?'

They looked at me with a cold gaze. 'That thing is no granddaughter of ours. She is contaminated by your demonic genes,' her father spat.

I clenched my jaw; shock and anger coursed through my body as they passed me. Her mother stopped and gave me an empty stare. 'She turned her back on her people, but for what? So you could have her killed.' She shook her head in disgust. 'I told her this would happen, but she insisted you were different. But now we all know the truth. A being created of darkness can only harbour darkness.' The spiteful words slipped from her mouth. 'It's your fault she's dead.'

I glared at them as they walked away. I would show them. Lily was my everything, and if it was the last thing I did, I would get her justice. Whoever sent those demons would pay. I'd hunt down and kill every single being that had caused this to happen. They would not get away.

I took a deep breath to calm my rage. It wouldn't do me any good. Especially not around Cassie. We spent a bit more time by the graves before making our way home. The cemetery was adjacent to the park Lily had loved walking in, and I couldn't help but remember all the beautiful summer evenings we had spent together here as a family. Cassie hadn't been to the park since the day we'd lost Lily. I hadn't had the energy, but she had a thing for beautiful flowers, just like her mother. And even though I was still struggling to reconnect with Cassie, I knew she would appreciate the scenery.

We made our way through the park and stopped to look at the nemesias and hydrangeas. As we got ready to leave, Cassie grabbed hold of the white hydrangeas, and I remembered how Lily had wanted to plant some in our garden. I cut a flower off and let Cassie play with it as I placed her in the buggy.

When we were on the home stretch, three guys in their early twenties approached us. Despite their human appearance, the hair at the back of my neck stood up, signalling that they weren't human. I stared at them in shock. Why were they here? Was it a coincidence or had they come to finish the job the other demons had failed at? My heart hitched in my chest as I pushed Cassie's buggy behind me.

Before I had a chance to do anything else, they threw a knife at us. I failed to deflect it, and it embedded itself in the upper part of the buggy, inches from Cassie's head. Rage boiled inside me. They could have killed Cassie. They could have killed the only part of Lily I had left.

The rage made me lose control of my fire. It spread up my arms, and before I could reel it in, it exploded and set all the demons on fire, just like it had the day Lily died. With a rapid heartbeat I turned to Cassie, worried I'd burned her too, but she remained unharmed. Relief flooded through me as glowing ash swirled around us.

After that encounter, I was too scared for Cassie's safety to take her outside again. It was clear the demons hadn't finished what they came for and I was still being targeted. I knew I needed to find out why, but I didn't know where to start.

Scrying in the fire was useless. Most of the time, no images would appear, and the few times one did, all it showed me was how I had failed to save her. I had all the demons memorised, but what good did that do when I couldn't even figure out if someone had sent them or why they had attacked us? I needed to do something. But I couldn't leave Cassie on her own, and it was too dangerous to take her outside. What if we got attacked by demons again, but this time they actually managed to hurt Cassie? I shook my head in horror. No. I wouldn't do anything that could put Cassie in danger.

I gazed down at her little body lying in the cot I'd placed in the living room so she could be close to me. Her breathing was soft and pure, almost angelic. This was not the life Lily would have wanted for her. She would have wanted her to experience the human world, not be stuck inside a house.

Maybe the best thing to do would be to give Cassie up, hide her away from anything supernatural and let her grow up in a loving human family. If I wasn't around, she would be able to be outside, to enjoy nature just like her mother did. My heart ached at the thought of giving Cassie up, but deep in my heart, I knew she would have a better, safer life without me – at least until I found out how to stop the demons targeting me.

I sat down by the fireplace and started scrying in the fire. A picture of Freya appeared. She was rocking back and forth in a chair with knitting in her hands and two large grey cats by her side.

'Freya, I need a favour,' I said into the fire. She stared straight at me, gave me a smile and held her hand up. The picture disappeared, leaving just the fire burning. What had she been trying to tell me?

A moment later, she appeared next to me in the living room. 'May her light be with you.'

I folded my arms, unsure what to do with my hands. 'Thank you.'

She looked around the room. 'I see your heart still belongs to this place,' she said as she made her way to Cassie, who was sitting up in her cot. 'Is this really what you want?'

Even though I hadn't told her my thoughts, it was like she already knew. Though I wasn't surprised – Jax had told me Freya always seemed to know about things. I nodded. 'Right now I can't give her the life Lily would have wanted. I'm too broken to give her the life and attention she deserves, and I can't guarantee her safety when demons are still after me. If she stays, she won't have a good life.'

'Are you sure? Even broken things can be mended with the right tools.'

My throat closed up. 'She deserves more than I can give her. I can't even take her outside without putting her in danger.' My stomach churned as I watched Cassie in the cot. Was I doing the right thing?

Freya placed a hand on Cassie, and her eyes glazed over. When she came to, she turned to me. 'I can place her with a family in the human world and erase any trace that she is your daughter. She will remain safe and appear human. But you cannot tell anyone about this until her powers start to mature – not even Jax – or it may change the future I have seen and put her in danger.'

'If you can see the future, can you tell me how I can avenge Lily?'

'I am afraid not. The future is not set in stone. If there are too many variables, the future is undetermined and even the best seer will be unable to see it.'

Of course it wouldn't be that simple, but at least I should have plenty of time to deal with my demon issues. My powers had started to mature at the age of seventeen and Lily's at eighteen. I picked Cassie up and held her tight before giving her to Freya. 'Make sure she's safe and loved. I'll come for her once I'm ready and know I can keep her safe.'

She took Cassie from me. 'I will leave her with a loving family. May you be reunited again when the time is right.'

I kissed Cassie on the forehead, and Freya gave me a warm smile. 'Do not forget, there is a reason for everything.'

A bright light blinded my eyes. When I could see again, Freya and Cassie were gone.

I went over to the fire and stared into the flames. It showed me Freya walking up to a house where a man was playing with a young toddler who couldn't be more than two years old. Freya handed Cassie over to the man. He smiled and showed Cassie to the toddler. The toddler stroked Cassie's face before handing her a toy car. Cassie seemed happy and content instead of her constant crying. Something stirred inside me, and it warmed my heart and strengthened my resolve that I'd made the right decision. At least for now. But it didn't hurt any less. What little love and heart that remained inside me had left with Cassie. I hoped one day she would be able to forgive me.

# NICK

## A Wish Granted

I took a seat on the bench in front of the forest, overlooking the cemetery, and gazed at the graves of my mother and Lily. Logically, I knew they weren't there, but it made me feel better to pretend they were. I told them about everything that had happened, including the tough decision to give Cassie up for her own protection.

My head and my heart were having a battle over whether I had done the right thing. Maybe I shouldn't have given her up. No – this was the best thing for Cassie. She'd have no ties to me and be able to experience the life Lily would have wanted for her.

A crow landed by my feet. I didn't need my senses to know it was Jax, my best friend. He transformed and took a seat beside me. 'I'm very sorry. Freya told me what happened to Lily. I can't imagine what you're going through.'

I turned around and acknowledged him. 'Thank you.' He hadn't aged a day. He still had the face and body shape of the teenage boy I had become friends with in school about forty years ago. The only difference was his messy brown hair. It looked like he'd just woken up and not given it a second thought.

He ran his hand through his hair and looked at me with his hazel eyes. 'I know I haven't been around much, but I'm here if you ever need me. Just like you were for me. No questions asked.'

I mustered up a smile. 'Yeah, I know. Brothers for life.' It warmed my heart knowing I could always count on Jax. He'd taken me under his wings and been by my side through thick and thin ever since I'd learned about my powers. I'd lost track of how many times we'd fought side by side, always having each other's back.

Jax conjured a lily and placed it on Lily's grave. He turned to my mother's grave and placed a black rose there, just like he had done so many times before. He came back and took a seat next to me again. We sat in silence. I wasn't sure what to say. I worried he would ask me questions, questions I couldn't answer, but he didn't. He remained quiet next to me, giving me unconditional support by just being present, like he had done when my mother passed away.

When the sun moved towards the horizon, I stood up. 'Thank you for the company. I really appreciate you coming by, but I think I prefer to be alone for a while.'

Jax patted my leg and got up. 'No worries, but know that I'm here for you.'

I watched as he transformed into a crow and flew away. I was grateful he had come and checked on me. It made me feel less alone.

I left the cemetery behind and made my way home through the park. Lily had always loved sunsets. When I got to the edge of the park, several demons turned up. They looked like a gang of hooligans with knives in their hands. At least they hadn't turned up while I visited Lily and my mum. I let out a sigh and scanned the park. A couple was walking further along. I reached out with my mind and planted a thought of urgency in their minds to make them hurry away. It was safer if there weren't any humans about, though most would probably think they had imagined it, which was why mind control worked as well as it did. It was harder to make them believe something that went against their logic.

I turned back to the demons as the first charged towards me with a knife. I released my blue flame, and the demon disintegrated before he reached me. I puffed up my chest, a plan forming in my head. I didn't have Cassie to protect this time, so maybe it was time to try to interrogate these demons so I could finally get a lead on who was targeting me. 'Anyone else want to meet the same fate? Or are you willing to back down?'

'Back down?' one of the demons said, his face full of disbelief. 'Why would we want to back down? A fight with you is worth a raise in rank.'

'Do you even know who I am?'

'Of course we do. A son of Surtr. Imagine how powerful we would be if we killed you.'

I rolled my eyes. 'In what world do you think you'll be able to kill me? You'll end up just like the others that tried – burned to a crisp.'

The demon tilted his head, evil glee in his red eyes. 'But we can feel your grief. Everyone can feel it. It makes you weak. Besides, you're alone. None of your siblings will come to your aid.'

'Didn't stop me the last time, and it sure as hell isn't going to stop me now.'

'We'll see about that.' The demon started to throw daggers at me, one after another. I dodged them fairly easily, but my actions caused me to lose track of the other two demons. The adrenaline pumped in my body, and the fire burned underneath my skin, ready to lash out and kill them all, but I needed at least one of them alive to interrogate. I tried to keep my fire under control, and I locked in on the one throwing the daggers. While I concentrated on trapping him in a ring of flames, a blade reflected the almost absent sun in the corner of my eye. I stepped back, narrowly escaping the strike, only to get knocked down by the other. I rolled over and threw my fire at them. Two down, one to go. I closed the ring of fire and stalked towards him, moving through the flames with no issues. I grabbed him by his collar. 'Who sent you, and why did you kill my wife?'

Fear shone in his red eyes, but his voice came out strong. 'I have no clue what you're talking about.'

'Don't lie to me.'

'I'm not.'

'Who ordered you to attack me?'

'No one. I saw an opportunity to become more powerful, and I went for it.'

'Don't test me. I know you're working for someone.' He refused to talk, and the anger inside me intensified, causing the fire beneath my skin to escape my hold. The demon's clothes started to smoke underneath my grip, and I was about to finish him off when the rustle of the bushes to my side distracted me. The demon broke out of my hold and teleported away. I took a step towards the bush, my fire burning in my hand. 'Show yourself before I set you and everything else on fire.'

A short demon that looked like a human in his mid-twenties, with dark skin and short white hair, came out with his hands held high. His eyes were wide with fear. 'I'm not with them. Please don't kill me.'

I sneered at him. 'Give me one good reason why I shouldn't.'

He looked up at me with his dark eyes. 'I ... I can ... I can help,' he stuttered.

I raised an eyebrow. 'Help how?'

'You're looking for information. I can get it for you. I can help you get your revenge.'

It caught me off guard. 'How do you know about that?'

He glanced around before clearing his throat. 'You're carrying an aura of grief. Crippling grief I could only imagine feeling if I lost my soulmate. It's causing your powers to spill over and radiate like a beacon, calling out to everyone. It's like a magnet for lower demons. They can sense your power and your weakness, and if they somehow manage to kill you, they will become powerful enough to rise in rank.'

I cocked my head. 'So that's why you're here?'

He shook his head. 'I have no intention of rising in rank. I was curious. This beacon shone so bright, I needed to see it for myself.'

I considered his words. 'Why should I trust you?'

He shrugged. 'You probably shouldn't. But I mean no harm. I'm sorry for your loss.'

Was he telling the truth? I didn't trust him, but I didn't have any other leads, and maybe he could give me the information I needed. I extinguished my fire.

'Thank you.' He bowed his head. 'What do you need?'

I wasn't sure I'd done the right thing or if I would ever see him again. After all, demons couldn't be trusted, but if there was even a small chance he could help, I had to take it.

'I need to know about the demons that attacked my family. Who sent them? Unfortunately, they all burned, so I couldn't question them,' I said with a wry smirk.

'I'll do my best to find the information you need.'

'Why would you help me? You're a demon.'

'I might be a demon, but so are you. Besides, I wouldn't know what I would do if I lost my other half, so the least I can do is try to help and ease the pain. And it wouldn't hurt to know a descendant of Surtr.'

'Thank you,' I said as he nodded and teleported away.

When I got home, I conjured a bottle of whisky and collapsed on the sofa. The house was so quiet without Cassie. I let out a sigh and looked at the mess around me. I needed to remove anything that could tie Cassie to me, but I couldn't bring myself to do it.

I went over what the demon had said – how I was a walking magnet for demons. I closed my eyes and sent out my energy to check on my barriers. They needed to be strengthened, but every time I strengthened them, it became harder and harder to clear my mind to visualise and build up the protective layers. What was I going to do? If I couldn't get my grief under control or keep the barriers functioning, it was only a matter of time before the demons would try to break into my house. And if they did, even if I could fight them, they would ruin the house and the only reminder of my family I had left.

I thought back to when Jax had taught me to create pocket dimensions that existed within their own dimension. He had helped me create one inspired by Dungeons and Dragons. We'd even used it as a prison a few times. It was technically in the basement but in its own dimension. Maybe I could do something similar with the house? No. It wouldn't work. Demons would still target me every time I left the house. Besides, I had no idea how to move an entire house into a pocket dimension, and I needed the house. I needed it to keep me anchored. So I needed to come up with another way to remove the beacon that made me a target for demons.

I let out a sigh and stared into the fire, replaying a memory of me and Lily during one of the early Christmases we'd had together. Lily had given me an old leather-bound book about the universe that year. She'd told me darkness needed to exist or there would be no light.

I marched over to the large bookcase and stared at my collection of books. Knowledge was a powerful thing, and books were also one of the few things that was almost impossible to conjure. To do so, one would literally need to know every single word in the book. That was one of the reasons I collected books, because you never knew when they may come in handy.

I ran my finger over the spines, reading the titles as I went. There were several books about different entities and religions, mixed with Lily's gardening books and my mother's favourite romance books that I hadn't had the heart to throw away. I let out a sad breath as I pulled out the book Lily had given me. It told a story of creation and destruction and how Kaliakwan had come to be. Kaliakwan was an entity, or rather, two entities in one body. One held the power of creation and the other the power of destruction. Together they used their powers to keep balance in the universe. They could create and destroy almost anything.

They were neutral and only did things that helped keep the balance. Even if they could help me, there was no guarantee they would, but it was worth a try.

I flipped through the old cream-coloured pages until I got to the part that explained how to summon them.

*Three drops of blood, sacrificed to a tree of the request,*

*During the strongest hour of day or night, depending on the quest.*

The problem with old books was that sometimes the translation turned out wrong or confusing. A tree of the request? What did that mean? Lily had sometimes talked about trees having magical abilities. Could that be it?

I searched the bookcase again until I found a small green book I remembered Lily reading about trees and their meanings. I flipped through it, skimming through the trees and their magical and inherent uses. Ash for connection, wisdom and surrender. Alder for endurance, strength and passion. Birch for beginning, renewal and youth. Elm for rebirth and the circle of life and death. I tapped my finger on the page. That should probably do the trick, since all this had happened due to grief and losing Lily.

After reading the description of what an elm looked like, I returned it to the bookcase but paused in the act. How many times had I leaned against the doorway, watching Lily as she stood in this very spot, or on the sofa with a book resting atop her pregnant belly, concentration written all over her face as she researched how to best care for some plant? An ache burned in my broken heart. This place was her home. I couldn't give it up or let the demons destroy it.

Determination shot through me as I picked up a large purple book about celestial bodies and their associated gods and goddesses to help me decide when to call on Kaliakwan. During the day or during the night? The sun usually stood for creation, whereas the moon stood for destruction.

I wanted the negative energy gone, so I decided to summon them during the night. I knew the phases of the moon also had different meanings. So I continued to flip through the book until I reached the part about the different moon phases. The new moon stood for new beginnings, a waxing moon for growing things, a full moon for protection and a waning moon for getting rid of things. I could spin most of them to work in my favour except the waxing moon.

I looked out of the window. A half moon was showing, but was it waxing or waning? All the days had merged into each other, and I couldn't recall the last time I'd seen the moon. In the end, I looked it up in the fire. Waning. That would work perfectly.

I waited until the waning moon was high in the sky before walking outside. It was a chilly evening, and I made my way to the nearby park. My senses remained alert, searching for any potential demons that might turn up. The park was deserted. The only sounds were the trees whistling in the wind and the distant traffic noises.

I scanned the trees as I wandered through the park, and after a while I found a tree matching the description of an elm, with ridged bark and oval leaves with serrated edges. I walked up to it and conjured a knife to prick my finger, letting three drops fall to the ground.

'Kaliakwan, I summon thee. Please hear my call.'

The trees swayed in the breeze, some leaves falling to the ground, but Kaliakwan did not appear. Had I missed something?

Doubt gnawed in my mind as I waited a bit longer before trying again. Still nothing. My heart sank. Did they not find me worthy?

I'd just turned around to head back home when a strong wind blew, forcing me to close my eyes. When I opened them again, an enormous shadow had appeared ahead of me. My breath caught in my throat. What type of demon was coming for me now? I summoned my fire and waited. The shadow became smaller. Eventually I could make out a being with two heads. Immense power radiated from them. I quickly extinguished the fire in my hand, relieved that Kaliakwan had finally answered my summons.

The body was divided into light and dark, along with the heads. The left side belonged to a beautiful female with long black hair, a dark complexion and generous curves, and the right side belonged to a muscular man with fair skin and white curly hair. They were a complete contrast to each other. Even though everyone referred to them as one entity, they were actually two.

They stared at me intensely, and my heart pounded in my chest. I knew they could kill me on the spot if they wanted to. Maybe this hadn't been such a great idea. Even my father would have been no match for them.

I lowered my gaze to the ground, took a calming breath and bowed towards the female entity. 'Kali,' I said before turning my head slightly to the man. 'Akwan.'

'What do you seek, descendent of Surtr?'

I remained quiet, not sure how to phrase my question.

'Speak your mind.' Their voice echoed through my head.

I looked up at them and started speaking. 'I radiate energy that attracts demons.'

'I see,' they said in unison. They took turns inspecting me, holding their hands out in front of me. 'We cannot destroy it. Your grief is yours to deal with.'

'If you can't take my grief away, can you make me forget?' As much as I loved Lily, maybe not remembering her at all would be easier. I'd forget the love of my life, but at least I wouldn't attract demons or feel paralysed by grief.

Maybe I could even bring Cassie back, show her the love she deserved, and we could become a family again.

'You are not thinking with a clear mind.'

I let out a sigh and did my best to keep the anger from my voice. Kaliakwan was not a being you would want to rub the wrong way. 'Is there anything you can do to stop the demons from seeking me out and attacking me?'

They tilted their heads, an empathetic smile appearing on the lighter one. 'We can create a haven for you where your negativity will not be detected. But disrupting the balance comes at a cost. Every action will create a reaction to keep the balance.'

'Can you move my house to this haven?'

'Yes, if you wish.'

I bowed my head. 'Thank you.'

'Then it's decided. Your house will be part of your ancestors' realm.'

My mouth fell open. 'What? That's hardly a haven. I still won't be able to go outside. If he knows I'm there, he'll force me to join his army.'

'It has been decided.'

I wanted to argue, but I bit my tongue. It was never wise to talk back to someone who could erase you with the snap of their fingers. 'At least can you promise I will remain safe?'

'We will keep it hidden from him. As long as you're in that dimension, your energy will not be detected.'

Great. So instead of worrying about demons attacking, I had to worry about my father. I'd almost failed to save Jax from him, and now I would have to live in the same realm without a chance of getting Cassie back. 'Can you not move me anywhere else?'

'No. Moving you to Muspelheim would cause the least disruption to the balance. You are a part of that realm. The hole will be smaller.'

I frowned. 'The hole?'

'Yes. To build a hill, there must be a hole. Destruction cannot happen without creation, and creation needs destruction to thrive.'

Knowing it was pointless to argue with them, or maybe even dangerous, I bowed my head. 'Thank you.'

'It is for the balance of the universe that we have granted your wish. Do not leave Muspelheim unless you have to. Remaining in the human realm will disrupt the balance, as your energy cannot be contained while you're here.'

The wind blew past, and a moment later they were gone.

I went over what Kaliakwan had said as I made my way home. I'd made a terrible mistake. This wasn't my wish. I had wanted the demons to stop attacking so it would be safe to get Cassie back, but somehow I'd screwed up even more.

When I reached my house, it was still in the human world. Relief flooded through me. Maybe they hadn't moved it after all, but as I opened the door and stepped inside, the air around me changed. It was different. Hotter, heavier, with a subtle hint of sulphur. Proof they had indeed transferred my entire house to another dimension. I let out a defeated breath. Hopefully they hadn't been lying about it being hidden from Surtr.

I went around inspecting the windows. They all looked out onto the human world. Visually, there was no indication the house had moved. A feeling of loss fell over me. I wouldn't even be able to enjoy the flowers Lily had planted in the garden anymore. I walked through the back door in the kitchen and entered the garden to enjoy one last look at it before following Kaliakwan's rule of staying in my father's realm, but to my surprise a reddish sky greeted me, devoid of any stars – a sky that could only belong to Surtr's realm.

I reached the edge of the garden and opened the gate leading to the alleyway. The human world was visible on the other side. My house and garden had been moved into Surtr's realm while it still sat where it normally did in the human world. I placed a concealment spell on the gate to stop unknowing humans from accidentally stepping into the hell realm. It would be a death sentence for anyone who didn't carry demon blood.

# NICK

## Amare Demon

I was stuck in a cycle of self-loathing. By summoning Kaliakwan I had only made things worse. I still couldn't leave the house, and now there was no chance of getting Cassie back. She wouldn't be able to enter this realm until her powers fully matured. I screamed in anger. Those demons had destroyed my life. Whoever was responsible would pay. I would get my justice.

I went over to the bookcase. Maybe if I could figure out what type of demons they were, I'd know where to start looking. I stared at the books at my disposal, cursing myself for never having taken an interest in demon lore. It was the downside of being married to a Vendari – a being of light that loved the human world. But for the first time in my life,

I regretted not learning more about the supernatural world and my origins.

I thought about reaching out to someone, but Lily and I had mostly kept to ourselves. Lily's friends had quickly abandoned her when they'd learned she'd married me – a being with demon blood. It didn't matter to them that I didn't act like one or that I had grown up human, learning the importance of love and trust. They only saw what was in my blood.

I wasn't doing much better on the friendship side. The few friends I'd once had were humans, and I'd had to leave them behind. That was the problem with not ageing like a normal human. I only had Jax. He might have been able to help me get information, but I knew he would never agree. He had always been righteous and forgiving. I had offered to help him get retribution for what my father had done to him, but he had declined, telling me an eye for an eye would only breed more darkness. But at that moment, I didn't care. Darkness had become second nature to me since I'd lost my light, and I would not rest until I had figured out and killed everyone who had been involved in my family's demise.

Failing to find any book that could help, I sat down on the sofa and stared at the fire. There must be some indication of who the demons were, who they were working for and why they had attacked us. I willed the fire to show me anything related to the demons that had attacked us, but it only showed the afternoon that had broken my heart and changed my life forever. I didn't need to be reminded. It was ingrained into my mind how the demon had materialised on the porch, towering over Lily. Its wicked smile as it thrust the blade into her. How I'd been too slow to save her.

I stood up and shook the image out of my mind. But something still lingered. They looked different from the demon I'd tried to interrogate. And they seemed too organised compared to the demons that had tried to kill me since.

I spent the next few days going through all the books I had at my disposal, but I wasn't getting anywhere. As I was pacing the room, debating what my next step should be, the doorbell rang. I paused. I wasn't expecting anyone.

I made my way to the door and opened it. In front of me was the short demon I had spared a week ago. I honestly hadn't thought I'd ever see him again.

He bowed his head. 'You were harder to find this time. I thought maybe you'd got your grief under control, but I can tell I've been wrong. '

I stared at him. 'How did you find me? I thought I was hidden.'

'You were. If it wasn't for the energy of the portal, I wouldn't have been able to find you. Why did you move to another realm?'

'You said it yourself. I was a beacon for demons, and I was tired of being attacked. Why'd you come back?'

'I always keep my word,' he said with a smile.

'And what did you find out?'

He looked down at the ground. 'No one's talking.'

'And why is that? I thought demons loved to brag about things.'

'You said it yourself. You killed everyone that attacked you. Maybe no one's left to brag about it.'

'I don't believe that. It wasn't a random attack. They were too organised. Someone must have sent them.'

The demon became thoughtful. 'Can you describe the demons that attacked you and killed your soulmate?'

'I can do you one better.' I conjured the pictures I had created of the demons and gave them to him.

His eyes became wide. 'I believe you are right. These are shadow demons, created by the blood of an upper demon. And these flying ones ... they're in league with Icarus.'

I frowned. 'Who's Icarus?'

His mouth fell open. 'You don't know who Icarus is?'

I shook my head.

'I'm sorry. I just thought a powerful demon like yourself—'

I cut him off with a glare. 'Don't think. Before my family was destroyed, I had no need to involve myself with demon scum.'

The demon in front of me took a step back and bowed his head. 'I'm sorry, sir. I didn't mean any disrespect. Icarus belongs to the Laces species.' I scratched my head, still lost as to what he was talking about. 'He's not an upper demon, so he wouldn't have been able to create the shadow demons,' the demon explained.

'So he must have been working with someone else?'

'I believe so.'

'Can you help me find out who?'

'I can try.' His eyes met mine. 'But if I do, you owe me a favour.'

'What favour?'

'I don't know yet. I'll let you know when I do.'

I nodded, unsure whether I'd made the right choice or if it was going to bite me in the arse. He smiled and held his hand out for me to shake. 'Great. I'm Ant.'

'Nick,' I replied shortly before shaking his hand.

'I'll see you around,' he said and disappeared from the porch.

I was about to close the door when my eyes landed on the spot where Lily had died in my arms. There was still some discolouration on the stone floor of the porch. Guilt boiled up inside me. I hadn't been to her grave since Kaliakwan had transported my house to Muspelheim, Surtr's realm. I took a step through the door but thought better of it. They had told me to stay put, and Lily's soul wasn't really at the grave; only her physical body was.

I went back to the living room to think about what Ant had said. It sounded like there was a lot more to the attack and Lily's death than I'd first thought. But why had some upper demon created shadow demons to attack us? And why hadn't they come back to finish me off?

A few days later, Ant was back at my door. He carried a stack of books. 'I thought while I tried to figure out who sent those demons after you, you could do with some reading material to actually learn a thing or two.'

I smirked. 'When did you become this brave?'

A grin appeared on his face. 'I assumed that if you were going to kill me, you would have done so by now. But you let me live. Besides, you told me last time your wife had been a being of light. She would never have married a monster.' He shifted his stance. 'Can I come in?'

'Why?'

'I know you want to avoid the human realm, but the time shift between the realms isn't ideal and we have much to discuss.'

I hesitated. I still hadn't got rid of all the things that belonged to Cassie, and I couldn't let anyone know about her – it would put her at risk. And even though Ant hadn't given me a reason not to trust him, he was still a demon.

I grabbed hold of Ant and teleported him to the back garden. He stumbled back, some of the books falling out of his arms. His eyes widened as he scanned the area. 'Where are we?'

I gestured to the garden. 'This is my own little personal part of hell.' He opened his mouth but closed it again. I ignored his reaction and took a seat at the picnic table. 'So, tell me about these books.'

He bent down to collect the books that had dropped on the ground before handing me one of them. It was thick with a black cover that felt like rubber. 'This book is called the codex and lists all the main species of demons that exist or existed.'

I flipped through the pages. There were weird symbols in ink that looked like blood. 'Is that ...'

He placed the rest of the books on the table. 'Yes. The cover is made from demon skin and it's written in blood.'

I closed the book. 'I can't read this.'

'I know it's not very hygienic ...'

I rolled my eyes. 'I meant that I don't understand what it says.'

Ant let out a breath. 'It was worth a try. Luckily for you, I have this.' He picked up a thick notebook off the top of the book pile. 'If we're going to figure out who killed your wife, you need to know what we may be up against. Everything I know about everything is in here.'

I took the book from him. It had drawings of different demons and information written underneath in English. My heart skipped a beat as a drawing of a fire being made of stone appeared. My father. Ant must have realised. 'Oh yes, the infamous Surtr,' he said thoughtfully, looking over my shoulder. 'Are we in his realm?'

'Sort of,' I said absently as I flicked through the notebook.

'How long has it been since my last visit?'

I frowned. 'It's been four days. Why do you ask?'

'Different realms have different time speeds. For example, in human time, it's been twenty days since I last saw you, so time moves a lot slower here. Better make sure my visit is short so my wife doesn't worry.'

'Are you in this book?' I asked, ignoring his previous statement.

Ant shook his head. 'I'm in the actual codex – well, my species is. No point in writing down my own history when I know it by heart.'

'What type of demon species are you?'

He smiled. 'I'm an Amare demon.'

'A what?' I asked with a frown.

He let out a sigh. 'You sure don't know much about your

own culture.'

'I was never interested in finding out.'

'Let me tell you a story. The first Amare demon was created after a goddess became jealous of her sister and her sister's husband. She tried to seduce him, but he only had eyes for his wife, so in a massive moment of rage, she cursed the sister, turning her into a heartless demon. The husband, knowing his wife was pregnant, sacrificed himself and cut his own heart out so his wife would be able to love and care for their child. The Fates, having seen what happened, took pity on them, and even though they could not reverse what had been done, they split the heart in two so the husband and wife had half a heart each and together could live as one. For this reason, the Amare demons have soulmates, and when we find them, our hearts become one and we gain a soul. So, you see, I may be a demon, but I'm not that much different from you, because I'm not soulless like most of our kind.'

I let out a grunt.

Ant gave me a sad smile. 'I know you have lost your one true love and you want the ones that killed her to pay. The reason I'm helping you is because the thought of losing my wife ... I wouldn't know what to do with myself, but I think once you've avenged her, it'll be easier to put everything behind you.' He collected all the books together and handed them to me. 'Anyway, I'll come and see you when I have more information, but in the meantime, read up about our kind. You don't want any surprises.' He looked around. 'Now, can you please get me out of here?'

# NICK

# A Favour Returned

Ant and I grew closer as time went on. I still wasn't sure if he had a hidden agenda, but I was thankful for the help and the company. He continued to teach me about demons and how things worked while trying to get information about who had been behind Lily's death. It gave me hope that maybe after I got my revenge, I could put it all behind me and start living again.

I'd been watching Cassie in the fire. She was growing so quickly. It made me restless, as we hadn't made any progress and I was worried she wouldn't remember me at all. The family she lived with had just celebrated her fourth birthday, even though in this realm it had only been nine months since I'd given her up.

I paced back and forth in the garden. The scent of fresh flowers filled the air, but I couldn't enjoy it. All it did was remind me of everything I had lost and how I was at the mercy of Ant's information. 'I'm tired of being stuck here,' I told him. 'I can't walk around in the human world, and I'd rather not take a chance walking around this realm. But I need to do something. Maybe I should help you investigate.'

Ant hesitated. 'It's not a good idea. I'm a nobody. No one cares if I'm around. I have no powers, so they don't see me as a threat, which means they aren't watching what they are saying. But you would raise suspicion. They would feel your power miles away. I never would have figured out that Icarus worked for someone higher up in command if you'd been with me.'

I let out a deep breath and joined Ant at the picnic table. 'I feel so useless. All I do is sit around doing nothing. At least now we finally have a lead. Maybe we should go and interrogate Icarus for more information about who he's working for.'

Ant shook his head. 'I don't think he'd talk.'

'We can make him talk,' I said as I took a seat next to him.

'There's a reason I've never confronted him. He's not like the demons that attacked you. He commands legions.'

'I don't care. He has information we need.'

Ant let out a sigh. 'It's not a good idea. I don't even know where he is.'

'I do. The fire will tell me.' He jumped as I made a fireplace appear next to us.

'How?' Ant asked, inspecting the fireplace as I ignited

the wood inside it.

'I can scry in the fire. It will tell me what I need to know.'

He scratched his neck. 'Can you use it to find out who's responsible for Lily's death?'

'I've tried. But all it shows is what happened that day.'

'I'm sorry. How do you know it will show you where Icarus is?'

'I just do.' I stared into the fire, willing it to show me where Icarus was.

Vegetation surrounded a huge demon with what looked to be an exoskeleton with black wings and horns sitting on a makeshift chair made of trees in a glade. 'Grab my shoulder and I'll teleport us to him.'

'I'm not sure that's a good idea. Especially without a plan.'

I let out a sigh, placed a hand on Ant's shoulder and teleported us.

We emerged in the glade. Ant gave me a disapproving shake of his head as he scanned the area. His eyes went wide as he pointed towards the insect-like demon I'd just seen in the fire. 'Your fire was right. That's Icarus.'

Icarus's gaze landed on us. 'Well, well. What do we have here?'

I marched up to him. 'I'm here for information.'

'Is that so?' he said as he stood up from his chair. He was taller than I'd expected. I didn't even reach his shoulders.

'You're going to tell me who you are working for.'

Icarus laughed. 'Unless you want to die, I suggest you leave.'

I clenched my fist as anger swirled around me. 'Do you

even know who you're talking to?'

'Don't know, don't care. Now leave before you become my next dinner.' He waved his hand at us dismissively.

Ant pulled at my jumper. 'I think we should leave.'

I shook my head and conjured up my sword. 'I need to do this. We need to figure out who he's working for.' I conjured the fire in my other hand. 'Are you going to tell us or not?'

Icarus tilted his head, a smirk playing on his lips. 'I'm thinking no.'

I rushed towards him with my sword held high, but he kicked me. I rolled on the ground. A sword appeared in his hand as he moved away from his chair. Anger coursed through me and I threw my fire at him, but he deflected it with his sword.

He took a step towards me and we danced around each other, meeting each blow sword to sword. Sweat formed on my forehead. I wasn't used to this much physical activity anymore. I swung my sword and slashed at his abdomen, but he blocked it and pushed me away before taking flight.

I couldn't reach him in the air with my sword, so I dropped it and conjured my fire in both hands. I threw firebolts at him in quick succession, but he dodged them with ease. It only ignited my rage, and I became careless. Gathering up as much fire as I could muster, I threw it right at him. He tried to move aside, but it hit his leg, and the smell of burning flesh filled the air.

He let out a shriek and dived towards me, thrusting his sword at my heart. I rolled out of the way, but the sword cut my back and caught my jumper, trapping me on the ground.

Icarus flew towards me again and kicked me hard – so hard, the fabric of the jumper tore. I landed a few feet away with a thump. I got to my knees and tried to catch my breath, but before I could recover, he punched me in the face, causing me to tumble once again. My vision went blurry, and as I looked up, he stood over me with his sword held high. I wasn't sure if I would meet the same fate as Lily, but as Icarus swung his sword, Ant grabbed me and teleported us to the alleyway. He opened the back gate and we stumbled into my garden. I collapsed in a heap on the grass.

'I told you it was a bad idea,' Ant said as he took a seat at the wooden picnic table. I grunted, not wanting to admit he was right. 'This is why it's better if I go alone. Information doesn't need to include fighting.'

'I almost had him,' I said as I got up into a seated position.

Ant tried to cover up a half laugh. 'It was a shitshow and you know it. Next time, you leave it to me.'

I rolled my eyes. 'Whatever.'

Ant looked me over. 'How's your back? Do you need help attending to your wounds?'

'I'm fine,' I answered, despite the burning pain in my back.

Ant studied me with a serious look on his face. 'If you say so. Then if you'll excuse me, I'm going to get going.'

I waved him away and lay down next to the sunflower bush. Lily had laughed so hard when I'd first conjured it. Apparently it was all wrong – sunflowers didn't grow on bushes. I let out a determined breath. I would avenge Lily even if it killed me.

I lay there for a while longer before I got up on unsteady legs, needing to tend to my injured back. I'd just got out of the bathroom when someone banged frantically on the front door. I rushed to get it. What the hell was going on?

What I saw when I opened the door broke my heart. Ant stood on the other side. In his arms was an unconscious woman with a big gash in her abdomen. I stared at them for a moment, frozen, as all the images of the day I lost Lily flashed before me.

Ant's voice brought me back to reality. 'My wife. You need to help her,' he said with tears in his eyes.

I blinked away the memories as grim determination set in. I grabbed hold of the two of them and teleported to the back garden.

'Nick. Please help her,' Ant pleaded.

'What happened?'

Ant didn't answer as he laid the woman down on the wooden picnic table. 'I'm so sorry. It's all my fault,' he mumbled to her as he put pressure on the wound in an attempt to stop the bleeding.

Despite the pressure Ant applied, the blood kept coming, and the same numbness and helplessness I'd felt when I'd lost Lily swept over me as blood started dripping down between the planks of the table. I brushed away some tears. 'I can't help. I don't have any healing abilities.'

Ant looked up at me, tears falling down his face. 'You can cauterise the wound. She's my everything. I can't lose her.'

'It might kill her.'

Ant bared his teeth. 'You owe me. Doing nothing will

kill her.' He gestured to where his hands were putting pressure on her wound. 'Use your fire to stop the bleeding.'

I stepped up to her and took a deep breath, conjuring my fire. Her shirt was nothing more than fragments. I held my hand and flame steady as I moved it towards the bleeding wound in her abdomen. The woman let out a scream before passing out again as the skin around the wound sizzled. The gushing stopped, but there was still some blood oozing out. 'I don't know if it will be enough. If she moves, the wound might open up.'

Ant stroked the woman's face lovingly. 'We may not have a lot of power, but us Amare demons heal quickly.'

'So what happened?' I asked.

He let out a defeated breath and wiped his hand over his face. He opened his mouth to say something but hesitated. 'I ...' He let out a defeated breath. 'I don't know. I got home and found Dalia unconscious with a big wound. It looks like she's been clawed by a demon. I didn't think it was safe to stay there, and I trust you.'

Dalia stirred, and Ant grabbed his wife's hand. Her other hand went to her charred abdomen. 'My baby,' she mumbled. Tears ran down her face and her voice got louder. 'My baby. I lost my baby.'

Ant blinked back some tears before placing his hand over hers. 'Shh. It's okay. You're still here. It's going to be okay.'

She shoved Ant's hand from hers. 'No. I lost my baby. Our baby is gone.'

I felt like I was intruding, and seeing her reaction to the loss of the baby made me think of Cassie. I wondered how she was doing. If she was still safe.

I started towards the living room and the fire but stopped midway. My clothes were covered in blood, and Lily had always hated when I sat on our sofa in dirty clothes. Like the time I had helped her sort out some flower beds for the garden. She had complained about how I had got dirt all over the sofa and what a pain it would be to clean it. I'd offered to just conjure a new one, but she insisted we use our magic as little as possible. She wanted to learn the human way of doing things. And she had excelled at everything she'd put her efforts into.

I went upstairs to have a shower. The door to our bedroom remained closed, just like it had been since the day Lily died. Even now, I couldn't bring myself to go in there. I'd been using the guest room, though I rarely slept anymore. Most of the time, I would just pass out on the sofa for a few hours. Nightmares still haunted my sleep, and they were somehow worse than the actual incident. Demons would be mocking me from afar, telling me I'd let it all happen because part of me had wanted it to happen. I shook my head. I didn't want to think about it.

After I had showered, I went back downstairs and looked out of the window that overlooked the garden. Ant and his wife were embracing each other. I felt a stab in my heart. Had he almost lost his wife because of me?

I didn't want to intrude, so I went into the living room and took a seat on the sofa by the fire. I stared into the fire and thought of Cassie. Her smile appeared. It showed her sitting by a table. Next to her was the girl who had given her a toy as a toddler, and on the other side were two young boys.

At the top of the table was a woman. Last time I'd checked on Cassie, she had been living with the man Freya had left her with. What had happened to him? Had he remarried?

I searched in the fire and learned he had died in a car crash. Doubt about whether I'd done the right thing gripped my heart, but Cassie seemed happy where she was. Besides, she wouldn't be able to live in this house with me anymore, not since Kaliakwan had moved it to the demon realm.

Maybe I could get Ant to check on her. He had trusted me with his family, but maybe it would be too risky. I dismissed the thought. It would pain me too much if I caused anything else to happen to Ant and his family, and even more if anything happened to Cassie because I'd told someone about her.

I entered the garden, and as I approached them, Daila gave me a weak smile. 'You must be Nick. It's a pleasure to meet you. Ant always speaks so highly of you.'

'I'm sorry for your loss,' I said.

'Thank you,' Dalia answered quietly as her hands went to her abdomen. She looked around the garden. 'Where are we?'

I thought about telling her that we were in a hell dimension, my own little secure hideout in my father's domain, but I thought better of it. 'You're safe. You're at my home. Nothing can touch you here.'

She turned to Ant. 'Our house. Our house isn't safe anymore. What are we going to do?' She brought her hands to her face.

'Our house was never safe. It was just well hidden.' Ant reached for her hands. 'But it doesn't matter. All that matters is that you're still by my side.' He caressed her face and kissed her forehead.

'You can stay here,' I offered. I couldn't help but think that all this was my fault for not listening to Ant and seeking out Icarus.

Dalia looked up at me. 'We wouldn't want to impose. It's your house, not ours.'

Ant placed a hand on her shoulder. 'I don't think he meant the house.'

'I was thinking about something else.' I conjured a small house, similar to a caravan, on the grass between some large trees.

A sound of amazement escaped Dalia's lips, and her mouth fell open as she stared at the house that had just appeared.

I gestured towards it. 'I know it isn't much, but as long as you're here, you'll be safe. No one would want to come here.'

She crossed her arms and looked at me with sceptical eyes. 'Do I want to know why no one would want to come here?'

I shrugged. 'It's probably better if you don't. This place is hidden from the inhabitants of this dimension. They don't know we're here. And demons, once they enter this dimension, can't escape without assistance.'

Her eyes went wide. 'But what if we need to leave?'

'Then use the alleyway. It leads back to the human world.' I gestured towards the end of the garden.

Dalia looked around with a deep frown. Ant patted her shoulder. 'I trust Nick. Just rest and get well.'

I smiled at them. 'Make yourself at home. I'll be in the house. Just knock on the door if you need me.'

Ant never spoke again of the attack on his wife. I offered to help him set everything right, but he just brushed it aside, saying he didn't care as long as Dalia was still alive. As much as I wanted a lead on who had killed Lily, I could tell Dalia needed Ant around, so I insisted he stayed to be there for his wife. My revenge could wait. I didn't want to have another broken family on my conscience. Dalia made a full recovery and, less than a year later, gave birth to a little girl.

They named her Nicole as a tribute to me for helping save Dalia's life, but it only made me feel more guilty. The attack on their house had happened after we had gone to interrogate Icarus. If it wasn't for that or the fact Ant had been snooping around, no one would have found their house and hurt his wife.

They seemed like a happy family, but I avoided spending time with them, as it was a painful reminder of what I had lost.

I was sitting on the sofa, staring into the fire and watching Cassie. She had got so big, and even though I was no closer to figuring out who had destroyed my family, my heart felt a little lighter knowing Cassie was having a good childhood. She seemed close to the other children, and she was often smiling. It'd been two years since I'd given her up and she was now eleven years old. She looked more and more like

Lily every day.

A knock on the back door interrupted my scrying, and I went to open it. Ant stepped inside. 'How are you doing?'

I shrugged. 'The same.'

'I'm sorry,' he said as he shifted some rubbish on the kitchen table and took a seat. 'I appreciate the time you've given me to spend with my family. I know you're restless, but I really appreciate you not going out on your own.'

I let out a breath. 'I feel like it was my fault Dalia got injured. If I had listened to you instead of being reckless, I wouldn't have put you and your family in danger.'

'You were, but it wasn't your fault. If anything, it was mine. I should have known better. Anyway, I wanted to let you know how much I appreciate everything you've done. And I haven't forgotten my promise. I owe my family to you, and it breaks my heart that I haven't been able to give you the information you seek. I need to take some extra precautions, but I'm ready to go back out there for you. We will get Lily the revenge she deserves.'

# NICK

## Summoning Jax

Though Ant had started to gather information again, we weren't any closer to finding out who Icarus worked for or who had ordered the shadow demons to attack me and my family that day. It felt like we were running out of time. It'd been more than three years since that awful day.

I stared into the fire, willing it to show me Cassie. For every day that passed here in this realm, five days had passed in the human world. And now Cassie was approaching her seventeenth birthday, and her abilities would manifest soon, and with that came the risk of someone recognising that she wasn't human.

Cassie sat at a dinner table with three other teenagers and a middle-aged woman, the same people who had been around since she was younger. She still seemed happy and safe. I willed the fire to show me what would happen if I didn't interfere. I wasn't sure if it would work, but slowly the image in the fire changed. Cassie was being tied to a chair in the middle of a circle, blue flame surrounding her. Someone was chanting, but I couldn't locate it. My heart speeded up. Would Cassie be kidnapped? Would my father find out who she was and take her? I took a deep breath, trying to calm myself. The flames had been blue, so it was unlikely to be my father, as his fire was amber. But there were a lot of beings that could be after her, especially if they knew who or what she was.

I stood up and paced the room. What should I do? Even though the fire only showed a potential future, it was clear Cassie wouldn't be safe unless I interfered somehow. As she was only part demon, she couldn't enter a demon realm until her abilities had fully manifested, which wouldn't be until she turned eighteen. And because I had sent her to live in the human world, she wouldn't even know about the supernatural world or who she was.

The thought of turning up and explaining myself crossed my mind. But that would probably make it worse. Even though I'd tried to come to terms with Lily's death, I still carried an aura of grief that attracted demons, and Cassie's safety was the reason I'd given her away in the first place.

Cassie needed someone who could watch over her in the human world and help her understand her abilities while making sure she was safe. But who?

I slapped my hand to my face. Why hadn't I thought of it sooner? Jax would be perfect for the task, and I trusted him wholeheartedly.

I thought back to when we'd first become friends. It had been a bad day and my bully, Owen, had been worse than ever. He'd shoved me into a locker and walked away laughing. Anger and rage ran through me, and the next moment, he was on fire. But before anyone had a chance to react, Owen was back to normal and everyone seemed to have forgotten what had just happened. The new guy, Jax, marched towards me. 'Dammit, Nick, you need to learn to control it.'

'Control what?'

'Your fire. I won't always be around to fix it and make sure no one remembers. Sooner or later your ability is going to kill him because I won't be around to stop it.'

I frown. 'Ability? I don't have any abilities.'

'Really? You think the fires that appear every time Owen bullies you are just random?'

I stared at him, trying to comprehend what he was saying. 'The fires are real? I thought they only happened in my mind. No one seems to notice them.'

Jax ran his hand through his hair. 'Only because I deal with it. But I won't always be around, and eventually they'll question what they've seen and whether it's real or not. So you need to learn to control it.'

'How do I do that?'

'By practising and controlling your emotions.'

'But how am I going to control it when I don't even know how it's happening?'

'It happens because you're part demon.'

I raised my eyebrows. 'Demon? You got to be joking. They don't exist.'

'Well, your ability says otherwise.'

I was about to tell him I didn't have an ability when my hands burst into flames. I screamed.

Jax observed me closely. 'Breathe and calm down.'

'Easy for you to say when I'm the one on fire. How do I know you're not the one causing this? You're always around when the fires happen.'

Jax chuckled. 'It's a part of you. It's not going to burn you. Your negative emotions are bound to your powers. By controlling your anger, your ability can be controlled.'

'How can you be so sure?'

'I can't,' he said with a smirk. He looked at my hands. 'But it looks like I was right.'

I followed Jax's gaze and realised the fire had gone out. I didn't know him, but he seemed to want to help, and what choice did I have? No one else would believe me, and I would end up in the nuthouse if I told anyone about it.

'How do you know all this?'

Jax ran his hand through his hair. 'Well, as you may have gathered, I'm not exactly human either.'

That was the start of an amazing friendship. He taught me how to control my powers, and I gained a brother. He told me never to give in to the hatred and anger, because it would feed the demon inside and cause me to have no control over my actions. I used to think he was exaggerating, but I knew better now.

I let out a sigh. Since I'd met Lily, I hadn't spent a lot of time with him, but what we went through, you don't just forget. I trusted him with my life. Maybe I could get him to look after Cassie. He'd been there for me in the beginning, when I'd first found out about the supernatural world. Without him, I would have been kidnapped or killed, or worse. He would know what to do.

Only problem – I hadn't seen Jax since he'd visited me at the cemetery. He didn't exactly carry a phone. I could scry for him in the fire to see what he was up to, but I wouldn't be able to call on him through it unless he was near a fire, and knowing Jax, he was probably flying around in a forest. He used to tell me stories about how he sometimes got so caught up in being a crow that several years passed between him taking his human form. I wondered if that was why he looked younger than me, though it could have been because I was half human.

As I thought about how I could reach him, I remembered he was bound to me – an unfortunate mishap that had happened while he was helping me find out who my father was. Just thinking about what Surtr had done to Jax broke my heart. It had been my fault.

I had been having nightmares telling me to come and stand by my father's side as he prepared for the end of the world, but at the time, I didn't even know who my biological father was. Jax had jeopardised his life searching for him. Surtr had imprisoned and tortured Jax to get to me. To convince me to join his army of my own free will. An army destined to fight and die during the end of the world, or more specifically during Ragnarök.

After I had located Jax and come face to face with my ruthless father, I learned only descendants of Surtr had the ability to move from the realm. In the end, I got Jax out of Surtr's prison without having to join my father's army, but he tricked me into binding Jax to me. He said it was the only way to get him away from this realm. I should never have believed anything Surtr told me. All I had needed to do was hold on to Jax as I teleported away.

I never wanted to exploit this bond between us. When I'd bound him to me, I'd bound part of his will to mine, and I could make him do things he didn't want to do. However, I would never have dreamed of using him like that. After it had happened, we'd tried to find some way of breaking the bond, but Freya said it was unbreakable and the only way to break it was for one of us to die. And neither of us was willing to pay that price.

I continued to pace the room as I zoomed into my mind and tugged at the bond that tied us together, summoning him to my side. How would he react to me summoning him? Would he be up for looking after Cassie? I knew it was a lot to ask.

Jax's energy appeared in the room, so I knew he had answered my summons. I continued pacing as he fluttered around, inspecting the room in his crow form. Eventually he transformed into his human form in front of me, but he was still studying his surroundings, so I cleared my throat to get his attention.

'Jax, it's good to see you,' I said as I offered him a smile. Despite not seeing him a lot over the last forty years, he was still my best friend. I thought about how to approach the subject but decided to be honest and speak from my heart. 'I'm sorry about summoning you like this. I realise how degrading it must be to be forced somewhere against your will, but I didn't know any other way to reach you.'

He met my gaze, and his face creased with worry. 'It's okay. What's going on?'

His stare became intense. I evaded it, taking a seat on the sofa. I gestured for him to do the same. The fire sparkled in the fireplace and I glanced into it, willing it to show me pictures of Lily. It was painful, but she gave me strength. I took a deep breath, pushing down the longing. 'I need a favour from you. You're the only one I can trust.'

The fire showed the last moments of Lily's life and how she had sacrificed herself to save Cassie. I turned to Jax and clasped my hands together in my lap. 'I never told you how Lily died.' Tears threated to fall down my face, so I turned back to the fire. I took a moment to collect myself before speaking. 'She was killed by a shadow demon.'

Jax's eyes went wide. 'What? Why? Do you know who made him?'

'Them.' I clenched my fist as anger rushed over me. 'And if I did, they'd be dead already.' I closed my eyes and reeled in my hatred. 'I think I was their target.' It was the only thing that made sense. They'd probably killed Lily to throw me off my game, only they hadn't realised I would burn them all to the ground for it. I shook my head. 'It doesn't matter. I can take care of myself. But I have a daughter, and Lily ... Lily died protecting her,' I said, choking on my words.

Jax shifted in his seat and jerked his head back in surprise.

I conjured a picture of Cassie in the fire. It was amazing how much she looked like her mother, and a sharp pain entered my heart. 'Her name is Cassie. She lives in the human world.' I took a deep breath. I still wondered if I had made the right choice.

'I had to hide her away. No one can know she's my daughter. Not until I've killed every single one of the beings responsible.' Anger and hatred filled me for what had been done to me – to my family. They would all pay one way or another.

I let out a sigh, calming myself down once again. 'She's turning seventeen soon. My source can only guarantee her safety until her powers manifest.' I continued to stare into the fire. 'She doesn't know what she is. She doesn't know about this world. If anyone tried to get her, she'd be an easy target.'

'What do you want me to do?' Jax asked.

A vision of Cassie being kidnapped appeared in the fire. I turned away and faced Jax. 'I want you to keep her safe. Watch her, befriend her if you must, and help her understand her abilities like you did for me.'

He hesitated. 'I'm not sure I'm the right person for the job.'

I stared pleadingly into his hazel eyes so that he understood the sincerity of what I was saying. 'You're the only one I trust. I may be overreacting. Maybe no one is after her, but I made a promise to Lily to make sure that she's safe.'

'Where can I find Cassie?'

My eyes went back to the fire. 'She lives in a town called Stonefield.'

'Where?'

I searched through the images in the fire again for more clues without any success. Unable to find what I was searching for, I shrugged. 'I'm not sure. I can't tell, but it's a small town. Let me show you.' I used my telepathy to send the images I'd just seen in the fire over to Jax. 'Sorry I can't be more helpful.'

'No worries. I should be able to find her based on this. Can't be too many Stonefields about.'

'Thank you. This means a lot to me.' I stood from the sofa, and Jax did the same.

'I guess I should be off,' Jax said and patted me on the back. I had expected him to walk towards the front door, but he remained in his spot for a moment before casting me a fleeting look. 'Why can't I teleport?'

'We're in Surtr's realm.'

Jax trembled. 'What? Why would you do something this stupid?'

I placed a hand on his shoulder. 'It's okay. Just breathe. My father doesn't know we're here. My house is concealed.'

Jax eyes fixated on the scar on my wrist his demon form had caused when I'd saved him from my father. He took a deep breath and glanced into my eyes. 'How? Why?'

I sighed. 'It's a long story. Short version, I grew tired of being attacked.'

Jax eyes widened in shock. 'Who attacked you?'

'Demons. Lily's death broke something inside me. My powers aren't contained. They're like a beacon telling everyone where I am. Can't you feel it?'

He shook his head. 'You feel the same as always.'

I furrowed my brow. 'What about when you came by the cemetery all those years ago?'

'I could sense you, just like now. I thought it had to do with me being bonded to you.'

'Was it like that when we escaped Surtr?'

'I don't know.' He shrugged. 'I've done my best to forget about it all.'

I couldn't blame him for wanting to forget. They had tortured him until he forgot who he was. Only his demon instinct had remained. He'd attacked me when I'd tried to save him, but it was my fault he had ended up there, and maybe it was partly due to guilt, but I couldn't give up on him. As soon as we had escaped, I'd called on Freya and she'd taken him back home.

Jax's voice brought me back to the present. 'How do I get out of here?'

I cleared my head and gestured to the hallway. 'Let me show you.'

Jax followed me to the front door, and as I opened it, he rubbed his chin. 'I don't understand. Why can I see the human realm?'

I chuckled, amazed how he could be so powerful in one instant but so clueless the next. After all, he was the one who had taught me about portals. 'I would have thought you'd know a portal when you see one. Just step through and you'll be in the human world.'

Jax patted my back. 'Look after yourself.'

'As long as you make sure nothing happens to Cassie. I made a promise to her mother to keep her safe.'

'I will protect her with my life,' Jax replied. He stared at the door and ran his hand through his hair before hesitantly slipping through it.

I smiled as he turned to face me, and I closed the door. It had been nice seeing my friend again. And if anything happened to Cassie, Jax would be there to protect her.

# NICK

## MYSTERIES

The knock on the back door woke me from my drunken state, and I got up from the sofa and stepped into the kitchen as Dalia entered the house with a casserole in her hands. 'Any news on my husband?'

'Not yet.' I felt bad for her, as Ant had been gone for a while. I hoped it meant he'd finally infiltrated the higher demon ranks and found out who had created the shadow demons.

She put the dish down on the kitchen counter. 'I made you some lunch – thought you might want to eat.'

Ever since Dalia had caught a glimpse of how neglected everything was, she had taken it upon herself to look after me and the house. I tried to be patient with her, as I knew she was only trying to be helpful. But it wasn't her job to keep my house clean or to cook me food, and it made me feel like she was intruding on Lily's memories. Lily had enjoyed the mundane household chores, even though we could easily have used our powers instead. Nowadays I couldn't be bothered, which was why Dalia was trying to be helpful.

I mustered up a smile. 'Thank you, but I'm not hungry.'

'No worries. I'll just leave it on the side in case you change your mind.'

'Thanks,' I replied as I grabbed a glass from the cupboard and opened a bottle of whisky.

'Do you need anything?'

I shook my head. 'I'm good.'

'Are you sure? Why don't you have a shower while I tidy up a bit?'

'I know you mean well, but I'm good.' I grabbed the bottle and took a large swig before heading back to the sofa.

She picked up a bucket and collected rubbish from the floor and tables as she followed me into the living room. 'I know you're hurting, but she wouldn't want this for you.'

I turned around and stared at her in disbelief. 'How do you know?'

She brought her hand to her heart. 'If anything happened to me, I'd want Ant to get on with his life. To be happy.'

I let out a sigh. 'It's not really that easy. It's not like I can flip a switch and forget that I lost the love of my life.'

'I know. But if I was in your shoes, I'd cherish all the time we spent together and watch as he lives on in our children.'

It felt like a jab, though I'd never told them about

Cassie. 'I can't do that until Lily has had her justice.'

She gave me a sympathetic smile. 'I hope you'll find yourself again once all this is over.' She walked to the door, leaving me alone.

I shrugged and went back to watch Lily and Cassie in the fire – to watch the happy moments we'd had as a family. The thought of being able to truly live and be happy again without Lily didn't seem possible. But once I had avenged her, I owed it to Cassie to try.

I woke up to the sound of the doorbell. I had no recollection of how long I had been asleep. The only relief I ever got was by drowning my sorrows in a bottle. It numbed the pain, left me in a haze and kept the nightmares at bay, allowing me a few hours of peaceful sleep.

The doorbell rang again. Hoping it was Ant coming back because he had discovered something, I pushed myself to my feet and stumbled towards the hallway to answer the door. Ant could use the alleyway, but since his little girl had arrived, he'd been careful about that. He said he didn't want to draw any attention to it in case someone decided to come for his wife and child. Though I thought he was being paranoid, I didn't blame him. I'd been exactly the same.

I wiped sleep from my eyes and did a double take. Jax was standing outside the door. My breath caught in my chest, and my heart rate speeded up. 'Why are you here? Did something happen to Cassie?' I studied him for any clue, but he appeared calm.

'Cassie's fine. At least for now.' He ran his hand through

his hair. 'There are some other issues I wanted to talk to you about.'

I opened the door further to let him in and went back to the living room. He followed. I kicked a bottle under the sofa and sat down. 'So, tell me about these issues. They must be quite serious for you to come and see me about it,' I said, cocking my head.

'The house Cassie lives in is shielded.'

I shifted in my seat. 'What d'you mean, it's shielded?

'The supernatural energy gets neutralised once people enter the house, and there's no way of telling if they are supernatural beings anymore.'

Did the shield have something to do with Freya? Had she placed one on the house because of Cassie? No – Jax would have known about it. It must be something different. 'How did you find this out?'

'Yesterday, when Leah, the girl Cassie lives with, came to pick her up, I sensed she was a witch, but her magical energy disappeared as soon as she walked into their house.'

'That's very strange.' I rubbed my scruffy beard, trying to make sense of it. 'What did Freya say about it?'

'She said an enchantment like that could only be done by ancient magic.'

So Freya hadn't placed it, but someone had. And it sounded like it had been placed to protect whoever was living there. From watching the fire, I knew there were more people living in that house. Maybe it was protecting one of them. Or maybe it had been placed to hide something more sinister. After all, I had seen Cassie surrounded by blue fire in my vision. Did this have something to do with it? 'What do you know about the other people that live in the house?'

Jax shrugged. 'I thought they were human, but now I'm second guessing myself. I'll have to ask Cassie about it. They've all lived together from a young age.'

I peered into Jax's eyes. Whatever the reason for the shield, he had one mission. 'Make sure she stays safe. I can't break the promise I made to Lily.'

Jax opened his mouth like he was about to say something but closed it again. Was he hiding something? I was about to ask him about it when he suddenly stood up. 'I must be off.'

I cocked an eyebrow, confused by his abrupt departure.

'By the way, Cassie seems to have developed an ability,' he said as he made his way towards the hallway. I got up and followed him as he continued talking. 'I'm trying to teach her, but I can't read other people's minds, so I don't know how much help I can be.'

Thoughts of how I had struggled to control my mind reading entered my head. For some reason, I couldn't read Jax's mind, even when I tried. But it was good that Cassie had confided in him. 'She trusts you, then.' I hesitated. It was something about the way he acted, like he wanted to tell me something but had thought better of it. But maybe I was reading too much into things. 'That's good. It'll make it easier for you. Just do what you can. The abilities will come to her when she needs them.'

Jax stopped at the door and turned to me. 'Like your abilities did?' he said with a grin.

I gave him a mischievous stare. 'They always seemed to work when we needed to get out of trouble.'

'Yeah, trouble that you caused by having them

malfunction.'

A smile appeared on my lips, and my heart felt lighter thinking back to all we'd been through together. 'You weren't that much better, if I remember correctly.'

Jax reached out and patted me on the back before opening the front door. 'Anyway, I better get back.'

'Let me know if you discover anything else. But Jax, next time just text me.' It seemed harsh, but the more he visited me, the higher the chance of someone finding out my connection with Cassie.

He frowned. 'Will that work?'

I smirked. 'You can turn into a crow and you're questioning why a phone works in another realm?' In all honesty, I had no idea how it worked. I knew my house was in Surtr's realm, but all the technology still worked like it did before the house had been moved. Jax shrugged and stepped through the door.

I closed it and thought about our conversation. This was a new development. Did the enchantments have something to do with the future I'd seen for Cassie? I went back to the fire and concentrated on finding out more about this enchantment, but no images appeared. Something or someone was blocking it. It made me uneasy. Was some ancient being after Cassie?

I reached out to Freya in the fire. As soon as I saw her face, I opened my mouth to speak, but she cut me off. 'I know what you are going to ask. But I do not know anything more than you do. It might not even be there for her.'

'But if anything happens to Cassie ...' I shook my head. I didn't even want to think about it.

'Was that not why you sent Jax to look after her?'

'Yes. But—'

'No buts. Trust that Jax can protect Cassie from whatever it is.'

'But what if someone is coming after her because of me?'

'Jax has given her a special necklace. As long as she is wearing it, her energy will be masked. No one knows she is your daughter. The being that placed the enchantment is there for something else.'

I wasn't sure if that was a relief or a worry, but I would do what Freya told me. I trusted Jax with my life. I just needed to trust he was strong enough to protect Cassie against whatever was coming.

The next day, Ant returned. 'I have some news to discuss with you. But I need to see my wife and child first. I've missed them so much.' He rushed through the house, the back door shutting behind him. I watched through the window as Dalia and Nicole came out to greet him with a smile. Nicole was only two and too young to understand why Ant wasn't around all the time. She was a lovely little girl, though I avoided her, mostly out of guilt, as she reminded me of what I could have had if Lily hadn't been killed and I hadn't sent Cassie away.

My phone vibrated, interrupting my thoughts. Jax had sent me a text asking if Lily had the ability of empathy and if she could feel others' emotions. I debated whether this had something to do with Cassie's abilities that had started to emerge and was about to text back when Ant came into the house.

'How much do you know about the keepers?'

I frowned. 'What keepers?' I tried to recall if there was anything about keepers in the books he'd given me.

Ant let out a sigh. 'The demon keepers. There's one for each direction. Ziminar of the north, Amayman of the east, Gaap of the south and Corson of the west. I thought you'd read up on the books I'd given you.'

I tried to recall what I'd read about them. 'They're guarding a seal.'

'It's not so much guarding as being forced to.'

'What do you mean?'

'The universe is made up of balance. In essence, there are two opposite forces, good and evil. During a mighty war that almost destroyed everything, the beings of light and dark agreed on a ceasefire. They implemented a balance structure and divided the universe into thousands of realms. These are the building blocks of our existence. The four most powerful beings, one on each side, would act as keys to four seals. If the seals were ever to open, it would cause all the different realms to collapse on each other and allow darkness beyond our imagination into the universe as well as the purest of light. It would be mayhem, as good and evil would fight for balance once again.'

'What does this have to do with who killed Lily?'

'I overheard some demons talking. One of them said something was put in motion to free one of the keepers. They mentioned Icarus's name and how he's a pawn in a game he doesn't understand.'

'So you think one of the keepers is responsible for Lily's

death?'

Ant shrugged. 'I don't know. But it's possible. Maybe it's worth reconsidering your revenge.'

'You're the one that said I needed to avenge Lily to be able to put my grief behind me, so whoever is behind it needs to pay.'

Ant rubbed his forehead. 'I ...' He shook his head and let out a breath. 'Okay. But if we're going down this road, I need to gather more information. I don't want to be wrong. Killing one of the keepers may not cause all the dimensions to merge, but it will have consequences. And it might be worth figuring out what those consequences are and who would benefit from it.'

# NICK

## THE KEEPERS

My hand hovered over the door handle to my and Lily's bedroom. It had taken me eight days since I'd received the text from Jax to work up the courage to enter the room. I tried to force myself to open the door, but my stomach felt hollow as I thought of what was waiting for me. A faint lingering aroma of Lily's perfume, freshly picked flowers that would now be dry and wilted. Not to mention Cassie's birthday gifts from when she turned one that she never got to enjoy. I took a deep breath. I had to do this. For Cassie. Lily had kept diaries about her life, her charges and her abilities, and as Cassie seemed to have taken after her mother in that department, I wanted her to have them. They might help her understand her abilities better and make her feel closer to her mother.

As I pushed the handle down, a crash sounded from the living room. What now? I rushed down the stairs, a fireball in my hand, ready to attack anyone that dared intrude into my home. Jax's voice sounded in my head as I reached the bottom of the stairs, and I extinguished the fire.

'What is this?' I asked, noticing the woman hanging over Jax's shoulder.

'This,' he said as he dropped the woman on the floor, 'is Cassie's foster mum. She's part of an organisation that's been stealing the powers of supernatural beings for a long time.'

Hatred filled me, and my darkness stirred, making my eyes shift colour. How had I not seen this before? She had been in Cassie's life since she was five, pretending to care for her and the other children. I wasn't sure what type of being she was, but I could sense the demon blood inside her. Was she the reason for what would have happened to Cassie in the future, had Jax not intervened and kept her safe? Why had Freya allowed her to be placed with this woman?

'You can't kill her,' Jax blurted out, picking up on my mood.

'Why not? It sounds like she deserves it.' Why was Jax being unreasonable? Any being that was out for blood deserved to be put down so they wouldn't do it again.

'She has information we need. I've got a shapeshifter that can't shift because of her and a whole group of witches that have lost their magic too.'

I took a deep breath to calm the darkness inside. 'I see. And Cassie?'

'She's safe,' Jax replied a little too quickly. He rubbed his head. 'She managed to escape before the fight.'

So Jax didn't know if she was truly safe. I glared at him before walking over to pick up the woman. 'I'll take her to the dungeon. I expect that's why you brought her here.'

Jax nodded, and I teleported away. Hopefully he'd get the hint and go to check on Cassie.

I walked along the stone hallway, passing doors as I went, and continued through the big wooden doors at the end. Jax had helped me create this place when he'd taught me about pocket dimensions. At the time, it hadn't been intended as a prison, but it had been useful during the early years when we needed to detain beings that were after us. Well, more likely me, but Jax never seemed to make that distinction.

I carried her into the dome-shaped enclosure that removed all magic – another thing Jax had taught me to create. She stirred as I dropped her onto the bed. I sneered. 'You're lucky Jax wanted you alive. If it was up to me, I'd make you pay.'

Fire burned in my veins. Jax hadn't said anything about her not being harmed, but I wasn't sure I could stop myself once I started. Besides, who knew how much pain a being like her could take before she succumbed? So, to avoid the temptation, I teleported back to the house.

I went over to the fire and searched for what had happened to Cassie. She was standing in what looked like a basement with another girl protectively behind her – the same girl Cassie had grown up with. The woman Jax had just dropped off threw an energy bolt towards them. Worry wrapped itself around me, but before the bolt hit them, the fire changed the scene. Cassie and the girl were now surrounded by trees. My worry eased, as she looked unharmed. Had Cassie teleported them away? I guessed that was what Jax had meant when he'd said they'd escaped before the fight broke out. I willed the fire to show me where Cassie was now. She was sitting on a sofa, her head on Jax's shoulder, surrounded by the other teenagers she had grown up with and a girl with dark features, about the same age, that I didn't recognise. It was so typical of Jax to protect everyone that needed it, whether they wanted it or not.

I paced the room. Ant should have been back by now. Had something happened to him? I tried scrying for him in the fire. There was an image of a stone castle, but he was nowhere to be seen. I threw my glass of whisky into the wall. Why didn't my abilities work when I needed them to?

When the doorbell rang, I hoped it was Ant coming back to tell me what he'd found out, but to my disappointment, I was greeted by Jax and the young lady I'd seen in the fire when Cassie and the others had been sitting on the sofa.

'Oh, it's you,' I said with a frown. It was less than two days since Jax had dropped the woman off. I left the door open and went back to the living room.

They took their time.

When they finally entered the living room, I sent out my senses to inspect the girl. I didn't detect any demon blood in her. How was that possible? She shouldn't have been able to enter this realm unharmed, though the lingering energy of magic probably had something to do with it. 'Who's this?'

'This is Sky, from the witch village,' Jax said.

I took a step towards her and her posture became rigid. She swallowed and followed my every move but made no attempt to talk. She appeared weak and powerless, but maybe she was hiding something or hiding her powers.

I turned to face Jax. 'Why is she here?' Even though I trusted Jax's judgement, it annoyed me that he had brought some random girl, a stranger, into my house.

'We've come to question Abigail. Sky is one of the children that had her magic sacrificed because of me.'

Abigail? Oh, he must be talking about the woman he dropped off. The one Cassie and the others had grown up with. I slapped his shoulder. 'Why didn't you just say so instead of wasting my time?' I didn't know what he had done to cause her magic to be sacrificed, but knowing Jax, he probably blamed himself for something that wasn't his fault. Once he'd got his wits back after being tortured by Surtr, he'd even apologised for that.

Jax rolled his eyes. 'What got your knickers in a twist?'

'I've got my own shit to deal with,' I mumbled, though I doubt he heard me.

'Would you mind taking us to her?' Jax asked.

'Give me a second.' I could have teleported them, but what if Ant came back while I was away? What if something had happened to him and I wasn't here to help? I made my way over to the closet door leading to the pocket dimension. 'She's in the room at the end, behind the giant doors.'

Jax nodded, and they both walked through the portal.

As I closed the door after Jax and the girl, the doorbell

went. I marched over to the front door and opened it. Ant's voice was full of excitement as he followed me into the living room. 'I overheard some demons talking about Corson, the keeper of the west, ordering the hit. Something about changing the future. I didn't understand exactly what they were talking about, but it was obvious he pulled the strings.'

'Thank you for letting me know. Do you know where we can find him?'

'Not yet. But maybe you should consider the repercussions of getting your revenge. It's not worth dying for.'

I frowned. 'Dying?'

'You struggled against Icarus. Besides, the keepers aren't your average demons. They're upper demons and just as powerful as your father. Normal weapons won't work on them. They are true immortals. They can't be killed.'

I scoffed. 'Everyone can be killed.' I headed toward the bookcase. 'You just need to know where to hit them and with what.'

Ant followed my gaze as he took a seat on the sofa. 'And how are you planning on finding that out?'

'I'm not sure, but there must be some weapon that can kill them.' I placed my fingers on top of the books, hoping to find one that might hold the answer.

'That won't be easy. Most of those weapons are a myth.'

'Doesn't mean they don't exist.'

# NICK

# THE DEAL WITH SURTR

I'd been pacing back and forth, trying to figure out how to find a weapon that could kill Corson, when my knees buckled under me and I struggled to breathe. It felt like someone had stabbed me in the chest, and it reminded me of the day I lost Lily. Cassie! I pulled myself up from the floor and dragged myself to the fireplace. Was Cassie okay? I took a deep breath, urging the fire to show me Cassie, while I prayed I was wrong.

The fire showed Jax in his demon form holding on to a lifeless Cassie. There was a wound in her chest and blood seeping out of it. Tears streamed down Jax's face as he looked at Freya, asking her to save Cassie. Freya rushed to his side and placed her hands over his claws. 'I cannot, but you can.

There is so much untapped power inside you. Open your heart and think about love, but whatever you do, do not give in to your hatred. I believe in you.'

I held my breath. I'd never seen Jax heal anyone. But slowly his form started to glow with a white light I was familiar with, and as it extended to Cassie, my body relaxed, knowing Jax had healed her. Her chest wound knitted itself together, and as she tried to get up, Jax embraced her and kissed her. She pulled back, seeming confused. 'Jax?' she asked, and when he nodded, she wrapped her arms around him and kissed him back. 'I love you,' she said.

'I love you too,' Jax replied.

I leaned back on the sofa, unsure how to process what I'd just seen. I should be angry. Jax was supposed to keep her safe, not fall in love with her. But seeing him conquer his demon and heal Cassie from the brink of death – well, I couldn't be anything but grateful. But it made me wonder about Jax's parentage. I knew he didn't know his parents, but demons didn't have the ability to heal. Only beings of light did.

I was half asleep on the sofa when the doorbell rang. I got up and went to answer the door. Jax stood in front of me. 'Social call or business?' I asked. I wondered if he was there to tell me about the fight that had gone down or to apologise for not letting me know sooner.

'Hi to you too,' Jax said as he looked around uncomfortably. 'I guess it's more of a social call.'

I smiled. 'Very well. I guess I have some time.' I opened the door further to let him inside. 'Sorry about the other day.

I wasn't expecting you to drop by, and I was waiting to hear back from my scouts. I'm getting closer, you know.'

Jax rubbed his neck. 'Closer to what?'

'To figuring out who was responsible for Lily's death. Just waiting for my source to confirm it.' I took a seat on the sofa. 'So, how is Cassie doing? Any new abilities I should know about?'

'Her main ones are still mind control and empathy. But she's been practising her telepathy and teleportation skills too.'

'Anything else you want to tell me?' I tried to remain casual to see how much he was going to share.

Jax stayed quiet for a while. 'We ran into some trouble with Hecate and I almost lost her.'

His eyes were on me. Maybe he expected me to get angry, but watching him conquer his inner demon to save Cassie had made me realise I'd made the right decision asking him to look after her. I wouldn't need to worry about Cassie. Jax would die to keep her safe. 'Well, it's a good thing you were there to protect her, then. Maybe I need to pay Hecate a visit.'

Jax shook his head. 'No need. She's gravely injured.'

I gave him a nod. 'So why are you here? Because we both know it's not just to tell me about everything that went down with Hecate, because if it was, you would have come sooner.' I remained serious as I gestured towards the fireplace, reminding him I did have the ability to see things in the fire. 'Don't think just because I'm not around that I'm not up to speed with what's happening.'

Jax seemed to be lost in thought, so I cleared my throat to get his attention. He glanced over at me and ran his hand through his hair. 'I have some news about me and Cassie.'

'Oh. You mean my daughter you were supposed to look after, not fall in love with.' I gave him a smile so he knew I didn't have any bad feelings towards him. 'I want her to be happy, and even though I'm not sold on the idea that my best friend is planning to spend eternity with my daughter, I can't blame either of you. The heart wants what the heart wants. After all, I would be foolish to tell you otherwise. I wouldn't have been with my beautiful Lily if I'd added logic to the equation.'

Jax's body relaxed, and he returned my smile. 'Thank you, Nick. It really means a lot to me.'

I glared into his eyes. 'However, if you hurt her, I will hunt you down,' I said in a stern voice. After all, it was my responsibility, as Cassie's father, to make sure she remained safe.

He placed his hand over his heart. 'I will protect her with my life.'

'Good.' I thought about Lily and how upset she had been when her parents had refused to give us their blessing when we got married. 'I do have one request. I would like to see my daughter first and personally give you both my blessing. It was a tradition Lily's people used to do, and as they denied her it due to marrying me, it would mean a lot to me if I can do it for you, to carry on the tradition in Lily's honour. It's what Lily would have wanted.'

Jax smiled. 'It would be my pleasure. Like you said, we have eternity together, so there's no reason to stress about anything. I'll bring Cassie with me once it's safe.'

She wouldn't be safe around me until I killed Corson.

I got up from the sofa, as I sensed Ant entering the garden from the alleyway. 'Duty calls. My scouts are back with confirmation and Corson's whereabouts.'

Jax froze, and his eyes went wide. 'Corson, as in the demon keeper of the west?'

'Yes.'

A look of concern crossed his face. 'The keepers are forces that shouldn't be messed with.'

'If Corson is responsible for Lily's death, they will pay.'

'You ... you can't kill him.'

I sighed. Jax was always the bigger person, but I wasn't Jax, and my wife deserved retribution. 'I'll find a way.'

'Please be careful. No revenge is worth ending the world for.' He patted me on the shoulder before stepping out of the door.

I clenched my jaw. Jax was wrong. I wouldn't end the world. I wasn't planning on killing all the keepers, just the one responsible for destroying my family.

I should have gone to see Ant, but Jax's last comment spun around in my head. *Ending the world.* My father was destined to end the world. He was forever forging his sword, which was foretold to be responsible for killing gods and burning the world down when Ragnarök took place. That sword was exactly what I needed to kill Corson.

I took a deep breath, summoning my courage, and teleported myself to the middle of the realm.

I scanned the area. The air made my eyes burn and my throat dry as I took in the red sky and wretched landscape around me. The ground consisted of black sand and porous rocks, a stark contrast to my back garden. Despite it having moved to Surtr's realm, Lily's plants and flowers were still flourishing and the grass remained green and healthy. Here, nothing grew, not even a single tree. There were just jagged mountains and volcanoes. At least none of them were currently active.

The clinking of stone on metal echoed in my head from Surtr crafting his sword on the anvil. The first and last time I'd been here, when I'd rescued Jax, he'd been working on the same sword. You would have thought he'd have finished it by now.

Surtr put down the sword and the hammer on a rock next to him that served as a table and glanced my way as I approached with caution. He was a mighty beast almost twice my height. His body looked to be made of molten rock, with amber lava floating underneath. He raised his hands towards me. 'My child. Have you finally come to join my army?'

I stopped and stared at him, wary of getting too close. 'I need to borrow your sword.'

Surtr laughed in my face. 'If you think I'm going to let you borrow my sword, think again.' His black eyes stared into my soul. 'The sword can only be wielded by me.'

I was worried he might lash out, but I refused to back down or show him any weakness, despite the quiver in my stomach.

Surtr had had a chance to kill me before, but he hadn't, so I had to believe he wouldn't kill me now. I swallowed and took a step forward, staring up into his black eyes. 'I need something that can kill a true immortal.'

He chuckled. 'That's a fool's errand. There is a reason

why we are called true immortals. You are better off staying here and training with my army until Ragnarök starts. Nothing else will matter then.'

'Avenging my wife matters to me. He killed my wife. He has to pay.'

Surtr remained quiet for a while as he poked around in the fire next to him. 'Emotions are nothing but a distraction. But I will tell you about another sword that has the power to kill a true immortal, but I want something in return.'

I crossed my arms. 'What do you want?'

'You know what I want. For you to willingly join my army.' He picked up his sword and placed it in the fire.

I didn't want to join his army. I never had. But I needed that sword. I let out a sigh. 'I will join your army and fight with you during Ragnarök as long as I get to kill Corson first.'

He raised his hands. 'Where's my guarantee? You know I cannot leave this place. Give me part of your flame so I can summon you,' he commanded.

The irony. I had been living in his realm, under his nose, for years without him having a clue about it. 'If I give you my flame, how do I know you will honour our deal and not summon me as soon as I leave?'

Surtr became thoughtful. 'Sinmara,' he yelled, making me jump.

Smoke collected on the ground and turned into a woman. Dark tendrils covered her like a dress, her face pale as a ghost. I recognised her from the dreams I used to have as a teenager – dreams that told me to seek out my father and take my rightful place in his army.

Surtr gestured towards her. 'Sinmara can create a flame oath. It cannot be broken by either party.'

Demons could not be trusted, but I knew even though Surtr wanted nothing more than for me to join his army, he had never forced me, and he had let me leave this realm before. He couldn't keep me there against my will, but this flame oath would change that. 'Tell me about the weapon.'

'Not until the flame oath is completed.'

If I went through with it, I'd have given up my freedom. Not that I had much freedom as it was, but I would have given up the opportunity to get to know my daughter. Maybe this wasn't such a great idea after all. But while my grief attracted demons, I couldn't see Cassie. It wouldn't be safe for her. And the only way to deal with my grief was to avenge Lily, so I needed that sword. I gritted my teeth and gave Sinmara a nod. 'Okay. I'll do it.'

She took hold of my hand and did the same with Surtr. 'Now summon your flames.'

I conjured my blue flame as Surtr's amber one appeared in his hand. If he thought anything about my flame being blue, he didn't show it.

Sinmara transferred the flames to her hands and brought them together. 'When Corson is hit by the Dauđans, the flame of Nicklause, son of Surtr, shall belong to our army, ready to march when Ragnarök starts. As the flames mix, so shall it be.' The two flames engulfed each other and became a green one. A glass orb appeared around the flame, enveloping it and sealing my fate away.

I turned to Surtr with a frown. 'Dauđans? Is that the

weapon I need?'

'Yes.'

'How can I get my hands on it?'

'The sword is hidden in the biggest volcano in the most hostile fire realm.'

I let out a sigh. 'So you don't actually know where it is? You said you'd get me a weapon that could kill a true immortal.'

A smirk appeared on Surtr's face. 'I told you I would tell you about a weapon that could kill a true immortal. I never said I'd get it for you. I am bound by this realm, so even if I wanted to, I cannot get it for you. Now let me get back to amending my sword.' He got the sword out of the fire and placed it on the anvil before picking up a hammer.

I slumped in defeat. 'Thanks for nothing,' I mumbled, teleporting myself home. This had been a waste of time.

# JAX

## Sky's Vision

A melody started playing in my head. It infiltrated my dream and became louder and louder until it woke me up. A moment later, I realised the sound was coming from my phone. I reached over to answer it, amazed Cassie was still sound asleep.

'Hello.'

Mark's desperate voice sounded on the other end. 'Jax. Something's wrong with Sky again, but this is different. She's in hysterics. I can't get through to her, and I don't know what to do. She keeps saying the world is going to end because someone has taken a sword. You need to help her.'

'I'll be over in a second.' I hung up the phone and rubbed the sleep from my eyes. Freya had told me to pay attention to

Sky's dreams, as some of them were visions. Last time Sky had got stuck in a vision, she'd struggled to wake up, but Mark had said she was in hysterics. Would a vision be able to do that to her, or was this related to something else?

Wanting to check on Sky as soon as I could, I kissed Cassie on the head and left her a note, knowing very well she'd have a go at me later for not waking her up and telling her about Sky. But she looked so beautiful in her sleep, I didn't want to disturb her. I got dressed and teleported over to the wooden cabin.

I arrived in the dark living room. Thick curtains covered the windows, but it wouldn't have made much difference to the light, as it was still dark outside. Mark looked up from where he was pacing back and forth, biting his knuckles next to a door that was ajar. 'Took you long enough.' The light from the bedroom illuminated his worried face.

'Good morning to you too.'

He grunted and led me into the bedroom. The ceiling light shone on Sky, who was sitting up on the bed, rocking back and forth and mumbling to herself, tears streaming down her face. Mark continued to pace as I stepped towards her. Her gaze was on me, but there was no recognition in her dark brown eyes, just a blank expression as she stared into space. 'How long has she been like this?' I asked as I sent out my senses. I detected nothing unusual, which probably confirmed that this was caused by whatever vision she was having.

Mark stopped moving and glanced over at Sky, the worry over his mate clearly visible in his pained gaze. 'I'm not sure. She was like that when I woke up. I tried to wake her. Shake her out of it. But she wasn't responding. So I called you.'

I placed a hand on her shoulder, stopping her rocking movement. 'Sky?'

'The world is going to end. Someone has taken the sword,' she mumbled.

'What sword?' I asked. I tried to give her some of my energy by visualising it flowing into her like last time.

'The sword in the volcano.'

I removed my hand from her shoulder and sat down on the bed next to her, taking her hands in mine to help the flow of energy reach her. 'What sword? And why is it in the volcano?'

'The world is going to end,' she whispered. 'Someone has taken the sword. The sword in the volcano.'

I looked over at Mark. 'I'm not getting through to her.'

Mark pulled at his short ginger hair. 'Try harder. You got her to wake up the first time she had a vision. Why can't you do the same thing now?'

I sighed. The first time she'd got stuck in a vision was after we'd come back from a hell dimension. I'd transferred some of my energy to her, which had woken her up. But this time around, it felt like something was blocking the flow of energy from reaching her, like she was too immersed in whatever vision she was having. 'I am, but it's not working.'

Mark let out a growl. 'You're obviously not trying hard enough.'

'Reel it in, Mark.' I knew he couldn't really help it, as he was a werewolf and his first instinct was to hate my kind, but I thought he would have come to trust me by now. 'I know you're stressed and worried, but I'm trying to help.'

'Sorry,' he mumbled.

I acknowledged his apology with a glance and readjusted Sky's hands in mine, determined to give it one more try. Taking a deep breath, I closed my eyes and concentrated on building up more energy inside myself. I visualised the energy moving out of me and forcing itself into Sky, like a stream merging with a lake.

She became quiet, and her movements stilled. I willed more energy into Sky and opened my eyes.

Mark pushed past me and shook her gently. Nothing happened. She still wasn't responding. A moment later, she started rocking again, repeating the same words over and over.

Mark hugged her tightly to stop her from rocking. 'Why isn't it working?'

'Something's blocking it.'

He looked at me with big, pleading eyes. 'Then unblock it. I'm begging you. She's my everything.'

'I can't.' I was already feeling the drain from giving away too much energy. If I were to give her any more, I would pass out. 'I gave her as much energy as I could manage.'

'No. It's not good enough. You need to fix her.' He slumped down by the bed, his elbows resting on the mattress and his head in his hands, soft sobs escaping him.

Mark's younger brother, Seth, opened the door. 'Is everything okay?' His eyes moved to Sky and then to Mark before meeting my gaze. 'What happened? What's wrong with Sky?'

'I don't know. She's stuck in a vision.' I glanced over at Mark. 'I'll go and see Freya. I'm sure she'll know what to do.'

Mark gave me a tense nod, brushing a strand of Sky's black hair away from her face. 'You're okay. I'm not going to let anything happen to you. We'll find a way to bring you back.'

I felt a sharp pang as I remembered almost losing Cassie, and I empathised with the agony Mark must be enduring. I blinked away a tear before teleporting to Freya's realm. The sun shone brightly in the sky. I turned into a crow and flew above the forests and lakes to reach her house. How I wished I could teleport directly to her house, but only Freya and her familiars could.

Up ahead, the forest opened up and revealed her wooden cottage with a large wooden veranda in a clearing surrounded by birch trees. As I approached, she stepped outside to greet me.

I landed on the veranda and transformed back into my human form. 'Something's wrong with Sky.'

'Yes, I am aware.' Her brow creased with concern as she placed a bracelet in my hands. 'Give this to Sky. It will help her. Now, what did she see?'

I opened my mouth to ask how she knew but closed it again. Of course she knew about Sky, just like she seemed to know about everything else that was going on.

Freya made her way to the chairs on the veranda. I followed her. 'She said someone has taken a sword that will end the world.'

'There are a lot of swords that could be said to play a part in the ending of the world. Did she say anything else?' She conjured up a teapot and two cups, filled the cups and handed one to me.

'She said the sword is in a volcano,' I said as I took the cup from her.

Freya took a deep breath, her eyes growing wide. She almost looked frightened, though I'd never seen her scared of anything.

'It might be the Dauðans.'

I frowned. 'What's that?'

'A sword created by the svartalfs, though they are better known as dwarfs, with the intention of killing Fenrir when his binding fails to hold him.'

'Why would they do that?'

She took a sip of her tea before she answered. 'Fenrir was originally chained because of Odin's recurring dream of Fenrir killing him. But the prophecy now states that when Fenrir breaks free of the chains placed on him, Ragnarök will be upon us and almost all the gods and goddesses will be killed as the world resets itself. But Odin thought that if there was a way to kill Fenrir as he broke through the bonds, Ragnarök could be avoided and the world as we know it would stay the same.'

I scratched my neck. 'Why was it hidden away? Wouldn't it make more sense to keep it guarded?'

'The future cannot be changed without consequences.' For a moment pain flashed in Freya's eyes, and I wondered if she'd learned that the hard way. She broke eye contact and started stirring her tea before she continued. 'The sword became too powerful and could not be destroyed. So the safest thing was to hide it away.'

'Do we know who took it or how to stop it?'

Freya's eyes glazed over. I sat back, drinking my tea as I

waited for her vision to finish.

Several minutes passed before she spoke again. 'The Daudans is yet to be stolen. So I might be wrong. Maybe there is another sword at play.'

'What other sword can it be?'

'I do not know. That is the only sword I know that is hidden in a volcano.' She put her hand over the one I was holding the bracelet in. 'Do not forget to give that to Sky. Hopefully she will give you more information once she wakes up. Remember, she had this vision for a reason. Everything is connected.'

I kissed her cheeks before transforming into a crow once more and setting out over the forest. The clouds were moving in and the wind ruffled my feathers, but it did nothing to help the overwhelming feeling that the fate of the world rested on my shoulders.

# NICK

## The Search

I got back from Surtr with a feeling of betrayal. I had gone there hoping to return with an object capable of killing Corson. Surtr had tricked me. I wasn't any closer to killing Corson. All Surtr had given me was the name of a sword hidden in the biggest volcano in a hostile realm. How would I even know which realm to search? There were thousands of them.

I reached for a leather-bound book in the bookcase that contained information about the realms. The book stated the universe was made up of more realms than one could count, from heavenly to hellish and everything in between, mirroring a delicate balance of light and dark, creation and destruction. I hoped it would mention specific dimensions that existed and how to reach them, but it didn't.

I cursed and threw the book on the floor. Useless. I ran my finger over the spines in the bookcase, searching for another book Ant had given me, hoping it held the answers I sought.

Several books later, a knock sounded at the back door. 'Come in,' I shouted as I threw another useless book onto the floor. I didn't need to read minds to know it was Ant coming to check up on me.

'Where have you been? I thought you'd come over when your friend left,' Ant said as he walked into the living room.

'I had something I needed to do.'

He stopped and looked around. 'What are you doing? Why are all the books on the floor?'

'I'm trying to find out about the different realms that exist.'

He stepped over some books and took a seat on the sofa. 'How come?'

'Surtr said the sword I need is hidden in another realm.'

Ant's eyes went wide. 'You went to see your father?'

I gave him a darting gaze. 'I needed answers.'

'And did you get them?'

I let out a sigh. 'Not really. Only that the sword is hidden in another realm.'

'And what sword is that?'

'The Dauðans.'

Ant's mouth fell open and he took a deep breath. 'The sword of fire. Also known as the Deathbringer.'

I looked up at him with hopeful eyes. 'You know about it?'

'I know the myth.' Ant's brow furrowed. 'I don't think you should go down this path.'

'Why? You're the one that insisted I need my revenge to put my grief behind me.'

'They don't call it the Deathbringer for nothing. Did your father tell you where to find it?'

'No.'

'I see. And that's why you've been going through the books?' He picked up some of the books scattered around the living room and placed them back in the bookcase where they belonged. 'I doubt you'll find the answer in any of these. If the Dauðans is real, the information you seek will only be known to a select few.'

I raised an eyebrow. 'Your point?'

'It's not going to be easily accessible. Exactly what did Surtr tell you?'

'He told me the sword was hidden in the biggest volcano in a hostile realm.'

Ant scratched his forehead. 'A hostile environment, you say? If the sword is made of fire and in a volcano, it makes sense it's in a fire realm. You're sure it's not hidden in this one?'

'He said he's unable to get it for me, as he can't leave his realm.'

'Could he be lying? After all, Surtr is a fire giant known to the dwarfs.'

I frowned. 'What do the dwarfs have to do with it?'

Ant shook his head in disappointment. 'The myth states they were the ones who created the sword.'

'If the dwarfs made it, why did they hide it away?'

'It's known as the Deathbringer, so I'm sure they had their reasons.'

'What realm do you think it could be in?'

Ant became thoughtful. 'A sword of that much power will be hidden somewhere people don't normally travel to. If I remember the story correctly, a group of dwarfs set out to hide it away from everything, but they never came back. So your guess is as good as mine. Know any realms that might fit that description?'

'None except this one.'

Ant's eyes widened. 'You haven't been to any other realms?'

I shrugged. 'I grew up human. Fell in love with an angel who loved the human world. And my friend got hurt finding out who my father was. I didn't want anyone else to get hurt, so I stopped caring about where I came from or why I was created. It wasn't worth it. I was happy just living my life until they killed my light.' I sat down on the sofa. 'I was hoping the books would give me some ideas about the different realms it might be in.'

'You don't need books to tell you about realms. You just need to think about where you want to go and then you're there.'

'But how can I go somewhere if I don't know where this somewhere is or what it looks like?'

'The same way you teleported to Icarus.'

'Scrying in the fire doesn't work. I've already tried.'

'I didn't mean that part. How do you normally teleport?'

'I visualise the place, imagine being there and then I am.'

'Exactly, so just think about where you want to go and

then teleport.'

'But I don't know where I want to go.'

'That's not true. You know you want to go to a hostile fire realm. How do you think I move around? I'd admit it's a little risky, because you don't really know where you'll end up, but it's a great way to explore new places or lose an enemy. Besides, most of the time you can just teleport home if need be.'

I frowned. 'Most of the time?'

'Well, I've had a few close calls, but as you can see, I'm still here. You should give it a go.'

'Okay, but you're coming with me.' I placed my hand on Ant's shoulder and thought about a hostile realm where the sword might be.

We materialised in an eerie landscape. Several suns were visible in the sky, giving out a low glow, almost like twilight. All the colours were off. Something that looked like black grass grew on the ground, and there were what looked like puddles of water, but they were dark maroon. It made me uneasy. The trees had blue leaves, and the branches hung low, almost like some invisible force had weighed them down.

I scanned the area. A group of large black creatures were sitting at the top of a tree. It was hard to make out their forms, but they reminded me of Jax's demon shape, with large black wings and beaks – maybe they were related? Jax had always wanted to know where he came from. Maybe this information could help him.

'Do you think it's here?' Ant asked, breaking me out of my thoughts.

I shrugged. 'I wouldn't know.'

'But you're a fire demon and the sword is made of fire.'

'That doesn't mean I can feel where fires are located.'

'But what does your gut tell you?'

I glanced over the landscape again. One of the creatures in the tree opened its red eyes and stared at us. It let out a shriek, and the others opened their eyes too. I took a step back and placed a hand on Ant's shoulder. 'I think it's time to get out of here.'

He followed my gaze. 'Good point. Let's try another place.'

I thought about a fire realm, hoping I'd have better luck. We arrived on rocky terrain, with several volcanos visible in the distance.

'This is a bit more promising,' Ant said.

I nodded in response as I looked around. 'Wow, look at those massive pinecones. It looks like they're on fire.' I edged closer to examine it.

'I don't think they're pinecones. There's no trees nearby.'

As soon as I touched one, it let out a shriek. Big black eyes stared right back at me. 'I guess you're right,' I said as I backed away from it. It rose up and brushed one of its front legs along the ground.

'Nick, we need to go.' Ant's voice was filled with fear. 'Run!' he shouted as the burning pinecone started charging at us, along with the others that had woken up.

I caught up with Ant. 'Was this what you were talking about when you said you'd had a few near misses?'

'Yeah. We just need to get away from them so we can

teleport away from here.'

We continued to run over the uneven terrain, pursued by the pinecone animals. I desperately looked around for a tree or something we could climb, but there was nothing. Then I spotted a boulder in the distance. I pointed towards it and shouted to Ant, 'If we can get to that boulder, we'll have time to teleport away.'

I overtook Ant, and we were almost at the boulder when he let out a scream. I turned around. He was lying on the ground, holding his leg. The pinecones were closing in. Without thinking, I rushed back to Ant and summoned my sword. There were too many of them for me to win, but I wasn't going to leave Ant behind.

One of them bit Ant's leg. He screamed in pain. I shot it with my fire, but it did nothing. I slid over and stabbed it with my sword, and it released Ant. He scrambled to his feet as the pinecones surrounded us. 'We need to get out of here. I'll hold them back, and you concentrate on teleporting us away,' I said to him as I stabbed another pinecone that tried to bite us.

It didn't take long for Ant to get the concentration he needed to teleport us back. We landed on my front porch. I let out a breath. 'That was a close call.'

'Yeah. We almost became food.' Ant sat down and ripped off part of his tunic to tie around his leg. 'Thanks for coming back for me.'

'That's what friends are for. Let's get inside before I attract more demons that want to kill us.' I offered him my hand to help him up, then opened the door and supported him to the sofa. 'Will you be okay?' I asked, looking at his leg, which was dripping with blood.

Ant gave me a smile. 'I told you, I heal quickly. It's really the only thing I have going for me. Just let me clean it so it doesn't become infected and I should be as good as new in a couple of days.'

I conjured up some gauze and chlorhexidine and handed it to him. 'There must be a better and easier way to find where the sword might be located,' I said.

Ant started to clean his wound. 'Maybe you need to go back to Surtr and ask.'

'No.' I shook my head, thinking about the oath I'd made to Surtr and what else he would demand from me if I asked for more favours. 'He could have told me where it was, but he didn't. There needs to be another way. I just have to figure it out.'

'I'm sure there is.' Ant finished bandaging up his wound. 'Once my leg is better, I'll see if I can find anything about the sword, now that I know it's not a myth.'

# JAX

## The Daudans

Cassie and Leah were sitting on the sofa with Seth when I arrived back at the cabin. I went over to the sofa to give Cassie a kiss, and Mark marched out of the bedroom. 'What did she say? Can she help?'

I held up the bracelet Freya had given me. 'She told me to give this to Sky.'

Mark shook his head in disbelief. 'How is that going to help her? I was expecting some magical potion or something, not a bracelet.'

Leah rolled her eyes. 'Don't be so dismissive. It's probably infused with magic.'

I nodded. 'Leah's right. Freya wouldn't have given it to me if she didn't think it was going to help get Sky out of her vision.'

He snatched the bracelet from my hand and hurried back to the bedroom. We all followed.

Mark stroked some hair away from Sky's face and gently held her hand as he placed the bracelet on her wrist. Despite the bracelet, Sky was still rocking back and forth, mumbling to herself.

'It's not working. Why isn't it working?'

Leah placed her hand on Mark's shoulder. 'You're being impatient. Have some faith. Sometimes it takes a bit of time to work.'

We stood in silence as we watched Sky. Slowly, her movements stopped, along with her mumbling. Her breathing slowed, and a moment later she opened her eyes and looked around. Mark embraced her and kissed her head. She pulled away and cleared her throat. 'We need to stop him.'

'Stop who?' Cassie asked.

'I'm not sure. They looked like they were made of coal or stone. Some sort of fire being. They didn't seem bothered by the rough terrain or the environment. Even in my vision, I struggled to breathe because of the smoke. But the fire being just plodded along and climbed up the volcano, unaffected by the smoke and lava surrounding them.'

'You mentioned a sword earlier. Do you know what sword it was? Or what it looked like?' I asked.

'No, but it was in a volcano, and when the being emerged with it, it was on fire.'

'Freya seems to think it's the Daudans.'

Leah furrowed her brow. 'The what?'

'A sword created to kill Fenrir,' I answered.

Seth looked at me with wide eyes. 'Fenrir's real? I thought that was just a story to scare children.'

Mark frowned at Seth. 'Who's Fenrir? And how do you know about them?'

'The wolves. They talked about him during story hour. He's the son of the god Loki, a monstrous wolf that most of the gods were afraid of. The wolves use him as a cautionary tale – never think you're invincible. Even the most powerful wolf can be chained.'

'Huh?' Mark said, scratching his head.

'Fenrir thought he was invincible. He let the gods chain him up, only to break the chains in a show of strength and power, but while trying to show off a third time, he got tricked and the gods used an enchanted ribbon to bind him that was impossible to break.'

Seth looked like he was about to say something more, but I waved my arms in the air to get everyone's attention. 'Guys, we're getting off track. We need to figure out who's after the sword so we can stop it.'

'I thought the sword had already been stolen,' Leah said.

'Freya said the Dauðans still remains where it was hidden. So either they haven't taken it yet or Sky's vision is about another sword.'

'How does she know the sword hasn't been taken?'

I shrugged. 'I don't know. But she always knows more than she lets on. I think she can see the future.'

'If she can see the future, why doesn't she just tell us what to do?' Leah asked.

I had asked Freya the exact same thing when Abigail had

taken Leah. I let out a sigh. 'I don't think it's that simple.'

'Jax is right,' Sky said. 'I overheard Freya and Hecate talking about something before the fight broke out in the temple at Whitelake village. How Freya had tried to intervene before, but it changed everything.'

I guess that explained a thing or two. I shook my head to get back to the task at hand. 'Cassie and Leah, check if the witch village has any books about fire beings. Maybe Sky will recognise one of them as the creature stealing the sword. And if it really is the Daudans, then maybe see if you can find any books about the myths.' I glanced over at Mark and Sky. 'Stay here. And when Sky feels up for it, write down everything you remember about the vision.' I turned to Seth. 'You said the wolves know about Fenrir. See what information you can find out from them.'

'Sure, I'll be back in a bit,' Seth said and left the cabin.

Mark frowned. 'Isn't that a bit pointless?'

I shrugged. 'I thought it'd make him feel like part of the team and feel like he's contributing without putting him in any danger.'

Cassie smiled. 'That's very sweet of you. What are you going to do?'

'I'm going to pay my friend Baqer a visit. If anyone knows about swords that can end the world, it's him.'

Cassie gazed into my eyes. 'Please be careful.'

'You too,' I said. I gave her a kiss before teleporting away.

I appeared in the industrial estate where Baqer kept his shop. When I stepped inside, Baqer came out from behind the counter and greeted me with the customary cheek kisses. He was wearing his signature white tunic and headscarf known as a keffiyeh.

'Jax, my brother. How lovely to see you again. Did your lady friend like the book?'

I smiled. 'Yes, thank you. It was very helpful. However, I have another favour to ask.'

'Of course. How can I help?'

'I have reason to believe a magical sword that's been hidden away is about to be stolen. I need to know which sword it is so I can stop the world from ending.'

'I need a bit more information. There are many swords that can end the world in the wrong hands. Caladbolg, Shamshire-e-Zomorrodnegar, Skofnung, Kusanagi-no-Tsurugi, Moralltach and Excalibur to name a few.'

I let out a sigh. 'You sound just like Freya.'

At the mention of Freya, his face lit up. 'How is the goddess? I haven't heard from her since the war.'

I shrugged. 'She's good. Just as secretive as always.'

He gave me a knowing nod. 'I'm glad she's doing well.' He cleared his throat. 'Tell me more about this sword.'

'It's hidden in a volcano and made of fire.'

Baqer sucked in a breath, his face pale and his eyes big. 'The only sword I'm aware of that's made of fire and hidden in a volcano is the Dauđans. How do you know it has not been taken already?'

'Freya.'

Baqer nodded in relief.

'What's so special about the Dauđans? Freya mentioned it was created to kill Fenrir. I understand having a sword that can kill anything is dangerous, but how's it causing the end of the world?'

'Ahh. I take it you haven't heard the whole myth.' Baqer walked over to a large bookcase and pulled down a scroll. 'This is the myth of the Dauđans. The sword created by the dwarfs. Odin demanded they create a sword strong enough to kill Fenrir so he can be killed once he breaks through the enchanted ribbons that hold him, in the hope of preventing Ragnarök and the end of the world as we know it. The dwarfs started crafting sword after sword, all infused with different magic, hoping one of them would have the ability to cut Fenrir, but they all failed. They were ready to give up when they came up with the idea of infusing the sword with the eternal flame, so they stole some from Surtr and created the sword. They tried it on Fenrir and cut one of his ears off. The bleeding eventually stopped, and the wound healed with time, but they knew they had succeeded. Surtr learned about the eternal flame they had stolen and became enraged.'

The thought of Surtr tormenting me entered my mind, and I shivered. 'Did he retaliate?'

'No, but he would have killed the dwarfs had he not been confined to Muspelheim. Surtr told them they had no idea about the forces they were playing with. The dwarfs didn't take him seriously and kept the sword, but the word had spread, and many creatures tried to get their hands on it. They gave it to Tyr, the god of war and justice. They knew he was fair and wouldn't let it get into the wrong hands. However, as time passed, Tyr became more ruthless and killed everyone around him, whether they deserved it or not. The sword seemed to have changed him. The dwarfs stole the sword back from Tyr and tried to destroy it, but it had become indestructible, feeding on the life forces of the people it killed, gaining more power.'

I listened with interest. 'So the sword is a being in itself?'

'Not really, but there's a reason why it got its name. Daudans means "of death", and it's also known as the Deathbringer, because no one has managed to wield it without losing part of their soul. That's why a group of dwarfs took it upon themselves to hide the sword away, so it couldn't cause any more harm. Because of its power, it needed to be hidden where no creature would stumble upon it. The group was never heard of again, but rumour has it they found an uninhabitable fire realm and threw it inside a massive volcano. Some say their spirits still guard it.'

'But how would anyone know where it is?'

'Sometimes I forget how young you are. The eternal flame calls to Surtr. He would be able to sense where it is. If you're looking for whoever is planning on stealing it, it may be worth asking Surtr about it.'

A chill went down my spine. 'I'd rather not. The last time I saw Surtr, he tortured me to get to my friend.'

Baqer tilted his head. 'That does not sound like Surtr. He only cares about his kind.'

'Well ... my friend is his son,' I said as I rubbed my neck.

'Then maybe he can help instead.'

I gave Baqer a pat on the back. 'Thank you for the history lesson.'

# NICK

## Eternal Flame

I stared at the fire in the hearth. The scrying was completely useless. All it showed me was the sword lying on a massive flat boulder surrounded by magma. It had a metal hilt wrapped in what looked like leather, with runes engraved on it, but it was impossible to see what the runes said. The pommel held a round fire opal and the guard appeared to be a wolf's head, and from its jaws, the blade emerged. It was a jagged blade, and the glow of the magma was reflected in the metal.

I tried to teleport to it, but nothing happened. Frustration welled up inside me. The idea of going back to my father filled me with dread. Who knew what he would demand to tell me more about the location of the sword? I'd already given up my freedom. There needed to be another way.

The doorbell rang, snapping me back to reality.

Jax stood on the other side of the threshold. I held my breath. Had he figured out what I was up to?

'Are you here to tell me Cassie has refused your hand in marriage?' I said, my voice laced with sarcasm.

Jax smirked. 'No. Me and Cassie are good, but I need a favour.'

I gestured for him to come inside. 'What favour do you need?'

'It's come to my attention someone is trying to steal a sword which has the power to end the world,' he said as he followed me into the living room. 'Ever heard of the Daudans?'

My heart skipped a beat. Did he know what I was up to? I swallowed and took a seat on the sofa, hoping my face wouldn't betray me. 'No, I never heard of it. Should I?'

'My source said Surtr could locate it and feel its presence, as it's made of his eternal flame. I need to talk to him so I can stop whoever is planning on taking the sword, but we both know I won't put a foot near Surtr.'

'What do you want me to do?'

'Have you spoken to Surtr lately?'

I shook my head, trying to keep my expression neutral. 'No. Last time I saw him was with you.' I hated lying to my best friend, but there was no way I could tell him what I'd been up to. He wouldn't understand. Instead of helping me get my revenge, he would stop me.

'Would you mind talking to him? Maybe he knows

who's after it.'

I hesitated, the conversation with Surtr replaying in my head. I wouldn't put another foot near him unless I didn't have another choice. 'Because it's you asking, I'll go and talk to him, but I doubt it'll be helpful. He doesn't seem to care about anything but his sword and his army.' Guilt gnawed at my insides for lying to him again.

Jax opened his mouth but closed it again. He ran his hand through his hair. 'You haven't picked up on anything unusual?'

I cocked my head. 'What do you mean by unusual?'

Jax shrugged. 'I don't know. I just thought. You're Surtr's son. If he can feel the eternal flame inside the sword, maybe you can too.'

Excitement bubbled up inside me at the thought of being able to find the sword, but I did my best to contain it. 'I haven't felt anything unusual.'

'Are you sure?' Jax's eyes searched mine. Their intensity made my heart race.

'I'm sure,' I said as another bout of guilt turned my stomach. But this time, I wasn't lying.

Jax stood up. 'I must get back. Let me know if something comes up.'

I gave him a smile. 'I will.'

He made his way out to the hallway, and I followed him to the door. 'Take care of yourself,' he said as he leaned forward into a hug and patted my back.

'You too,' I replied.

After Jax left, I let out a breath of relief and went back to plotting. I hadn't managed to find information about the sword in any of the books, and we hadn't had much luck trying to search through realms for it. Going back to Surtr was my last resort, but maybe I didn't need to. Jax had said I was connected to the flame inside the sword somehow. Maybe I could use that to track it down.

I recalled what Ant had told me about teleporting to other realms and took a deep breath before closing my eyes. Reaching inside myself, I visualised the core of my being. I was a fire giant made of eternal flame – the same eternal flame that was infused in the sword.

The flame in my core branched out, like ropes on fire – one massive one and hundreds upon hundreds of smaller ones. In my heart, I knew they represented Surtr and his army. It wasn't what I was looking for. I dug deeper. A thin cord started to form. It was different from all the other threads and made of white fire. I followed it in my mind and felt myself shifting. When I opened my eyes, I wasn't in my house anymore.

The air was thick with smoke, causing me to cough, and I struggled to get enough air into my lungs. I fell to my knees, my legs burning as they came into contact with the hot, rocky ground. It was almost unbearable. My body started to itch. My skin rapidly darkened and became hard until it looked and felt like stone. A feeling of panic lay just below the surface as I stared down at myself, mesmerised. My skin grew hot and cracked before my eyes. Small fissures appeared on it, like spider webs weaving their way across the surface. As they grew in size, blue fire rose from inside my body and shone through the cracks. I screamed, but no sound escaped my mouth. What was happening to me?

# JAX
## WITCH VILLAGE

By the time I got back to the house, it was already nighttime. I'd replayed the conversation with Nick in my mind several times. Something about it gnawed at me. Had Nick been telling me the truth? I didn't see why he would be lying, but I couldn't wipe the doubt from my mind. I flew over to the house to see if Cassie and Leah were back from their trip to the witch village. They were sound asleep, so I took to the sky again. I needed to think and decompress.

When the sun emerged over the horizon, I made my way back home. I transformed into my human form when the smell of cooked meat engulfed my senses, and I followed my nose. In the middle of the kitchen island was a plate full of bacon.

'Morning, Jax.'

I looked up as I heard Leah's voice and gave her a smile. 'Morning. Where's Cassie?'

Cassie came up behind me and wrapped her arms around me. 'I'm right here.' I turned around and kissed her. 'Did you only just get back?' she asked.

'No, but you were asleep, and I needed to clear my head.'

'So you were out flying?' Leah asked.

'Yeah.'

'I'm starting to see why you're still so young.'

I tilted my head. 'What do you mean?'

'Well, you're several hundred years old but still look like a teenager. I bet you've spent more time as a crow than you have as a human.'

I shrugged. 'Time moves differently in different realms, so I'm not really several hundred years old. But yeah. I've probably spent a large amount of my life as a crow. Being a crow is easier.' I smiled at them. 'But now I have you two to look after.'

Leah chuckled. 'We all know we're the ones looking after you, Grandpa.'

I picked up a piece of bacon and gave her a wink. 'Whatever you say, granddaughter.'

Cassie cleared her throat. 'Did you find out anything useful at your friend's?'

'Yeah, but no one knows who might be after the sword. Did you find any useful books?'

'We found some, but most were destroyed when the temple collapsed.'

'Has Sky had a chance to look through them yet?'

Cassie shook her head and opened the cupboard. 'Not yet. It was late by the time we got back, and we didn't want to disturb them.' She handed Leah a plate.

Leah dished up some sausages onto the plate. 'We've invited them all for breakfast.' She hit my hand as I tried to pick up another piece of bacon. 'If there's anything left when they arrive.'

'What do you expect? It's right in front of me and smells amazing.'

'I thought you didn't need to eat,' she said as she got a tray of hash browns out of the oven.

I gave her a goofy grin. 'Just because I can't die of malnutrition doesn't mean I don't enjoy food.'

Cassie hid a smirk. 'You two are ridiculous. Jax, why don't you set the table?'

'Anything for my lovely fiancée.' I kissed her cheek, took the plates from her hand and carried them to the table.

She rolled her eyes at me. 'When did you become so cheerful?'

'What? I can't enjoy the company of my two favourite ladies?'

Leah glanced over at me. 'Speaking of ladies, Leaf was asking how you were doing. Why don't you go and spend some time with her?'

Guilt ate me up from the inside. 'I should, but ...' I'd been an awful father. First I'd had my memories of her existence erased, and then when I'd found her, I'd had to leave. Even though the witch village was easily accessible since Freya had moved it, I still hadn't spent much time with her. Every time I did, I felt ashamed. I should have fought for her. I should have known it was a trick. I'd promised her mother I would protect her with my life, but I had failed.

'But what?' Leah asked.

Cassie put her arm around me. 'You have nothing to feel guilty about. It wasn't your fault. But now you have the chance to get to know your daughter.'

'I guess you're right.'

'She is,' Leah said. 'And maybe it would help to get her off my back.'

'I don't see why you're so annoyed by it. I would have loved to have my mother around,' Cassie said.

'Yeah, but she expects me to take over the High Priestess role.'

I turned my head to Leah. 'What's wrong with that?'

She sighed. 'Nothing. Only I don't know what I'm doing. I never grew up as a witch, and I don't want to let anyone down. I'm not cut out to be in charge of an entire village. I can hardly look after myself. Besides, we still don't know if the old High Priestess is going to make it.'

'After she allowed the witches' magic to be taken, I doubt anyone still wants her to rule,' I answered.

'You'd be surprised. After all, she did what she thought was right, giving up some witches' magic for the safety of the entire village. It's not really her fault Hecate manipulated her into thinking you were a threat and that it was the only way to keep the village safe from you. But I don't think it's right that one person gets to dictate all the terms.'

'Then bring back the Elders.'

Leah frowned. 'The Elders?'

'When I lived in the witch village with Katie, they had Elders that ruled with the High Priestess. Anything important had to go through them.'

Leah let out a defeated breath. 'This is why I shouldn't take over. I didn't even know they had Elders. There's so much I don't know. What if I mess up?'

I'd just opened my mouth to tell her that she wouldn't mess up and her heart was in the right place when the back door opened. A massive white wolf came running toward us.

'Sorry we're late. Sky got a bit sidetracked,' Mark shouted from the door.

The white wolf disappeared in a ball of light and Sky appeared in its place. 'It wasn't my fault. I never realised how entertaining it is to chase something.'

Leah raised an eyebrow. 'Do we want to know?'

Mark shook his head. 'She's still working on ignoring the instincts and urges of the wolf.'

'I still can't get over the fact Freya gave you the ability to turn into a wolf. It's amazing,' Cassie said to Sky.

'It makes sense,' I said. 'This way she can still be out in the sun, despite being bound to Hecate, and be part of the pack with Mark.'

Sky smiled. 'Yeah, I'm forever grateful for Freya. I thought my life was over after Hecate tricked me into being bound to her.'

Cassie looked around. 'Where's Seth?'

Sky shrugged. 'Night came over. They're still in the cabin. Ever since we got electricity, all they do is play games together. They asked us to bring some food back for them.'

Mark handed me a notebook. 'I hope this will help. Sky wrote down everything she remembered from the vision.' He made his way over to the dining table and sat down.

'Speaking of your vision,' Cassie said as she turned to Sky, 'we got some books from the witch village that might be helpful. They were saved from the ruins of the temple, so they're a bit damaged, but if we're lucky, the creature you saw in your vision will be in one of the books.'

'Fingers crossed,' Sky said as she took a seat next to Mark.

'Leaf was going to have a look at the farm too, just in case,' Leah said as she brought over some plates of food to the table. 'Speaking of the witch village – Jax, would you mind teleporting me over after we've eaten? I'd like to talk to Leaf about the Elders idea, and I know she wants to see you.'

'Sure. Anyone else want to come?'

Cassie bit her lip. 'I think I'll stay home. Being the reincarnation of Katie and having all her memories and feelings about the place and how she felt holding Leaf for the first time is confusing. They aren't my memories, so I don't know how to act around her.'

'We're good too. We're going over to my parents' once the sun sets,' Sky said. 'I think they're still getting over that I can transform into a wolf, so no need to rub it in their faces.'

I teleported Leah and myself to the witch village after breakfast. We arrived in front of the newly rebuilt stone temple. Leaf came up to greet us. 'It's so good to see you. I have a surprise for you.' She took us to the waterfall in between the stairs leading up to the stone temple.

'I see you rebuilt it the same as it looked before,' I said as I thought about the fight that had gone down between the witches and Hecate. I was glad I'd injured her, but her abandonment of the place had caused it to become unstable, and if it hadn't been for Freya moving it into her realm, it would all have collapsed.

'Almost; there is one change.' She pointed to an inscription above the waterfall. *Always be true to your heart, for love has no boundaries.*

I blinked away some tears as I thought of Cassie's previous reincarnation. Memories of me and Katie flooded through my head, and I was reliving our wedding day again, when she walked down those steps in her beautiful white gown. 'How did you know?'

Leaf smiled. 'Everyone in the temple that day saw the visions and the love you shared for each other. And I wanted people to know that no matter who they are or who they love, everyone is welcome, especially now, when the wolves are a part of us too.' Leaf placed a hand on my shoulder. 'I talk to her sometimes. Being in the temple makes me feel close to her. I know she's not really here and her soul got reborn in Cassie, but her essence is here.'

There was a moment of silence before Leah gave me a nudge. 'I just got an idea that might help Cassie.'

I turned and looked at Leah. 'Help Cassie?'

'She's been thinking about her mum a lot lately. Do you know if Cassie's mother had a grave?'

'Yes – she's buried in the cemetery near Nick's house.'

'Why don't you take her there? I'm sure she'll appreciate it. And maybe it'll help her feel closer to her mother. Especially as it's too dangerous for her to see her father.'

I hit myself mentally. Why hadn't I thought of that earlier? With everything that had been going on, it made sense that Cassie had been thinking about family. I couldn't bring her mother back, but it would be easy to take her to the cemetery so she could feel closer to her.

# NICK

## The Fire Realm

I stared down at my body, which had turned into rock. What had this realm done to me? Muted panic mixed with uncertainty slithered around my mind, and without a proper glance at my surroundings, I teleported back to my house. Back to safety.

As I arrived in the living room, my head almost touched the ceiling and I realised how much taller I had become. Ant let out a gasp. His eyes met mine and he took a step back, his mouth wide open. 'N-Nick?'

I nodded.

'Wow. I've never seen you in your demon form before. You look terrifying.'

Demon form. Why had I not thought about that? It was

obvious now Ant had pointed it out.

'I didn't know I had one. This has never happened before. I used to try to turn into my demon form when I was younger, but it never worked, so I just assumed that because I'm half human, I didn't have one.' I thought back to what Jax had taught me about changing forms in my youth and willed myself to become human once more. As I visualised my human body, I could feel myself changing and shrinking, and slowly, the horrible beast I had become turned back into my normal human form.

Ant frowned. 'If you didn't know you had a demon form, how did you turn into it?'

'I don't know. The realm did something to me. One moment I was human and struggling to breathe, and the next moment I turned into something else.'

'What realm?'

'The one where the sword might be.'

Ant put his hand to his chin. 'Maybe the realm is too hostile for your human form, so your body went into survival mode.'

I shrugged. 'It's possible. But it was terrifying. When my skin cracked open and turned to stone, I thought I was going to die. I'd much rather change on my terms.'

'How did you find the realm?'

'My friend Jax came around. He said Surtr can feel where the sword is because it contains his eternal flame, and as I'm his son, I should be able to feel it too. So I just followed a strand in my mind that I thought was the eternal flame and ended up in another realm.'

'That's awesome. Did you sense the sword?'

'I'm not sure. I was too caught up with what was happening to my body to think about anything else. But I need to go back there. I just need to mentally prepare myself first.'

'Be careful.'

'Thanks. Anyway, why are you here? Do you have some news?'

'I did. I found some information about which realm the sword might be in, but I guess it doesn't matter now.'

I stared at myself in the bathroom mirror and willed my body to take my demonic form. It took a few tries, but eventually I began to change. My body grew and turned into the same molten rock Surtr had, but instead of red lava running through the cracks, mine was cyan. It made sense, really. Ever since I defied Surtr when I was younger, my fire has been blue. I changed back and forth a few times until I was satisfied I could change easily at will.

I closed my eyes, searched for the string of fire inside me that belonged to the sword, and teleported myself back to the fire realm.

A layer of dust covered the sky, causing the suns to give off an eerie orange light. It wasn't all that different from Surtr's realm. I scanned the area. Porous igneous rocks covered the entire landscape. There were several mountains around but no vegetation. The air was dry, stagnant and filled with smoke. But in my demon form, the air didn't bother me much. I took a step. The ground was hot, but it didn't affect me in this form.

The ground shook, creating cracks in the rocky terrain. In between the cracks, lava was flowing freely. I made a mental note to tread carefully. I was a being of fire, but how would the lava affect me if I touched it?

Taking a deep breath, I bent down and lowered my hand into it. There was heat but no pain. I smiled to myself. *This may be easier than I first thought.*

I scanned the landscape for volcanoes. There were several, but which one held the sword? I closed my eyes and opened my senses, searching for the string of white light. Slowly, a magnetised force connected to me and showed me which volcano I needed to reach. I tried teleporting to it, but it didn't work.

I walked towards it. Small amber dots appeared in the air around me. I waved them away. They became more insistent, like mosquitoes hovering in my face. At first it was just a buzzing noise. But it turned into whispering words. 'You do not belong here. Go back to where you came.' I inspected the amber dots more closely. They appeared to be some sort of flying insects. Maybe fire spirits?

'I'm not going back until I get what I came for,' I told them.

'You will regret this,' they answered.

I ignored them and started trekking up the volcano. The climb was strenuous, and it was hard to find anything to hold on to. The shaking ground did not make it easier. I fell several times, but I was determined. Nothing was going to keep me from that sword – from avenging my wife. I slammed my fist into the steep incline to make dents and used the dents as makeshift steps to continue my ascent. It was slower and more tiring, but the dents provided better traction and reduced the risk of slipping. It felt like I'd been climbing for hours, but the suns had hardly moved positions.

When I was halfway to the top, the whole volcano shook and small rocks fell from above. It took all my strength to hold on to the surface of the volcano to prevent myself from falling. A loud roar sounded above me and echoed throughout the entire realm. I looked up. The volcano had erupted, and lava was making its way towards me. My first instinct was to run. But then I remembered the lava didn't affect this form. I smiled to myself and kept climbing. My hands slipped on the rock as the lava flowed down the volcano. It reminded me of dough; there was nothing solid to hold on to, and finding a solid place to step on became a challenge. After what felt like an eternity, I finally pulled myself up to the rim at the top. I lay on my back and caught my breath, happy the volcano had stopped erupting.

The fire spirits swarmed around my face, making it hard to see anything beyond them. 'You do not belong here. Go back to where you came from,' they said in angry, high-pitched voices.

I ignored them and swatted them away as I got back to my feet. I looked around. There was a ring of mainly flat ground around the crater. I made my way over to the edge. There at the bottom, several hundred feet down, I could see the sword. It was calling out to me, begging me to possess it.

I was debating the best way down when the ground rumbled and heavy footsteps echoed behind me. How was that possible? I was supposed to be the only being here. I turned around. In front of me was a creature made completely out of grey granite. 'I am the guardian of the Daudans. Go back to where you came from or face my wrath,' he said in a deep voice.

I smirked. Had I been in my human form, it would have been a different matter, but in this form he didn't seem like a threat. He only reached up to my chest. 'No one is going to stop me from getting my revenge. Not even you. So please step aside. I don't want to hurt you unless I have to.'

He charged at me. Despite his size, the impact of the collision made me lose my footing, and he landed on top of me. I swung my hands around, hoping to get a good hit in, but it didn't seem to hurt him. It didn't even make a dent in his rock body. I pushed him off and rolled away. As I got up, I conjured a flame and sent it at him. He embraced it, and I could have sworn there was a smile on his face as the fire did nothing. But why would it? The stone creature was used to the heat. This entire realm was made up of fire and stone. I had to change my tactics. I rushed at him and at the last moment, I swerved and swept his legs from under him. He stumbled and fell to the ground. *Think.* How could a rock be broken down?

I thought back to when Lily had first attempted to cook. She had broken one of my mother's ceramic trays by pouring cold water into it while it was still hot from the oven. And this realm was hot, along with all its surroundings. So it was safe to assume the rock creature was too. But would I be able to conjure any water in this realm? Wouldn't it evaporate before I could hit the stone creature with it?

I thought of a massive ice block. It materialised in my hand. I threw it at the creature. By the time it reached him, it had become water. Steam appeared on his stone body. As he charged towards me, I stepped to the side, conjured another ice block and threw it at him. I wasn't sure if it was working, but it seemed to have slowed him down slightly. Clenching my fist, I struck him as he hit my side with immense force. I fell and rolled over. A small piece of stone had fallen off him. Maybe this was my chance.

I got up and conjured another ice block, threw it at his head and ran towards him. I jumped on top of him and snapped his neck. It cracked, and a moment later, the crack severed his head from his body. The stone creature's head fell, and the rest of his body collapsed with it until he resembled nothing more than a pile of stones. Guilt flared in the back of my mind, but I shoved it down.

'I'm sorry,' I said as I turned towards the crater to retrieve the sword.

# JAX

## A Drawing of Surtr

Leaving Leah with Leaf to discuss the idea of the Elders, I teleported myself home. Cassie was sitting on the sofa watching TV.

'Are you okay?' I asked as I made my way over to her.

'Yeah. I'm fine. Why?'

'Leah said you've been thinking about your mother. Would you like to go to her grave?'

Cassie perked up and turned the TV off. 'You know where she's buried?'

I averted my gaze. 'I'm sorry I didn't think of taking you there before.'

She got up from the sofa and wrapped her hands around mine. 'It's okay. You've had a lot on your mind.'

I embraced her and kissed her forehead. 'That's not an excuse. I should have realised.' I gazed into her eyes. 'You're the most important person in my life, and I will always be here for you.'

'I know. But I don't want to bother you with trivial things when there's much bigger things that need your attention.'

'You're my other half, my soulmate. It's your job to bother me. No matter what it is, I want you to come to me. We're in this together.'

'I love you too,' she said as she squeezed me in a tight hug.

'Do you want to go now?'

'Only if it's not a bother.'

I teleported us to the cemetery. It wasn't very big. A forest bordered it on one side, and the other side had a large hedge that separated the cemetery from a park. Nick's mother and Lily were buried next to a patch of grass separating the graves from the forest. In front of the forest was a bench overlooking the cemetery.

I gestured towards two light-grey gravestones right next to each other. 'This is your mother and your grandmother.'

Cassie wandered over to Lily's grave and hunched down. 'Tell me about my mother.'

'I wish I could, but I only met her a few times.'

'Tell me about those times.'

I ran my hand through my hair. 'She loved nature almost as much as I do, and she was loving and kind. I could see why Nick loved her. You look a lot like her.'

'I do?'

I nodded in response.

Cassie brushed her fingers over the engraving. 'We should have brought some flowers.'

'What flowers would you like? I can conjure them for you.'

'White lilies,' Cassie said with determination.

I smiled. 'According to Nick, they were your mum's favourite.' I gave Cassie the flowers and turned to Nick's mother's grave.

I conjured a black rose and placed it on the ground, like I'd done so many times before. 'I hope you watch over him and make sure he doesn't do anything stupid.' A feeling that Nick was up to something he shouldn't still lingered in my mind. I only wished I knew what it was.

Cassie looked over at me. 'Why did you put a black rose on the grave?'

'It stands for loss but also rebirth and new beginnings. I like to show her that I honour her choice of becoming a guardian angel while still mourning the loss of the person she was.'

'It sounds like you knew my grandmother quite well. Can you tell me about her?'

'Your grandmother had the most caring soul. She spent her life working as a nurse to help people. When I started to hang out with Nick, she cared for me like I was one of her own. She always saw the good in everyone, so when Nick told me she had chosen to become a guardian angel after she passed away, it didn't come as a surprise to me.'

'Is she still around?'

'Her soul is, but she doesn't have a physical form.'

'Do you think she's looking out for us?'

'I don't know.' I let out a long sigh. 'But I like to think she is.'

Cassie squeezed my hand. 'I like to think so too.'

The next morning, as we made our way downstairs, Leah greeted us from the kitchen table, where she was flipping through an old leather-bound book.

'When did you get here? We didn't hear you come home last night,' Cassie asked.

'Leaf dropped me off not too long ago. She liked the idea about the Elders. I just thought I'd try to modernise it a bit.'

Cassie approached Leah and ran her hands over the book. 'This is Katie's spell book, isn't it?'

Leah nodded. 'Do you remember writing in it?'

'Not really. It's strange. I don't know how to explain it. I have the memories of being Katie, but I know they're not my memories, not really. The intensity of them seems to fade every day.'

Leah gave Cassie a hug. 'I'm sorry they make you feel conflicted.'

'It's okay. They make me realise just how precious our lives are.'

When they pulled away from each other, Leah turned to me. 'Sky texted me earlier. She didn't have any luck finding the creature in any of the books.'

I let out a sigh. 'I guess it was a long shot.'

Leah closed the book on the table. 'I was thinking. Maybe we should have another look around Whitelock

Unlimited.'

'Why? Would they have books there?' Cassie asked.

Leah shrugged. 'I don't know. It's worth a look, though. Besides, I want to find out what that company was all about. I feel like it's more than a front, and we didn't really get a chance last time we were there. I want to know if there're more houses like ours. Are people still out there doing Hecate's bidding and stealing other beings' powers?'

I glanced at her. The last time we had been there, we had found a hidden portal that led to the witch village, and we had learned that their adoptive mother, Abigail, worked for Hecate and was involved with stealing magic from supernatural beings. That was how Mark had lost his wolf. But Hecate had been defeated, and Abigail was currently imprisoned with Nick. The magic that had been taken from Mark and the other witches had been restored, courtesy of Leah and Sky. 'Let's focus on one problem at the time. Figuring out who's after the sword seems a little more important.'

Cassie became thoughtful. 'Maybe I can draw it.'

I scratched my head. 'The creature?'

'Yeah. If Sky tells me what it looked like, I should be able to.'

I shrugged. 'It's worth a shot.'

She picked up her phone before walking over to the bookcase and grabbing a sketchbook and pencil.

Her phone buzzed. 'She's happy for me to come over.'

'Do you want me to teleport you?' I asked.

She smirked. 'No need. I can do it myself.'

A moment later she was gone.

I looked over at Leah with admiration. 'When did she become this good?'

She smiled. 'Don't look at me. She's your fiancée.'

I shook my head. 'I'm going to stretch my wings.'

I patrolled the neighbourhood for a while before landing outside the cabin. When I walked in, Cassie and Sky were sitting at the table. I went over and gave Cassie a kiss. The drawing of a stone giant in the sketchbook in her hands caught my attention, and my blood ran cold. 'Is this the creature you saw?'

'Yeah, that's what it looked like.'

I sucked in a breath, taking a small step back as visions of the torture he'd put me through flashed in my mind. 'That's Surtr. But it's impossible. He can't leave his realm.'

Sky tilted her head. 'You know this creature?'

'Yeah. He had me imprisoned, but Nick saved me.'

'Is that why you have a special bond?' Cassie asked.

I met her gaze. 'Partly. That's how Nick ended up being my master. Surtr tricked him. He told Nick the only way to get me out of the realm was to bind me to him.'

'He must be a very evil creature,' Sky said.

I ran my hand through my hair. 'I think so, but Freya told me he doesn't care about much except mending his sword and being ready to march with his army and burn the world to the ground when the time is right. So it doesn't make sense he would be after the Daudans.'

'What type of being is he?' Cassie asked.

'He's a fire giant. One of the first beings to exist.'

Sky held up her hand. 'Wait ... Isn't Cassie's father a fire demon?'

'Yeah. Surtr is Nick's father.'

Cassie stood up. '*What?!* My grandfather is an ancient fire giant? Why doesn't anyone ever tell me this stuff?'

I reached over and placed a hand on her shoulder. 'Because it doesn't matter. Your lineage doesn't determine who you are.'

'Maybe not, but it would have been nice to know. And you still haven't taken me to see my dad.'

'Because it's still too risky. Maybe even more so now. I wouldn't know what to do with myself if I lost you.'

Cassie crossed her arms. 'But you let Sky see him.'

'Against my better judgement, and only because we needed him to take us to Abigail.' I hugged her. 'I promise I'll take you to meet him once it's safe.'

I woke up in the morning and turned to face Cassie. 'Morning, beautiful.'

She stretched her arms above her head and gave me a kiss. 'Good morning.' I returned the kiss before getting up from the bed. 'You're leaving?'

'I'm sorry. I need to talk to Nick. It worries me that Sky saw Surtr take the sword. He shouldn't be able to leave his realm.'

'Maybe the sword was hidden in his realm to start with.'

I became thoughtful. *I guess that could explain a few things.* 'Maybe. But why take it now?' Cassie shrugged and I gave her another kiss. 'I'll see you later.'

I teleported to Nick's front door. Something hadn't felt right the last time I'd talked to him. Was he covering for Surtr?

I knocked on the door, but Nick didn't open it. Was he in the middle of something, or was he not home? I let out a breath, debating what to do. I didn't want to invade Nick's personal space, but this might be my chance to figure out what he'd been up to.

I put my hand on the door handle and opened the door. 'Hello. Nick, are you home?'

No answer. I stepped into the living room and looked around. The fireplace was cold. Several whisky bottles were lying on the sofa. Even though Nick hadn't been the same since Lily's death, I'd thought he had at least been coping with it – that his talk of killing Corson and getting his revenge had been the grief and anger talking and that he wouldn't actually go through with it – but maybe I'd been wrong. Maybe he was away doing something stupid that would get him killed.

My head spun with thoughts of what he might be up to. I leaned into our bond. I could feel he was alive, but I wasn't able to locate him. Concern for my friend surged within me, and I made a promise to myself that after I'd stopped whoever had taken the sword, I would help Nick. Maybe not to get his revenge – who knew what killing one of the keepers would do when killing all of them would end the world? – but I would do what I could to help him get closure.

I left the house and teleported back home. Leah and Cassie were out in the garden. Leah was holding a flame in her hand.

'What are you doing?' I asked.

'Well, if Cassie is a descendant of a fire giant, then surely she should be able to conjure fire. I'm trying to teach her.'

'Unfortunately your magic doesn't work the same way, so it won't work.'

A flame erupted in Cassie's hand, and she shrieked. 'Wow. Look at this. I did it.'

Leah gave me a smug smile. 'You were saying?'

I rolled my eyes before glancing at Cassie. A bright amber flame was burning in her hand. 'That's amazing. How did you do that?'

'I thought about it and it appeared,' Cassie said.

Leah chuckled. 'Not during the first hour.' Seeing them safe and happy made my body relax.

Cassie examined the fire in her hand. 'Can you conjure fire?'

I smirked. 'Sure.' I conjured a single flame in the air that slowly floated towards the ground.

Leah rolled her eyes. 'That's cheating. You're meant to control the fire, not just make a flame appear.'

I shrugged. 'Not everyone has the ability to call on fire from their innate magic.'

'It's a shame we don't all have the same ability. I would love to be able to fly,' Cassie said.

I gave her a hesitant smile. 'If you really want to fly, I can take you sometime.'

Cassie perked up. 'But doesn't that mean you need to be in your demon form?'

I gazed into her eyes. 'For you, I will do almost anything. But there may be another way.'

She gave me a passionate kiss. Leah made a vomiting sound. Cassie broke away with a laugh. 'You wouldn't complain if it was you.'

'Oh, I would very much complain if I was kissing my grandad.'

Cassie made a fire appear in her hand and threw it playfully at Leah. 'You know what I mean.'

Leah deflected it without a thought. She gave us a grin. 'Of course I do, but it's so fun winding you up.'

I let out a sigh. 'How about we go inside?'

'I'd like to practise a bit longer,' Cassie answered.

I kissed her on the cheek. 'I'll see you both inside in a bit.'

Cassie's sketch lay on the kitchen table. Only it was coloured in this time. Instead of Surtr's red fire, the fire was blue. The hair raised on my skin as a chill went down my spine. The picture wasn't of Surtr – it was of Nick. As far as I was aware, Nick was the only one that had blue fire. I didn't know he had a demon form, but if he did, that would explain why he'd been acting so strangely. Was that why he hadn't been home?

Panic surged in my body, and my heart raced. I gripped my hair with trembling hands. I needed to talk to Freya. I couldn't let the sword consume Nick. I wouldn't. There had to be a way to destroy the sword before it took over Nick.

# NICK

## Guardians of the Daudans

'You will regret this,' the fire spirits shouted, but I ignored them.

The stone creature had been taken care of. Now all I needed to do was climb down inside the volcano and grab the sword. Piece of cake. I let out a deep breath and started the descent.

It was tedious, and I had to be careful. The magma couldn't hurt me, but if I fell and landed in it, I wasn't sure I could stay afloat. I climbed to the lower level of the wall, creating holes by slamming my fist into the rock wall as I went, the impact sending tremors up my arm.

When I was almost at the bottom, I jumped onto solid ground made up of a large rock surrounded by a sea of magma. I wasn't sure how it stayed afloat, but I didn't question it. The intense heat shimmered in the air, distorting my vision slightly, but I could still see the sword lying flat on the ground in front of me. It looked exactly the same as when I'd seen it in the fire, with its jagged blade and wolflike guard. The blade reflected the amber light of the magma.

I hurried towards it and grabbed the hilt. A powerful surge went through me, awakening all my senses. A triumphant smile spread across my lips. The sword was finally mine.

The rock underneath shifted and the magma around it became wild, like a terrible storm at sea. I hunched down to keep my balance. I needed to get out of there before I stumbled and slipped into the magma. Closing my eyes, I tried to teleport away, but something blocked it. Maybe the volcano was enchanted. It would make sense, as I hadn't been able to teleport to it.

I conjured a scabbard, placed the sword in it and slung it over my back. I tried to ignore the movement of the rock from the surrounding storm as I started sprinting, trying to gain enough speed to make the jump back to the volcanic wall.

My hand slipped, but I managed to grab hold of a crevice in the wall and slowly regained my balance. I climbed upwards as quickly as I could, using the holes I'd created on the way down. The ground vibrated, probably indicating another eruption was soon to follow. And I wanted to be out of there when it did.

The vibrations became stronger. Pieces of rock broke off and plummeted into the magma. I was halfway up when a massive boulder hit me on the shoulders. I dug my hands into the rock wall, but the force was too strong, and I lost my footing and fell. Panic ripped through my body, and the air was forced out of my lungs as I crashed into the magma.

Why was I not sinking? My hands felt the hard surface. It was smooth, almost like scales. Had I landed on top of an animal? What animal would live in magma? I looked up and gazed right into a pair of golden eyes almost as big as my head.

'The sword belongs to me.' The dragon reared its head back, opened its mouth and sprayed me with fire, forcing me to take a step backwards to steady myself against the onslaught. Though it didn't hurt me, it felt like I was being splashed with a powerful jetstream, and it was hard to remain upright.

The ground underneath me shifted and a moment later I was in the air, holding on for dear life to the lower back of the massive fire dragon. The wings flapped on either side of me, their force making it even harder to remain on the dragon's back. I let out a deep breath. Great. Another being I needed to fight for the sword. Only this time I had the sword and could use it to my advantage.

The dragon spun around, and between its movement and gravity, I lost my grip on the beast and fell. Luckily, I landed at the top of the volcano, next to where I had killed the stone creature.

Before I had a chance to get up, a massive foot descended to crush me, but I rolled to the side, drew the sword and stabbed it into the scaly skin. Using it as an anchor, I propelled myself upward and onto its paw.

The dragon roared and flew straight up towards the suns. I was holding on for dear life, one hand on the sword and the other wrapped around the leg of the dragon. Sheer determination was the only thing keeping me attached to it. With the help of the sword, I slowly climbed up the leg of the dragon, and when I got to the chest, I plunged the sword straight in between the ribs to where I believed the heart would be. The dragon let out a shriek and, despite its best efforts to remain in the sky, began falling. When he was close to hitting the ground, I jumped off. The entire realm shook as the dragon crashed headfirst into a small mountain that exploded into a million pieces. Magma shot up through the cracks in the ground and swallowed the dragon whole.

Who knew it'd be so easy to kill a dragon with this sword?

The fire spirits swamped me again. I turned around and smirked at them in triumph. *I may not belong here, but I got what I came for.* Lily's revenge was finally set in motion. I tried teleporting away. But it still didn't work.

'You cannot leave with the sword. Our magic protects it,' the fire spirits said.

'I've got this far. You will not stop me.' I placed the sword in the sheath and hung it over my back as I started walking. 'What type of beings are you, anyway?'

'We're fire beings, created by the core of this realm.'

'Does the core connect to the magma around the realm?'

The fire beings became quiet. A plan formed in my head. If the fire beings' magic was what stopped me from teleporting with the sword, then maybe if I engulfed myself in the magma the fire beings were created from, I could trick them into believing they had the sword, and that way I would be able to teleport away. It was a crazy idea. I could get stuck in the magma with no way of escaping, but it was the only idea I had. I took a deep breath and plunged the sword into the ground. The rock cracked, opening up a puddle of magma. I stepped into it, holding the sword, relaxed and let the magma engulf me. When it had completely covered me, I teleported away.

Exhilarated, I arrived at my house and fell to my knees in a coughing fit, coughing up the magma that had got into my mouth and lungs. It left tiny specks of burn marks on the floor. After I'd caught my breath, I looked over to my side. There, in all its glory, lay the Daudans.

I had been victorious in bringing the sword back.

I went to check on the sword. It was still lying in the fireplace, the illusion of a flame hiding it from view. The need to go to the cemetery overwhelmed me. I needed to talk to Lily – to tell her I'd got a weapon that could kill the being that had destroyed our family. But when I got to the front door, I stopped. I hadn't gone into the human realm since the house had been moved. Who knew if demons would still be able to find me? Maybe I should take the sword with me. Just in case.

I took it from the fireplace, placed it in its scabbard and buckled it around my waist before concealing it from any onlookers, then teleported to Lily's grave.

I patted her headstone. 'I'm sorry I haven't been here in a long time. After Kaliakwan told me to stay inside, I didn't want to disobey them. But I regret now that I didn't come to see you.' A tear rolled down my cheek. 'Ant figured out who's responsible for your death, and now I have a weapon that can kill him.'

I looked down at the ground. Someone had placed a bouquet of white lilies there. But who? I turned to my mother's grave. A single black rose lay on the ground. Jax.

I let out a sigh. I hadn't meant to lie to him. 'I'm sorry, Mother,' I said in a broken whisper. 'I don't think you would be very proud of the man I've become. But I couldn't let Jax know. He would never understand.' I swallowed the lump forming in my throat. 'I'll do better after Lily's been avenged.' The wind caressed my skin, and I could almost smell my mother's perfume in the air.

I placed myself between the two graves and traced my fingers over the engraving on Lily's headstone. 'I'm sorry for giving our daughter up. It was better, safer this way. Jax has fallen in love with her. He will never let anything happen to her, so even if I'm not there to keep her safe, I'm keeping my promise. I hope you can forgive me and understand that I didn't abandon her. She's had a good childhood.'

I let out a sigh and looked to the horizon. It was starting to get dark. I could have teleported home, but Lily had loved this time of day, when the light gave way to the dark just so it could rise again in the morning and chase away the darkness.

As I strolled through the park on my way home, I thought about all the times we'd had a sunset or sunrise stroll together. It had always fascinated her. She'd told me how it had been growing up. Everything was always white and bright. There was no balance, no nighttime, no nature. I guess that's why she always loved a hike in the human world. My heart ached at her absence. Oh, how I missed her.

I was imagining Lily admiring the hydrangeas when an energy bolt flew past me. I looked up. Three demons stood before me. I gave them a grin. This would be my chance to try out the sword. 'You have no idea what you've just walked into.'

One of the demons met my eyes. 'There's one of you and three of us.'

'Never stopped me before.'

A smirk appeared on the demon's face as several more demons appeared in my peripheral vision. Despite using glamour to appear human, it wasn't enough to completely blend in, and their appearance looked somewhat distorted. Not to mention the red eyes and jagged teeth completely gave it away. Most of the time they would cover up to better blend in around humans, but there weren't any humans around.

The demon that been talking conjured an energy bolt and threw it right at me.

I wasn't prepared, and it hit me in the chest, burning a hole through my skin and the shirt I was wearing. Lily had got me that shirt and now it was ruined. Anger and hate gathered inside me and burned its way to the surface.

The demons stepped back, and I realised I'd transformed into my demon form. 'You'll regret this,' I said as I unsheathed the Daudans. In one sweep, I cut the mocking demon in half. That would teach him for ruining a gift I got from Lily. I challenged the others.

They stumbled backwards, their eyes wide with fear, but that only fed my strength. 'He made us do it,' one of the other demons said.

I sneered at them. There would be no mercy. I swung the sword again and again until all of them lay dead on the ground. I smiled to myself and sheathed the sword. Power vibrated inside me. With every breath I took, the feeling amplified, making my skin tingle as the raw, untouchable force engulfed me. This newfound strength made me feel invincible.

I teleported home and ran out to the garden. 'Ant. Ant. You'll never believe what happened.'

The door of Ant's house flew open. 'What happened? Were you attacked? Are you hurt?' He pushed Nicole behind him and stepped out, closing the door.

'I'm fine.'

He let out a breath. 'Maybe you should turn back to human. You wouldn't want to scare Nicole.' I willed myself back to my human form.

His eyes went wide with worry as I became human. 'I thought you said you weren't hurt.'

I shrugged. 'It's nothing.'

He stared at the wound. 'It doesn't look like nothing. Your chest is burnt. Who hit you?'

I waved my hand. 'It doesn't matter. I took care of it. It was amazing, and the power ... I've never felt this strong. I think once we find him, we have a shot at killing him.'

'Corson?'

'Yes.' I held up the sword. 'This blade ... its power ... You should feel it.'

Ant's gaze fixed on the sword and he reached towards it. Possessiveness overtook me and I stepped back, moving the sword away from him. 'Actually, I'd rather you didn't.'

He examined the sword with his eyes for a while longer before meeting my gaze. 'It's probably for the best.' He let out a sigh. 'Let's get you cleaned up.'

# JAX

# I Should Have Known

I didn't have the heart to tell Cassie the truth about her father, not until I had more information, so I wrote her a note telling her where I was going before I teleported to Freya's realm.

The wind rustled through the trees, taunting me for being so naive. I should have known. Nick had mentioned he was after revenge on one of the cardinal keepers – beings that were true immortals and could not be killed, at least not with normal weapons. I guess I hadn't realised just how badly he was hurting. I should have been there for him, helping him get through it.

I landed on the veranda as Freya exited the house. She gave me a sad smile. 'You cannot be responsible for someone else's actions.'

I met her gaze. 'It's Nick. He's the one that's after the sword.'

Freya gave me a sad smile. 'I know. Unfortunately, he is not just after the sword anymore. He retrieved it.'

'Why didn't you tell me?' I clenched my fists as frustration bubbled up inside me. How could she have kept something that important from me?

'Darling, I did not know until I felt you entering the realm. Even the future is disguised sometimes.'

'What should I do?' I started pacing.

'It is not for me to tell you.'

'The sword needs to be destroyed,' I said as I stopped and looked into her eyes.

Freya squeezed my shoulder. 'I am not sure it is possible. The Dauðans is made from the eternal flame. Maybe Surtr would know a way, but he wants nothing to do with it.'

'Can't you help me? You're powerful enough to take the sword from Nick.'

'It is not that easy. The sword feeds on the darkness inside, and I have spent a long time trying to right my wrongs. I have too many people depending on me. I cannot risk taking the sword.'

'Then what am I supposed to do?' I asked, desperation lacing my voice.

'Listen to your heart. Use the bond that connects you and Nick. Maybe it will be enough to get through to him.'

'And if it isn't?'

Freya let out a sigh. 'Even I do not have all the answers. Tyr fought the power of the Dauðans for a long time. We can only hope Nick will have the same mental resilience to the sword as he did.'

'I don't think he does. Tyr was the god of justice; Nick is half human.' I stared off into the distance, thinking about how his whole demeanour had changed. 'Besides, I think he gave up after Lily died.'

Freya placed a hand over mine. 'You might be right. But we need to have faith he can resist its pull. If not, it might be the end of him.'

My eyes went teary. 'I can't ... I can't let it take him over. It drove Tyr mad.' I froze, an idea starting in my head. 'How did the dwarfs get the sword back from Tyr?'

'I do not know. Maybe it will be wise to ask the dwarfs.'

'The dwarfs? How can I do that?'

'The dwarfs live underground in Svartalfheim, or more correctly, Nidavellir.'

'How can I get there? Can I teleport?'

'Not without being invited. You will have to go the long way there, through the opening in the ground. I have a cloak of feathers that can help you move between the realms of Yggdrasil. But be warned, the dwarfs are very cunning and deceiving.'

'If it can help Nick, then I need to go.'

'Very well.' Freya entered the house and re-emerged with a feather in one hand and a gold and amber necklace in the other. 'This necklace is very dear to me, but I have a feeling you will need it when you visit the dwarfs.'

I looked at her in confusion. 'Why?'

'I already told you. The dwarfs can be deceiving. It is unwise to accept a gift from them without giving one in return. I know you are only going there for information, but it cannot hurt to be extra careful. They may try to offer you amazing things. You will do best to decline. You do not want to owe them anything. And remember they are not your friends.'

She handed me the feather and the necklace. 'Please be careful. Do not lose this feather. It is the only way you can leave that place on your own.'

'Thank you.' I looked at the feather in my hand. It was a mix of browns and blacks with white mottling, typical of a falcon's plumage. On closer inspection, it appeared to be a primary feather, long and tapered. 'I thought you said it's a cloak?'

Freya chuckled. 'You know magic exists and still you get confused by the smallest of things. It needs to be unfolded.' She took the feather from me. 'Here, let me show you.' She unfolded the feather, so it now looked like two feathers next to each other. As she continued to unfold it, the feathers turned into a massive cloak. She gave me a smile and folded it all back together again.

'Here you go,' she said as she handed it over to me. 'Please be careful.'

I kissed her cheeks and said goodbye before transforming into a crow and making the journey back.

When I arrived at a place that allowed teleportation, I teleported over to Nick. I needed to stop him before I completely lost my best friend. I couldn't let the sword corrupt him, and, knowing how fragile his mind was, I was running short of time.

# NICK

## STOP TRYING TO SAVE ME

I sat in the living room with the sword in my lap as Ant tried to clean my wound. 'Nick, this would be a lot easier if you just put the sword down,' he said as he dabbed alcohol on the wound on my chest.

I grunted and shifted away from him. 'Just leave it. It doesn't hurt.'

'I can't just leave it. There's a hole in your chest. You can see all the way to the muscle layers. It needs to be covered until it heals. You don't want it to become infected.'

I shrugged. 'Demons don't get infections.'

Ant sighed. 'You're part human, so why take any chances?' He leaned back over to tend to my wound again. 'Please put the sword down.'

'Fine. But don't try to steal it from me.'

'I have no interest in the sword,' he said as he held up his hands.'

I eyed him for a while. Could he be trusted? He was a friend. He'd helped me get the sword. I reluctantly placed it on the floor next to me. As soon as I let go of the hilt, the fire from the blade faded and my body felt cold.

Ant smiled. 'Much better. Was that so hard to do?' He reached for the bandage.

I didn't answer. After the rush of using the sword on the demons, something inside me had changed. It was like the sword had become part of me. It needed me, and I needed it. I eyed the steel blade as Ant finished bandaging my wound.

I conjured a fresh shirt when the doorbell went off. I stood up from the sofa, ready to hide the sword, when the door opened. 'Nick. I know you're home.' Jax's voice echoed through the house before he marched into the living room.

I glanced over at Ant. He nodded and left. I followed him with my eyes, making sure he didn't try to steal my sword.

Jax stopped in front of me, his face flushed. 'I know you lied to me.'

I looked at him, hoping he wouldn't see the sword on the floor. 'Lied about what?'

'The Daudans.'

My eyes went to it. Had he waited for me to open the door, I would have had time to hide it instead of being caught red handed.

Jax followed my gaze. 'You need to fight its pull. You're strong.'

I scoffed. Didn't he realise that without the sword, I was weak? I'd never been strong. Maybe he didn't know me as well as he thought. Anger burned in my veins. He had no right to tell me what to do. 'No, Jax, I'm not. Not like you. You have always been able to fight what you are for yourself. Me? I've been fighting what I am for the sake of others. But there's no one left to fight for. The only thing holding me together is the thought of getting revenge for my Lily.'

Jax swallowed. 'Don't say that. You still have Cassie.'

I shook my head. Jax would never understand. 'I don't have Cassie. I gave her away. I promised Lily I'd keep her safe, something I wasn't able to do with all the demons attacking. And I only made things worse by trying to fix it. Corson destroyed my family. He has to pay.'

'There needs to be another way. Nothing good comes from violence.'

Anger brewed inside me. 'There isn't, and with this sword, I'm powerful enough to kill him.'

'There will be consequences. He's the keeper of the west.'

'I guess he should have thought of that before he targeted my family.'

Jax's jaw stiffened. 'This isn't you. You need to fight it.'

'I am fighting,' I shouted back. 'Just not the way you want me to.'

Jax took a step towards the sword. My heart beat faster and I swiftly positioned myself in front of him, hiding the sword from his field of vision. Did he really think I'd let him take it from me?

He stared straight into my eyes. 'You know I can't let you go through with it.'

I stifled a laugh. He really didn't have a leg to stand on. 'You can't hurt me. I'm your master.' The hurt on Jax's face pulled at my heart, but I couldn't let him stop me.

'I don't want to hurt you.'

'Then let me kill Corson with the sword, and then we can go back to normal.'

'There won't be a normal. There's a reason the sword was hidden away. Its magical properties will consume you until there's nothing left but darkness. It's already changed you.' He looked at me with pleading eyes. 'Please don't do this, Nick. There needs to be another way for you to move past your grief besides vengeance.' He reached out his hand towards me.

I pushed it away. 'There isn't.' I stalked over to the sword and picked it up.

Jax took a deep breath and ran his hand through his hair. With his jaw set, he tried to reach for the sword. I didn't want to hurt him, but I couldn't let him take it. I reached out with my free hand and grabbed his arm in an iron grip. His eyes met mine, filled with a pained watery gaze that threw my emotions into turmoil. I knew Jax didn't want the sword for himself, but the lingering feeling of betrayal wouldn't go away. 'Jax, stop trying to save me. I have to do this,' I said as I dropped his arm and pushed him to the floor.

Jax opened his mouth to argue, but I waved my hand and sent him back to his house before I did something I would regret.

I hugged the sword. No one was going to take it from me. The altercation with Jax had left me restless. There was a knot in my stomach I couldn't shake.

I walked out into the garden and knocked on Ant's door. 'Can I come in?' I asked as he opened the door.

He shook his head. 'Not with the sword. And I would appreciate it if you sheathed it, at least while you're around me and my family.'

I sighed and sheathed the sword. 'Better?'

Ant grimaced. 'What's up?'

Nicole wandered up to the door. Ant turned towards her, blocking her from my view. 'Hi, sweetie. Why don't you go and see if your mother needs a hand?' She nodded and walked back into the house.

Did he not trust me anymore?

Another knot formed in my stomach. I'd gone over to Ant hoping he would tell me I'd done the right thing sending Jax back, but now I wasn't so sure. I felt trapped. The memories of the invincible feeling I'd had after killing the demons entered my head. 'I need to kill some demons,' I blurted out.

Ant studied me for a while. 'I'm pretty sure that's the sword talking. Why don't you just relax? Meditate? You got the sword so you could kill Corson. No need to use it for anything other than that.'

'Then find Corson for me,' I said as I clenched my fist in anger. Why couldn't he see that I needed to use the sword?

Ant let out a sigh. 'It's not that simple.'

'Then make it simple.' I stormed off, anger boiling in my veins. Why wasn't anything straightforward? Or maybe Ant didn't want me to succeed.

# JAX

## NIDAVELLIR

I ended up at my house. *Did Nick really just teleport me back here?* Anger flashed through me, and I took a deep breath to calm myself down.

Cassie entered the living room. 'There you are ... What's wrong?' She gave me a hug.

'It's Nick ... he just teleported me away. He has the sword. Freya said to try and get through to him, but it didn't work. I don't know what to do.' I put my head in my hands and sighed. 'He used to be the strongest person I knew, at least before he lost your mother, but seeing him now, consumed by revenge ... I don't know how to get through to him. His need for revenge has taken over. I don't understand why he won't fight it.'

Cassie's eyes went wide. 'I thought Surtr had the sword?'

'I thought so too until I saw your drawing coloured in. Surtr doesn't have a blue flame.'

'But my father does?' She bit her lip. 'Why didn't you tell me?'

'I was hoping I was wrong,' I said, meeting her gaze. 'But I saw the sword with my own eyes.'

Cassie caressed my face. 'I'm sorry. But you shouldn't hide things from me. We're a team, and I can't help if I don't know what's going on.'

'I don't know if there's anything we can do to help anymore,' I said as I looked away, a sense of helplessness coming over me. 'He already seems consumed by the sword.'

Cassie placed her hands on her hips. 'I'm his daughter. Maybe I can get through to him. It's worth a try.'

'Not a chance. He's not himself. It's too risky. Even more so now.'

'But I want to help. He's my dad.'

I stroked her hair. 'Don't worry. I won't give up until I find a way. The dwarfs managed to get the sword back from Tyr. I just need to ask them how.'

Cassie's eyes lit up. 'We're going to see the dwarfs?'

I sighed. 'I'm going to see the dwarfs. You're going to stay here where it's safe.'

Cassie crossed her arms. 'I can't stay here doing nothing.'

'Yes, you can.' *I could lock her up to keep her safe.*

'I'll never forgive you.'

I remained quiet as I considered my options.

'I swear to the gods, Jax, I am not as helpless as you make me out to be,' she said, and her nostrils flared.

I let out a deep breath. 'Fine. You can come with me to the dwarfs, but you do exactly as I tell you and stay by my side the entire time.'

Her face brightened. 'When are we going?'

'Tomorrow. I need to think.'

I kissed her and stepped outside before turning into a crow. I hoped to the Fates the dwarfs had some good news for us. I took to the sky and let the movement of flying relax me, wishing that when I got back, everything would be fine, normal.

I got back to the house and transformed into my human form. The flight had made me feel a bit better – more clear headed. I opened the back door and stepped inside.

Cassie came running to me. 'Where were you? I thought something had happened when you didn't come home last night.' She embraced me in a hug.

I frowned. 'Last night?'

'Yeah. You've been gone for a whole day.'

'I'm sorry. I didn't mean to worry you. I guess I lost track of time.' Though it wasn't uncommon for me to lose my sense of time when I was in my crow form, I couldn't believe I'd let it happen this time. I should have paid more attention. I had people depending on me now.

'It's okay. You're here now.'

I scanned the room. 'Where's Leah?'

'She's with Leaf. Shall we go?'

'Sure.' She would be safer if she stayed home, but she was as stubborn as her father.

'How are we getting there?'

I held up the feather Freya had given me. 'With this.'

She tilted her head. 'With a feather?'

'It's not just any feather. It's a cloak.'

She smiled. 'So we're travelling with a magical feather?'

I returned her smile with a nod and started to unfold it. 'Ready?'

'Yes,' she said as she took my hand.

I wrapped the cloak around us and thought of Nidavellir. A moment later, we appeared next to the mouth of a cave.

Cassie turned away from the cave and looked around with her mouth open. 'What is this place?'

I folded the cloak and put it in my pocket before stepping closer to her. Around us was rocky terrain with massive tree roots spreading from one enormous trunk. The tree was gigantic, its trunk resembling an uneven wall more than a tree. When I looked up, I saw massive branches covering the sky above. 'I think that's Yggdrasil, the tree that carries the nine realms,' I said as I pointed at the tree.

I turned back to the cave opening. 'According to Freya, this is the entrance to Nidavellir, where the dwarfs live.' I took hold of Cassie's arm. 'Come on, let's go and see them.'

We entered the cave and continued along the passageway. It became smaller and narrower until we could barely walk upright. It was damp and dark. Eventually, we reached a point where light was visible at the end of the passageway. I turned to Cassie. 'Remember what I said. Stay by my side, keep quiet, and do exactly what I tell you.' She squeezed my hand in response.

We emerged from the passageway into a massive space. Gold patterns adorned the walls next to burning torches, sending amber light around the dark cave. Several dwarfs were walking among various buildings further inside. Right in front of us were two firepits and two dwarfs holding weapons that looked like something between spears and axes. The dwarfs were short, compact beings with greyish skin and white hair. They crossed their weapons, blocking our way. 'You're trespassing. What is your business here?'

'My apologies. We're here to seek information.'

'Omni does not take kindly to trespassers.'

'We've come a long way. We're seeking information about the Daudans.'

The guard narrowed his eyes. 'It is just a myth. We cannot help you.'

'You're the only ones that can.'

'Go back to where you came from.'

I tapped my foot in annoyance while attempting to keep my voice calm. 'No. I'm not going anywhere until I get the information I seek.'

'The Daudans does not exist.'

I ran my hand through my hair. 'It does, and I know exactly where it is. And that's why I need your help.'

They became quiet. A moment later, they were shouting at some other dwarfs in a language I didn't understand.

A few dwarfs came up to us and ushered us along through the massive cave and into a system of tunnels. Eventually, they stopped and pushed us into a metal cage. One of them closed and locked the door and turned to us. 'We will inform Omni you are here.'

We watched them leave. Cassie looked up at me with worried eyes. 'What are we going to do now?'

I stroked her hair. 'Shh. Everything will be fine. We just need to wait to speak to this Omni person. I'm sure it's just a misunderstanding.'

I embraced her, and she leaned her head against my shoulder. 'I hope you're right.'

# NICK

## WHERE'S CORSON?

I was deep in thought, imagining how it would feel to finally take out Corson, when Ant knocked on the door and entered my house. I gripped the sword lying by my side and pulled it into my lap. 'What happened to waiting until I let you in?'

'I thought we were past that. Why so paranoid?' Ant's gaze slid from me to the weapon in my lap.

I eyed him for a moment. 'I'm not paranoid. I just prefer it if you and your family don't come into the house unannounced anymore.'

'Okay.' Ant took a seat on the sofa opposite me. 'I have some news I thought you'd want to know.'

My interest was piqued. 'What news?'

'I've located Corson.'

My adrenaline started pumping, and I stood up, sheathing the sword at my side. 'Why didn't you just say so? Let's go.'

He opened his mouth to say something else, but I cut him off. 'What are we waiting for?' I started walking towards the front door.

He caught up with me. 'I don't know exactly where he is, only where he's normally at, but he can't leave the realm.'

'Well, let's go and find out.' I stepped through the front door leading to the human world, and Ant followed. 'You can teleport us now.' I placed a hand on his shoulder.

We arrived at a cliff that overlooked a dense forest of tall, bright trees. In the distance was a stone castle with a tower at each corner. It seemed familiar. I tried to recall where I had seen it before. Then it hit me. I'd seen it in the fire when I was looking for Ant.

Ant pointed to it. 'That's where he's supposed to be.'

'You've been there before?'

'No.'

I cocked my head. Was he lying to me? 'Are you sure?'

He hesitated. 'I haven't been inside. But I came here to check if the information I had got was sound.'

I accepted his answer, despite a lump of doubt in my stomach. We were so close now. I could almost feel the triumph as the adrenaline ran through me. 'Can we teleport over?'

'Probably better to walk it. It might have enchantments, and we don't want to let anyone know we're here.'

I used the sword to cut through the thick vegetation as

we hiked through the foliage. With each step, my resolve strengthened. Soon the forest opened up, revealing the grey stone castle. We stopped by the tree line to reassess. A long stone bridge stretched over the moat. That would be the easiest way in.

'It looks empty. Doesn't he have any guards?'

Ant shrugged. 'I don't know. It looks the same as when I saw it last.'

'And Corson is in there?'

'According to my source, he should be.'

'That's all I need to know.' I raised my sword and approached the bridge. Everything remained quiet. Almost too quiet. I took a step onto the bridge. From the corners, the shadows grew. Before I'd placed the other foot down, six shadow demons were facing me.

I smirked, already feeling the power of the sword. This was going to be a field day for me. 'Are you going to attack or just let me walk past?'

That was all the prompting they needed; they charged towards me.

I swung my sword and cut the first demon in half, and he fell to the ground. The fire burning inside me mirrored the flames on the blade. It didn't take much to kill them, at least not with the sword. If only I'd had this sword when they'd attacked us and killed Lily. Things would have been different. They wouldn't have stood a chance, and I would still have had my Lily.

I dodged a dagger thrown my way, and as I stabbed another demon in the chest, power surged through me, strengthening my connection with the sword until it became an extension of my body.

Two demons ran towards me. I grabbed one and swung him into the other, and they both fell to the ground. I smiled to myself as I slashed their heads off and spun towards the demon hurling daggers. Deflecting the daggers with the sword, I advanced on him. Another demon got in my way. I danced around him as he tried to get some hits in with his weapon, but in the end, I got bored and sliced him in half.

Creating a fire in my hand, I hurled it towards the one throwing daggers at me. He dodged it by rolling to the side, but that enabled me to reach him and cut him with my blade.

Ant came running up behind me. 'A warning would have been nice.'

'What's the fun in that?' I said with a smirk.

'You don't know what you're walking into. How can I have your back if you don't tell me the plan?'

I chuckled. 'There is no plan. Did you not see how easily I took them down?'

'Still, it doesn't hurt to be careful. We both know what happened when you tried to go up against Icarus.'

I gave Ant a smug smile. 'But I have the sword now.'

'I know the sword is giving you strength, but Corson is very powerful.'

'So am I.'

'Look. I think we have more company.' Ant pointed towards the sky, where several black dots appeared. They were moving towards us. 'Someone knows we're here.'

I shrugged. 'Let them come.' They were still too far away for us to do anything about it for now.

Ant picked up a dagger from one of the shadow demons I'd killed. 'It always amazes me. It's made from shadows, but it doesn't disintegrate when the demon dies.'

'It's because the dagger has already been created. All you have to do is bend the molecules around you to what you want. Like the house I made for you. Even if I die, it will still be there.'

Ant sheathed the dagger. 'Good to know. Are you planning on dying?'

'No. But if that's what it takes to kill Corson, I'm not opposed to it.'

Ant remained quiet as we continued over the bridge. More shadow demons appeared as we stepped through the entrance and into the small courtyard. We fought them as we made our way to the building at the back. Ant stayed in the background, for what reason, I didn't know, though I didn't complain. It meant I got to kill more demons. With each kill, the power of the sword rose and gave me more strength. My heart rate speeded up as we started up the outer stairway leading into the main part of the castle. Soon I would have my revenge.

The flying beasts appeared above our heads. They were harder to kill, maybe because they were up in the sky. I remembered them from when Lily had been killed. Ant had said they belonged to the demon Icarus, so he was bound to be around somewhere. But I was ready for him this time.

I threw fire bolts at most of the flying demons. On a few occasions, I used the newly dead shadow demons as stepping stones before they disintegrated so I could gain momentum and swing myself up into the air to stab the flying beasts.

Eventually, the beasts stopped coming, and we advanced up the outer stairwell. Icarus stepped out of a doorway as we reached the top of the stairs. 'You again? Did I not teach you a lesson the last time?'

In my human form, I didn't even reach his shoulders. We couldn't have that. I willed myself to turn into the fiery giant I was.

Icarus took a step back, a frown appearing on his face. 'What do you want?'

I gave him a smug smile. 'I want revenge – to kill everyone that had anything to do with the death of my wife. And that includes you.'

'I don't know what you're talking about.'

I cocked my head. 'But don't you? Aren't those flying beasts your legion of demons to command? They were there that day.'

'If you want a rematch, let's have at it.' He conjured a sword in his hand.

He had no idea what he was in for. I held my flaming sword up, deflecting his blow. His sword broke in half, both edges glowing amber.

Icarus seemed taken aback. 'What is that sword?'

I smirked. 'You really thought I wouldn't come prepared this time? This is the sword that will kill Corson.'

Before he could say anything else, I swung the sword at him.

He moved, and instead of hitting his chest, I cut off his right hand. It fell to the ground as he cried out in pain. He flexed his wings and tried to fly away. We couldn't have that. He would have the advantage if he was in the air.

I threw my fire at his wings and they burst into flames, preventing him from flying away, and I swung my sword again, this time leaving a massive cut in his abdomen. He fell to the ground, hunched over. *Time to get this over with.* I marched up to him and severed his head from his body. Decapitation was by far the easiest way to kill demons. I grinned to myself in triumph.

I turned to Ant, who had stood watching it all from a distance. 'Come on. We're almost there.'

I strolled through the doors, Ant following hesitantly behind. At the other end of the room was a throne made of stone, but the whole place was empty. Disappointment overwhelmed me and slowly turned into rage as I paced around the throne room. Corson should have been there. Was Ant conspiring with him? Was that why he'd kept in the background since we'd arrived?

Indecisiveness laced my mind. Ant had been nothing but supportive about my revenge, but there was a seed of doubt telling me he couldn't be trusted, telling me he was plotting to steal the sword from me.

I stalked towards Ant and threatened him with my sword. 'You said he would be here. You lied to me.'

Ant swallowed. 'I said my sources had confirmed he was here. There was no way for me to know he wouldn't be. As far as I'm aware, he can't leave this realm.'

Were all the powerful beings confined to a realm? 'Then he must be here somewhere.'

I searched the entire castle, every level, every room, but everywhere was empty. There wasn't even a low-level demon around. My rage was burning under my skin, ready to be released, when I entered the throne room again and snarled in Ant's face, 'Tell me where he is!'

Ant's legs were shaking. 'I don't know.'

'Are you lying to me?'

Sweat covered his face as he met my gaze. 'No. I owe you my wife's life.'

'Then let me motivate you. If you lie to me again, your wife will pay the price. Don't come back until you have a solid lead.'

Ant teleported away.

Fire burned in my veins, but guilt left a hollow feeling in my stomach. I shouldn't have threatened Ant or his wife. They had been nothing but nice to me. But he was hiding something from me. I knew he was.

# JAX

# What Happened to Tyr?

It felt like forever before the group of dwarfs came back to get us. On the positive side, they didn't restrain our hands. Maybe they didn't think we were a threat. We trudged through several tunnels until we came to a large secluded room. A dwarf with long white hair that almost reached the ground approached us with the help of a walking stick. He looked ancient. His face was covered in wrinkles, and he wore a monocle. The dwarfs around us bowed to him. It would be wise to stay on their good side, so I nudged Cassie and we both bowed to him, just like the dwarfs. The dwarfs stood up. One of them approached us. 'This is Omni, our elder.' He glanced over at Omni. 'They are here because of the Daudans. They said they've taken it.'

My throat constricted. 'No. No, we haven't taken it. I said I know where it is.'

Omni stroked his long white beard. 'I see. And why are you here?'

'We need information on how you managed to get the sword away from Tyr,' I said.

'And why is that?'

'Our friend, he has the sword. It's changing him.'

'You'll be wise not to get involved. The universe has a way of balancing itself out.'

'So you're saying we should just stand by and do nothing?'

'Eventually the sword will consume him completely and he will no longer be. The eternal flame will burn through him.'

I took a deep breath to keep my frustration under control. 'The eternal flame already runs in his veins. How do you think he got hold of it in the first place?'

Omni's face revealed a shocked expression before he carefully put together his mask of indifference. 'Then he will have to be stopped.'

'That's why we're here. We need to know how you took the sword from Tyr so I can take it from my friend and destroy it.'

'The sword is too powerful to be destroyed.'

'How did you get the sword away from Tyr?'

'By turning him to stone.'

I drew a breath and released it. 'I want to save my friend, not kill him.'

'He won't be dead. If he's as powerful as you say he is, he

will merely be asleep.'

'Can I talk to Tyr?'

Omni shook his head. 'It is not possible. He is still a stone statue.'

I ran my hand through my hair. This was useless. We needed to come up with something else. I bowed my head. 'Thank you for the information, but I'll find another way. I'm not turning my friend into stone with no way to reverse it.' I grabbed Cassie's hand, and we had started walking away when the dwarfs stopped me.

'We have given you a gift of information. It's only fair we get one in return,' one of them said as they all ogled Cassie. She stared at me with wide eyes, panic written all over her face.

'I would be happy to give you information in return for information, but Cassie is not a bargaining chip.'

'Was that not why you brought her?'

'No. I brought her because she wants to help my friend as much as I do.'

'I see.' Omni stroked his beard again. 'Then what can you offer us in return?'

I let out a sigh. Had Freya seen this coming? I reached into my pocket and pulled out the necklace Freya had given me. 'I'm willing to trade this for the information and for safe passage for me and Cassie to get out of here.'

The dwarfs' eyes went wide. 'The Brisingamen.'

I looked around, confused. I'd thought Freya had just given me a random necklace, but by the way the dwarfs acted, I realised there was nothing random about it.

Omni studied the necklace. 'How did you come across

this?'

'My dear friend Freya gave it to me when she learned I planned on coming here to get more information about the sword.'

'She must hold you very dear. She did a lot to acquire this necklace.'

One of the dwarfs whispered something in Omni's ear. He looked at me with a smug smile. 'We will accept your gift. Please tell Freya that if she wants it back, the price is the same as last time.'

He reached over to grab the necklace, but I hesitated. 'If I give you this, do you promise that me and Cassie will be given free passage away from here?'

Omni nodded.

It felt too easy. Maybe I was being paranoid, but better safe than sorry. 'I need you to say the words.'

Omni let out an annoyed breath. 'I promise to give you and your lady friend safe passage in exchange for the Brisingamen.'

'Thank you.' I handed over the necklace to Omni.

He gestured towards an opening leading back into the tunnel system. 'You are free to leave. My men will not bother you.'

I grabbed Cassie's hand and moved towards the tunnel. I made a clear point not to ask anyone for directions. They would see it as a favour and expect one in return. I'd almost lost Cassie once before; I wasn't going to risk it.

After a lot of dead ends, we finally saw the glow of a torch at the end of the tunnel. We became hopeful, as we thought we had finally managed to get back to the big hall where we had first arrived, but as we reached it, we realised we'd been wrong. This area was smaller. A wall remained on our right side as we continued further in. Torches hung on the wall, and several metal barrels containing fires had been placed on the ground.

A sound that reminded me of snoring echoed through the chamber. There were several stone statues of dwarfs ahead, and, as the wall at our side stopped, a massive beast chained up in a ribbon made of some sort of metal greeted us. The beast was enormous and took up the entire space. It resembled a wolf in shape and had black fur and a head as big as me. The tip of one of its ears was missing. A sword attached to its upper and lower jaw held its mouth open with its massive teeth clearly on display. Its canines were easily the size of our legs.

Cassie let out a whimper, and I turned to comfort her. 'What is this creature?' she asked, biting her lip.

I grabbed her arm. 'Come on. Let's leave before he wakes up,' I said as I pulled her towards me.

She dug her heels into the ground. 'He's scared and angry at being betrayed.'

She approached him, and my heart sank to my feet. He might have been chained, but he could still be dangerous. 'What are you doing?'

'He might look like a beast, but I don't think he is. Maybe we can free him.' Cassie reached out to him and stroked his muzzle. His eyes opened.

Panic flooded me. 'Cassie?'

'Relax. He wouldn't hurt me even if he could. He has a good heart.'

A young dwarf with short white hair walked up to us. 'Try telling that to Odin that he's destined to kill.'

My eyes went wide with realisation. 'This is Fenrir?' I covered my mouth, instantly regretting the question. We had nothing else to bargain with.

The dwarf waved his hand. 'We aren't all the same. I don't mind answering your questions. We rarely get visitors, so I will take your company as a gift. But to answer your question, yes. It's Fenrir. We keep him here so we can keep an eye on him.'

He held out his gloved hand to me. 'I'm Sekje.'

I shook his hand. 'Jax.'

'So why are you here?'

'We came to get information about the Dauđans.'

'Why?' Sekje asked, studying us.

'Our friend has the sword, and we're looking for ways to get it away from him before it's too late.'

'I see. My great-great-something-grandfather created the Dauđans. But I'm not a blacksmith. Too much hard work. I prefer the alchemy part of the creative process.' He pulled a pouch from his pocket and opened it. It looked like glittery sand. 'Feel free to use this.'

'What does it do?'

'It turns a being into stone.'

'You've turned all these beings into stone?' Cassie asked, pointing at the line of statues.

Sekje smirked. 'No. Some of them were just stupid enough to get caught by the sun. I'm really working on a way to reverse it, but I haven't had much luck. Apparently the fiery breath of Fenrir will break them free, but I would be foolish to try. Odin himself placed the sword through his jaw. Not to mention Fenrir was deceived by the gods and, in essence, the dwarfs eons ago, and I wouldn't want to play with fate, so until I can come up with another solution, they will have to remain stone statues.'

Sekje looked behind him. 'You shouldn't really be here. So I'll show you the way back to the hall if you promise never to speak about what you've seen here.'

I bowed my head. 'Thank you.'

Sekje led us through several tunnels and eventually back to the main hall. He pointed to the exit and disappeared back into the tunnel system.

Cassie let out a breath of relief as we made our way to where we had first met the two guards by the two firepits. Before we could pass, they crossed their weapons to stop us from leaving.

I opened my mouth to say something, but they cut me off. 'Tell Freya we'd love to have her come and visit.'

I nodded, and they moved their weapons.

As we made our way along the dark passageway leading up to the surface, Cassie grabbed my hand. 'I can't believe they almost took me away from you. I'm sorry I gave you a hard time. It's just ... he's my dad and I feel so useless.'

I squeezed her hand. 'It's okay. I understand. Though I'd rather you were safe. The thought of losing you ... I don't think I could take it.'

She turned to face me and wrapped her arms tightly around me in a hug. 'I'm sorry. I know you mean well, but I'm not as fragile as you make me out to be.'

# NICK

# AN UNEXPECTED VISIT

I sat on my sofa and watched some memories of me and Lily in the fire. How I wished I could hold her just one more time. It'd been several days since Ant had gone to get a lead on where Corson might be, and he still hadn't shown his face. I owed him an apology for doubting him and losing my temper. At least he still trusted me enough to let his wife and child remain in the house I'd conjured for them in the garden.

Someone knocked on the door. I went to see who it was, and a short man with grey skin and white hair greeted me. I scanned the twilight outside. What was this being doing here? 'Can I help you?'

'I believe you have something that belongs to us.'

'And what would that be?'

'The Dauðans.'

I took a step back. How did this being know about it?

I had placed the sword by the fire and hadn't taken it with me to open the door. If I had, I could have killed this intruder in a second. Maybe he was just guessing. 'I'm not sure what you're talking about. What's a Dauðans?'

'Don't play dumb with me.' He sprinkled some sort of dust on the threshold and took a step into the house. 'I can feel its power from here.'

What was that powder he used? And how did he just walk into my house without any repercussions? I never invited him in. The binding on the house should have stopped him. 'Who are you?'

'I'm Sekje.'

I rolled my eyes. 'Let me rephrase. What are you and why are you here?'

'I'm a svartalf, or what most beings refer to as a dwarf. And I've already told you why I am here. To retrieve the Dauðans.'

I clenched my fist. 'How can you just walk into my house without being invited?'

He smirked. 'We all have our ways. Now, can you be so kind as to fetch me the Dauðans?'

I didn't like this one bit. Maybe I could get the sword and annihilate him. I plastered a smile on my lips. 'Stay here. I'll get it for you.'

I retrieved the sword. When I was back in the hallway, Sekje blew some sort of powder on me. It seemed different from the one he'd used on the threshold. It stung my eyes, and my whole body started to itch. Rage bubbled up inside me. 'What have you done to me?'

Sekje smirked. 'It's just a little precaution. Did the same to Tyr when we needed the Daudans back from him.'

My skin started to harden, similar to when I changed into my demon form. 'Why am I turning to stone?' I asked as I glared into his eyes.

He shrugged. 'Relax. It won't kill you.'

I willed myself to take my demon form. After all, it was made of molten rock.

Sekje's eyes went wide. 'You're a descendent of Surtr.'

'No shit.' I grabbed him around his throat and lifted him off the ground. I was tempted to strangle him. 'Who sent you?'

'I sent myself.'

My impatience got the better of me and I sliced him in half with the sword before he even had a chance to scream. No one was going to take my sword away from me.

I called out to Ant but realised he wasn't home. After all, I had told him not to come back until he had more information. I let out an agitated sigh. What was I going to do with this dwarf? I kicked the two parts of him out of the house and onto the porch. Let the humans deal with it. They'd probably think it was a prank, a Halloween prop, rather than something supernatural.

I strengthened my wards around the house. How had he been able to get in? It made no sense. As I was about to close the door, Ant materialised.

He took a step towards me but kept his distance. His facial expression was guarded, and he avoided eye contact with me. His eyes fell on the body that had been cut in half. 'What's a svartalf doing here?'

I perked up. 'You know what it is?'

'Yeah, but they usually keep underground. They're not really keen on the sun.'

'He came for the sword.'

Ant narrowed his eyes. 'So you killed him?'

'He gave me no choice. He tried to turn me into stone.'

'So that's why you're in your demon form.'

I willed myself to take my human form again. 'Better?' Ant nodded, though his eyes were full of apprehension.

I scratched my head, debating how to apologise for my outburst the other day, but instead I changed the subject. 'Any news?'

'Some. But don't you think we should deal with this first? They may send more after you, and next time you may not be so lucky.'

I shrugged. 'Let them come. After I've killed Corson, none of this will matter. They can have the sword. I made a fire oath with Surtr that can't be broken.'

Ant's eyes went wide. 'A fire oath?'

'Yeah. It was the only way to get him to tell me about the sword. He tricked me. I thought he actually had the sword, but it doesn't matter now. Once I've killed Corson, I'm bound to Surtr and his stupid army.'

'Maybe we can find a way around it.'

I sighed. 'What's the point? The only chance I have to ever see Lily again is if I meet her in the afterlife. Which isn't very likely. Besides, maybe dying during Ragnarök won't be that bad.'

Ant took a step towards me but hesitated and stepped back. 'I'm very sorry for everything that's happened to you. In another life, our friendship may have been based on happiness.'

Guilt flooded my gut. 'I'm sorry for how I acted before. I was just frustrated. We were so close. Of course I won't hurt your wife. I wouldn't want to put you through what I've been through.'

Ant gave me an unsure smile and walked through the house and out into the back garden. Did he not believe me?

# JAX

## RUMINATING

When we arrived back at the house, I let out a sigh. 'Now what? I'm not willing to turn Nick to stone just so we can get the sword from him. There must be another way.'

'My offer to talk to him still stands. I'm his daughter. Maybe he'll listen to me.'

'No. It's too dangerous.'

Cassie had opened her mouth to say something when Leah entered the living room. 'You're back. Where did you go?'

'To the dwarfs,' Cassie said.

'As in the dwarfs that made the sword?' I nodded. 'Did you find any answers?'

'Not unless we want to turn Nick to stone.'

Leah placed her hand on her hip. 'That's not the worst idea. Turn him to stone, grab the sword and turn him back into a human.'

'You make it sound so easy, and I really wish it was, but we have no clue how to turn him back. Tyr is still a stone statue.'

Leah rolled her eyes and let out a sigh. 'Sucks to be Tyr.' She scratched her head. 'I forgot to tell you, Sky came by. She said she'd had another vision. She wasn't sure what it meant but thought you might know. I told her I'd let you know when you came back. Anyway, I'm happy you're safe, but I'd better get back to my studies.'

'What are you studying for?' Cassie asked.

'Just how the Elder committee would work and how to make it fair.'

'So you've decided to become the High Priestess?' I asked.

Leah shrugged. 'I don't know. Leaf said she'd stand in until I'm ready, as long as I train for it and learn their ways. It's a bit ironic, really, as Leaf hasn't had any training to be a High Priestess either. But the people seem to accept her.'

Talking about Leaf always brought guilt to my heart. 'I don't think the training matters too much. It's more what's in your heart. If you want the best for the people in the village, then you should claim your rightful place as High Priestess.'

'But I don't know if that's what I want. I have a life here. Or at least I had one before all of this. I was going to finish college and apply to university and become a doctor.'

'I'm sure you can train as a healer in the village.'

She let out a sigh. 'Not if I'm the High Priestess.'

Cassie placed a hand on her shoulder. 'I'm sure you'll figure it out.'

'Yeah, and if you decide the magical world isn't for you, I'm happy to supply proof of graduation,' I said with a smirk.

'You mean you're happy to conjure up a certificate?'

I smiled. 'Anything for my girls.'

Leah rolled her eyes. 'You'd better get over to Sky. Hopefully it's not another end of the world situation. One is more than enough to deal with.' She started to walk away but stopped and turned to me. 'Would you mind teleporting me to Whitelock Unlimited at some point? I want to check it out again.'

'Sure. Let me just see Sky first.'

'No problem.'

I teleported over to the cabin where Sky and Mark lived and was heading to the front door when Cassie appeared next to me. 'I can't believe you teleported away without me. We're a team. Where you go, I go.'

I grabbed her hand. 'I'm sorry. Leah mentioned Sky wanted to talk to me. But I guess you're right. If whatever Sky wants to talk about includes your dad, you deserve to know.'

'Thank you,' she said and walked past me to knock on the door. A moment later, Mark opened it. 'Good, it's you.'

We stepped inside. Sky greeted us in the living room, where Seth and Night were sitting on the sofa playing video games.

Seth looked up and gave us a nod before pausing his game. 'Come on, Night, let's go for a walk or something. I can show you around the wolf pack grounds.'

Seth and Night walked past us and out the door. I looked around, confused. Why had they left?

'Night doesn't know about my visions,' Sky said as if to answer my question.

'Why not?' I asked.

'I don't want him to tell our parents. They've been through so much, and I don't want to worry them. It's bad enough that I can't see them during the day.'

'What about what Freya said to you? "Love can conquer even the worst of curses." I thought she was telling you your mate bond with Mark was stronger than the bond Hecate had on you. And that you would be able to go out in the sun again without having to be a wolf,' Cassie said.

Sky turned to me. 'What do you think? You know Freya best.'

I hesitated. 'I don't know. She always speaks in riddles. It's hard to interpret until after something has happened.'

She shivered. 'Until we're sure, I'd rather not attempt it.'

We stood in awkward silence until Cassie spoke up. 'So what was this vision you wanted to talk about? Did you remember something else from when the sword was taken?'

'No. I haven't had that vision since I woke up. This one was different. It was Nick and the sword. He was slaying demons.'

'That doesn't sound too bad.'

'Maybe not, but the sword changed colour. The blue flame faded and got replaced by an amber one. I wasn't sure what it meant, but as I saw it, I thought it would be important. And maybe you would know why.'

'I'm not sure. His fire started out amber but changed after he met Surtr for the first time. I have no clue why it would change again.'

'Maybe Freya would know,' Cassie said.

'She probably does. I can ask about the wolf thing at the same time.'

Sky smiled. 'Thank you. If anyone would know if I will ever be able to walk in the sun again, it would be your grandma.'

I tilted my head. 'My grandma?'

'Oh, I thought you knew she was your grandma.' Sky reached up to twist her hair. 'Me and Mark overheard Freya and Hecate talking during the witch fight in the temple. How she can see the future, but when she tried to change it to rescue her daughter, she ended up with you, her grandson.'

This was news. Why hadn't she told me I was related to her? Was she ashamed of me? She never talked about a daughter. I didn't even know she had one. No, they must have heard it wrong. I kissed Cassie goodbye and teleported to Freya's realm.

Thoughts of what Sky had told me spun around in my head. A feeling of betrayal twirled in my stomach. If Freya really was my grandma, then she knew more about my childhood and who my parents were than she let on. Was that why she'd told me I was a god?

I took the scenic route to her cottage and landed on the veranda. I'd expected her to be sitting outside with a teacup in her hand, waiting for me, but she wasn't.

I walked inside and looked through the downstairs before going upstairs to the bedrooms. She wasn't in hers. My eyes landed on the door of my childhood bedroom. I opened it just to realise it was exactly the same as I'd left it. She hadn't changed anything. I smiled to myself. As long as I'd been alive and as much as I could take care of myself, it was nice to know some things didn't change. Even after all these years, I still had a bedroom to come home to.

I let out a sigh. Freya wasn't in the house. It would be impossible to find her; she could be anywhere. I could wait, but I had no way of knowing when she would be back. Maybe it was best to head home again.

As I turned to leave the room, my eyes landed on a pile of five quartz crystals in the corner. Freya had used them to restrain my demon while she was trying to get through to me when my demon side had taken over after the torture by Surtr. Maybe I could use them on Nick.

I arrived back home, and Cassie greeted me in the living room. 'What did she say?'

I shrugged. 'She wasn't there.'

She bit her lip. 'Oh. Do you have any other way of contacting her?'

'Not really. I've never been in this situation before. She's always been around when I needed her.'

'Do you think something's happened to her?'

'No. She's more than capable of taking care of herself. You've seen how powerful she is. I don't think we need to worry.'

'Maybe you can try again tomorrow.'

'I guess you're right.' I felt defeated. It was obvious Nick was getting out of control. But I didn't know how to stop him. Cassie must have felt my hopelessness.

'How about we do something else? Stressing about things we can't change is pointless.'

I leaned in towards her, a smile tugging on my lips. 'What did you have in mind?'

'You said you'd take me flying.'

I met her gaze. 'Are you sure you want to do this?' Cassie nodded. 'Okay. I'm going to try something, but if it doesn't work, I'll need to fully transform to be able to take you flying.'

'Your demon form doesn't scare me.'

I gave her a lopsided smile. 'Does anything scare you?'

'The thought of losing someone I love does.'

'You never fail to amaze me.' I reached out and tucked a strand of hair behind her ear. 'Ready?' I asked before I reached deep inside myself. A chill went through me as I connected to my demon. I hated the icy feeling it caused, but it was all worth it for Cassie. I concentrated on my wings, visualising them spurting out of my human form. Hopefully I could control the transformation enough to only partly transform. A gasp escaped Cassie's lips, and I opened my eyes.

'That's amazing.'

I looked at my hands, which had remained human, and moved my muscles connecting to the wings. 'Please tell me I'm mainly in my human form.'

Cassie smiled. 'You look like a dark, handsome angel.'

I let out a sigh of relief and lifted her up in my arms to carry her outside, flexing my black-feathered wings. I was happy it had worked, but I'd never flown like this before. I hesitated.

Cassie had her arms wrapped around my neck. She leaned in and spoke in my ear. 'It's okay. I trust you.'

I closed my eyes, moved my wings, and the next moment, we were airborne. Cassie laughed as the breeze engulfed us.

We flew over the forest and town. 'The view is amazing from here,' Cassie said in awe. 'Look, there's my house.' She pointed at the house she used to live in with Abigail. 'And there's our school.'

I continued to drift around in the sky until the sun started going down.

'That's the restaurant you took me to for our first date,' Cassie said.

I smiled as memories of our first date played in my head. 'Are you hungry? We can always take a break and go for a meal.'

'But what if someone sees you?'

'The trees and the twilight should shield us from view. Besides, most of them won't believe it. But if anyone actually sees us, we just need to make them think they didn't.'

'I can read their mind to check.' Her confidence made me smile.

We descended, and I made my wings disappear before walking into the restaurant. We asked to be seated out on the terrace, at the same table as last time. The soft melody of the adjacent river was soothing as we ate and enjoyed a normal, quiet evening. My thoughts sometimes turned to Nick, but each time they did, Cassie distracted me with something mundane.

'I think we should bring Leah and Leaf here sometime.'

I jerked my head. 'Huh?'

'Like a family meal. You haven't seen much of Leaf lately, and I know they're not really my family—'

I cut her off. 'Family is not determined by blood. You grew up with Leah. She will always be your sister. And I know Katie's memories are confusing for you, as you're not her, but they are your family as much as they are mine.'

Cassie bit her lip. 'I don't think Leaf likes me.'

'How can anyone not like you? You're amazing. Besides, I think it's me. Every time I see Leaf I'm overcome with guilt at how I abandoned her.'

'But you didn't know. And she forgave you.'

'It doesn't make me feel any better about it. Besides, I can't even save my best friend.'

Cassie stroked my cheek. 'Neither of those things are on you. With Leaf, they made you forget, and with my dad, I've seen how hard you're trying. You're not responsible for everyone.'

I let out a breath. 'Then why does it feel like I've failed them?'

She placed her hands over mine. 'You haven't. Come on. Let's get out of here.'

We paid for our food and left the restaurant hand in hand. 'Do you want me to conjure my car?'

Cassie shook her head. 'I want to show you something. Close your eyes.'

I did what she said. The air shifted. I could tell she'd teleported us somewhere. 'Can I open my eyes?'

'Yes. you can open them.'

I took in the scenery. We were standing on the cliff that overlooked the town. The cliff where she'd first told me she loved me. Warmth filled me. 'Why did you bring me here?'

'I thought you needed a reminder.'

'A reminder of what?'

'Of how far we've come. It's hard to believe it hasn't even been a year since you took me up here for a date.'

I gave her a kiss. 'You don't know how happy I am to have you.'

Her cheeks turned pink. 'I thought we could spend the night out here. I debated bringing a tent, but then I thought I could just ask you to conjure one.'

I smiled. 'I can do you one better,' I said and conjured a four-poster bed.

She rolled her eyes – 'Always a show-off' – and got into the bed. 'So, you said I'd be able to conjure things one day. Can you teach me?'

I joined her in the bed and wrapped my arms around her. 'Of course. All you have to do is imagine that it's there. Picture it. Every single detail. It's usually easier to imagine something that already exists and just make it move between the fabric of the universe. But you should be able to conjure things from thin air too. It's all about willing the molecules around you to do your bidding.'

Her forehead creased with concentration as she held her hand out, closing her eyes.

She opened her eyes and let out a defeated breath. 'It's not working.'

'Like with all abilities, it takes time.'

'You always make it seem so easy.'

'I've had a lot of practice.'

She scoffed and got under the covers. I joined her and she cuddled up to me. I kissed her head. 'Don't worry, you'll get there.'

# NICK

## THE BETRAYAL

My fingers were tingling and my body was restless. I needed to use the sword again. My soul screamed for its power. But where could I find demons to slay? Wait – what about the woman Jax had brought over? He'd said I couldn't kill her, but that was before they'd gone to talk to her. Surely he wouldn't need her anymore.

I picked up my sword, teleported to my dungeon and walked through the big wooden doors leading to the room where she was kept. Though I'd kept prisoners there before, it had stood empty for a long time – since before I'd met Lily. I had considered getting rid of it, but I wasn't sure how to remove this realm. Besides, it carried a sense of nostalgia, reminding me of what Jax and I had been through together, and it had come in handy for Jax.

I approached the dome of light that removes magic from everyone inside it, expecting to see the woman who was imprisoned, but it was empty. Where was she? Had Jax taken her? No, Jax wouldn't have done that. He'd given her to me because he thought she was a threat. I scanned the area. No one was there. But the dome wasn't a place you could just walk out of. Jax must have taken her.

Anger boiled up inside me. He must have sneaked her out when I wasn't around. So much for being my best friend. Jax would pay for this. I kicked an object lying on the floor, only to realise it was a knife. I picked it up and examined it. Blood covered the blade. But whose? And why had it been left behind?

I moved it from hand to hand while walking around the dome, thinking. An abnormality in the dome made me stop, and I stepped closer to examine it. It looked like someone had cut through it. Was that even possible? Had Jax given the knife to the woman so she could escape? No. It didn't make sense. Jax had helped create the dome and set up the force field around it. He could have dismantled it if he'd wanted to move the woman somewhere else. Something else must have happened. Maybe I needed to warn Jax.

I teleported back to my house, removed the sword from my waist and placed it on the couch, but as soon as it was out of my reach, a feeling of emptiness came over me and my body felt drained. I eyed the sword, my hands itching to pick it up again. Maybe I should just keep it on me. It gave me energy, and every time I used it, I felt more powerful. But who could I use it on?

A plan formed in my head, and I straightened up. I still emitted energy that drew demons to me. I picked up the sword belt, secured it around my waist and covered it with a coat before walking out of the front door into the human realm. I thought about going to Lily's grave, but it wasn't ideal for what I wanted. Instead I went to the nearby park – the park where I had summoned Kaliakwan. I took a seat, hoping the demons would come.

I stayed there as the spring breeze danced on my skin. Lily always loved walking here. She loved everything human. Hatred filled me as I thought about her. I'd been so close to avenging her, but Ant had given me the wrong information.

Before long, several demons turned up. I smiled. 'I hope you brought reinforcements.'

I fought them, taking my time, playing with them, letting them think they almost had the upper hand before killing them with the blade. It felt good. The power from the sword seeped into my body, making me feel alive.

As demon after demon fell at my hands, something inside me changed. The flame of the sword changed colour. It was no longer blue but a bright amber.

*That's weird.* It had always mirrored the flame inside me. I summoned my own fire to see if anything had changed, and, to my confusion, my fire had turned amber too. The blue fire had been sacred to me. Lily had appreciated the blue fire. She'd told me it showed just how special I was. But now it was gone.

I lashed out, screaming and setting everything, including the trees around me, on fire. I watched the devastation for a moment before realisation hit me. Lily had loved this park. I extinguished the flames, sheathed my sword and walked home.

As I entered my house, I heard talking and laughter from the garden. I went to investigate. Ant was out there playing with his daughter while his wife watched them.

I stepped outside, and the laughter died down. Ant's wife picked Nicole up and disappeared into their small house. Ant looked up at me. 'Where have you been?'

'I was out.'

'You don't go out.'

'I needed to blow off some steam. Took a walk to the park.' Ant looked at me with worried eyes. 'Don't worry. I didn't hurt any humans.'

'I didn't ask.'

I studied Ant. He was acting strange, worried. Like he didn't trust me anymore. I couldn't understand what I had done to break his trust. Unless he was worried I would find out he had betrayed me. I shook the thought out of my head. He wouldn't do that to me.

'Do you have some information for me?' I asked.

Ant scratched his neck. 'Yeah. I reached out to my contacts. They all say the same. Corson can't leave his realm. I know he wasn't in the castle when we went, but he has to be somewhere in that realm. So I did some digging.'

'What did you find out?'

'The realm isn't too big, but there's a fortress hidden in the forest. Maybe that's where Corson is.'

I considered this for a while. 'Okay. Let's go.'

Ant gave me a look. 'Now?'

'Yes. The sooner I get to kill Corson, the sooner you can

stay at home with your family.'

He let out a sigh. 'Let me at least say bye to my wife and kid. Besides, you could do with getting cleaned up.'

I gave him a glare. I wanted to leave right away. But he was right. My clothes smelled of burnt demon, and there was mud and black blood all over them. 'Okay. I'll see you back here after my shower.'

He nodded, and I walked back into the house. I thought about leaving the sword downstairs in the living room, but it would be safer if I took it with me. I left it on the bathroom floor as I stripped my clothes off and got into the shower.

I met Ant in the garden and teleported us to Corson's realm. We stood on the cliff overlooking the castle we'd stormed the last time we were there. Grey clouds covered the sky, but from the cliff, it was still easy enough to see the castle in the distance.

'Why would he have a castle if he's not staying in it?'

'Maybe he knew we were coming,' Ant said.

I turned to Ant and narrowed my eyes. 'And how would he know that?'

Ant shrugged. 'I don't know. But it's not completely impossible. According to rumours, he is one of the most powerful demons in existence.'

'And I'm the descendant of one of the first demons on Earth. Don't believe everything you hear.'

Ant turned and scanned the forest. 'We have to go through there to get to the fortress. It's a bit of a trek. And it's hidden in some sort of cloaking spell. You can't see the fortress until you're almost right on top of it.' I gave a grunt and followed him.

We were deep in the forest, vegetation everywhere, when Ant stopped walking. 'We're here.'

I looked around. There was a glade up ahead, and I recognised the makeshift wooden throne Icarus had sat on the first time I'd fought him. 'Isn't this where I first fought Icarus?' I asked as I pointed to it.

Ant scanned the area. 'I don't think so.'

Was he lying to me? 'That throne of branches looks exactly the same to me.'

'I'm sure a lot of places look similar.' Ant took a few steps in the opposite direction and pointed to the ground. 'See these rocks?' I followed his gaze to a group of rocks laid out in a circle. 'I left them there to remind myself of the path to follow, and if we follow the line from the circle, we should get to the cloaked fortress.'

'What line?' I said in a huff, only to realise there was actually a line of stones creating a path, starting at the stone circle. 'You did this?'

'I didn't want you to think I'd deceived you, so I made sure I knew how to find the fortress,' he said in a strained voice.

We hiked in silence for a while until the air vibrated around us, and the next moment, a fortress appeared in front of us. I raised my sword as we entered. Ant's eyes flickered to the sword, and he gasped but stayed quiet.

No one stood at the gigantic arched entrance. The entire area seemed deserted. 'Are you sure this is the place?' I asked

Ant sceptically.

'I've searched the whole realm. This fortress and the castle are the only buildings that exist. And I saw him with my own eyes when I was here last.'

'Well, he's not here now.' The fire burned inside me. 'There's nothing here but a large empty room.'

Ant took a step back. 'I don't know what to tell you.'

I grew into my demon form and towered over him. 'That's not good enough. I told you to find out where he is.'

'I did. He was here, and he can't leave this realm.'

I raised my sword. 'Are you having me on?'

Ant took a step back. 'I've been trying to help you get your revenge since I met you. I wouldn't lie to you.'

A fire erupted inside me. Before I knew what I was doing, I blasted a fireball towards him.

Ant disappeared.

I couldn't believe he'd left me. Hatred boiled in my veins as I teleported back to the house. I wouldn't let him get away with this.

When I arrived in the garden, he was holding his daughter with one arm and dragging his wife with the other. 'Come on, we need to leave,' he told them as he ran towards the garden gate. I materialised in front of him. He handed Nicole to his wife and shielded them with his body. 'I thought we were friends.'

I tilted my head. 'I thought we were too, but friends don't abandon each other.'

He took a step towards me. 'Friends also don't try to kill each other.'

I shrugged. 'You betrayed me.'

'I didn't. I've told you everything I know. I might have had my own agenda when we first met, but after you saved my wife, I've given up everything to try to help you.'

'Not everything,' I said, turning my eyes to his wife and child.

'If you hurt them. I'll ...'

'You'll what? You're no match for me.'

He said something to his wife in a language I didn't understand. Tears welled up in her eyes when she replied.

'If you want to fight me, then let's fight, but leave my wife and child out of it.' He picked up a stick from the ground.

I laughed. Did he really think he could take me? We circled each other, moving away from the gate.

*'Now,'* he screamed as he rushed towards me with the stick in his hand. I set the stick on fire and it fell to the ground. I caught movement in my peripheral vision. Dalia, carrying Nicole in her arms, was running towards the exit. I teleported in front of the gate and swung my sword, driving it into her abdomen. Dalia dropped Nicole and crashed to the ground. Everything went quiet.

Ant stared at me. 'What have you done?' Pain filled his voice.

I faced him. 'At least now you'll feel the same agony I do.'

Ant scooped Nicole up in his arms and rushed past me, disappearing through the gate before I could react.

Horrified, I stared down at Dalia's lifeless body. What had I done?

# JAX

# A Visit from Ant

I woke up the next morning to Cassie sitting up in the four-poster bed I'd conjured on the cliff. She had her hand out and her eyes closed.

'What are you doing?'

She opened her eyes. 'I'm trying to make something appear, but it's not working.'

I put my hand on her shoulder and gave it a squeeze. 'You'll get there.'

She turned towards me with a smile, then climbed on top of me and kissed me. I put my hands on her back and pressed her against me, deepening the kiss. 'I love you.'

'I love you too.'

After spending some more time in bed, we teleported

back to the house for a shower. When we came downstairs, Leah was eating cereal at the kitchen table. She looked up as we entered. 'You're home.' She smiled. 'I'm starting to feel like I'm the only one living in this house. I even had to do some grocery shopping to make sure I could feed myself.'

I chuckled and gave Cassie a kiss on the cheek. 'What would you like for breakfast?'

'Can I have some eggs and bacon, please? These cereals suck.' Leah pushed the bowl away.

Cassie giggled. 'I'll have the same.' I conjured three plates of food.

'So, what's on the agenda for today?' Leah asked.

I shrugged. 'Not a clue. I wanted to talk to Freya, but she's not home.'

'Do you have time to take me to some places?'

'Where do you want to go?'

'I found this list when I went to Whitelock Unlimited. It has ten addresses on it, one of which is ours. So I want to check out the others to see if the people still live there and if they're also supernatural beings.'

I ground my teeth. 'You went to Whitelock Unlimited by yourself?'

Leah's shoulders slumped. 'Yeah. I asked you to take me, but I got tired of waiting, and I know you have a lot on your plate.'

'I'm sorry. But you really should have let us know. What if something had happened to you?'

Leah shrugged. 'Well, it didn't. The place was deserted.'

I let out a breath. 'Where did you want to go? We can start by checking out one address. But we don't know what to expect, so we need to be careful.'

Leah smiled. 'Thank you.'

'Can I come too?' Cassie asked.

'Sure.'

There was a knock on the door. I looked at Cassie and Leah in confusion before I got up to answer. Outside stood a man, though by the energy he radiated, I could tell he was a demon. A little girl of around two years old was hiding behind his leg.

He wore an expression of panic. 'I'm sorry. I didn't know where else to go. I need help.' He wiped a tear from his cheek. 'I know you don't know me. I'm Ant, a friend of Nick's. Well, I was.'

I thought back to my conversations with Nick. Had he mentioned someone called Ant? I gave Ant a closer look. He seemed familiar. 'You were there when I tried to talk to Nick.'

'Yes. I'm seeking refuge for my daughter. Nick has completely gone off the rails, and I fear for her safety. He killed my wife.' Tears fell down his face, but he brushed them away. 'I understand if you don't want to invite me in. I haven't proved to you I can be trusted, but I'm begging you. Please keep my daughter safe.'

Cassie walked up to the door. 'He's telling the truth.'

I turned to her. 'How can you be so sure?'

'His emotions, his grief is overwhelming. The fact he hasn't broken apart is astonishing.' She bent down to the little girl. 'What's your name?'

Still hiding behind Ant's legs, she looked up at Cassie. 'Nicole,' she mumbled.

Cassie reached out her hand. 'Why don't you come inside while the grown-ups talk? I think we may have some ice cream in the freezer.'

Nicole's eyes went wide. 'What's ice cream?'

Cassie smiled at her. 'You'll love it. Come on.'

Nicole looked up at her dad, her face a mixture of confusion and worry. Ant nudged her towards Cassie. 'It's okay. You can trust her.'

Cassie and Nicole walked into the house hand in hand. Before they disappeared out of sight, Cassie's voice sounded in my head. *He's being sincere.*

'Cassie seems to believe you're telling the truth and that I should hear you out.'

He let out a sigh of relief. 'She's an angel in disguise.'

I smiled. 'She sure is. So tell me what happened. The Nick I know wouldn't kill an innocent being.'

A mix of sadness and anger appeared on his face. 'The Nick you know is gone. It's like the sword has completely taken him over. He used to be sweet, though depressed. He even saved my wife once after she was severely injured. That's why we named our daughter after him.' He took a deep breath. 'I've been trying to locate Corson for him, but he slipped away. Nick became paranoid, thinking I'd set him up. We argued. I tried to get my wife and child away from him, but he caught on and killed her. He said he wanted me to feel the same agony he did.'

Tears were streaming down his face. 'I picked Nicole up and ran. I didn't know where to go, but I remembered you from Nick's and thought maybe you could help.'

Hearing him talking about how Nick had changed

broke my heart. Gone was the goofy boy who would do anything for his friends and family. He'd been broken and depressed after Lily died, but I'd still had hope. But now, because of the stupid sword, there didn't seem to be anything left of the Nick I knew. The sword had destroyed him.

I gestured with my hand. 'Do you want to come inside?'

Ant looked around. 'Are you sure? I don't care what happens to me as long as my daughter is safe.'

'Please come inside. I would hate to be the reason your daughter grows up without a father.'

Ant took my hands in his. 'Thank you. You don't know how much this means to me.'

As we reached the kitchen, Nicole came up to Ant. 'Cassie gave me ice cream. It's yummy. Can we bring some home?'

Ant ruffled her hair. 'You may need to stay here for a while. Daddy needs to find us a new place to live.'

She looked up at Ant with wide eyes. 'What about Mummy?'

Ant took a deep breath. 'Why don't you go and play some more?' Nicole disappeared into the living room with Cassie and Leah.

I glanced at Ant. 'Does she not know her mother's dead?'

He shrugged. 'I'm not sure. She's been acting like nothing happened. Maybe she's just in denial. It all happened so fast. I haven't even allowed myself to think about it yet. Because once I do, I know I'll break apart. And we need to stop Nick. But more importantly, I need to get my wife's body. She's the other part of my soul.'

Everything clicked into place. 'You're an Amare

demon?' Ant nodded. 'Okay. What do you suggest we do?'

'I'm not sure. Maybe you can distract him while I get my wife.'

I ran my hand through my hair. 'You think that will work?'

'I don't know. But I know you share a special bond.'

My eyes widened. 'He told you about that?'

'I'm sorry,' he said with a pained expression.

My shoulders slumped. 'Don't be. If I had a choice, I'd do it all again. Anything to get away from Surtr's torture.'

'It must have been horrid.'

I grimaced. A silence developed. I cleared my throat. 'You really think I can get through to him? It didn't work very well last time.'

'I'm not sure. It depends on what mood he's in. It's like he's two different people at the moment. Sometimes the real Nick shines through.'

I rubbed my hands together. 'Okay, let's give it a go. Nicole will be safe here with Cassie and Leah.'

'Nick can't visit?' he asked with a frown.

'No. He's never been invited in. I haven't lived in this house very long.' Ant let out a sigh of relief.

We went into the living room to say our goodbyes. I kissed Cassie. 'We'll be back soon. I love you.'

She gazed into my eyes. 'I love you too. Please be careful.'

'I will.' I squeezed her shoulder and turned to Leah, giving her an apologetic look.

'It's okay. This is more important,' she said.

I nodded and joined back up with Ant.

# NICK

# WHAT HAVE I DONE?

I stared at the lifeless figure lying on the ground, my body frozen in place. What had I done? I hadn't meant to use the sword. I hadn't meant to kill her. The deceit from Ant just hurt, and in that moment, I wanted him to hurt as much as I did, but that wasn't an excuse.

I cleaned Dalia up and placed a sheet over her. Ant would hate me now, but I couldn't take back what had happened, just as I couldn't bring Lily back to life. I hung my head in shame. I'd become as cold hearted as the demons I killed. Was it really worth the revenge I was seeking?

The doorbell rang. Who could it be? Maybe it was another dwarf trying to take the sword away from me. I teleported into the hallway and opened the door.

'Jax?' I said. A smile reached my lips at the thought that I hadn't pushed him away. 'I never thought I'd see you again.'

He huffed. 'You're not getting rid of me that easily.'

'I'm glad. Please come inside. How can I help?'

He hesitated before stepping inside. 'I really wish you'd get rid of the sword. It's changing you and you don't even see it. But I know that's not going to happen until you've killed Corson. Ant told me you were having trouble.'

'Did he now?' My gut became heavy. What was Ant doing with Jax? Were they plotting against me? I tried to suppress the feeling, not really sure why I was having these thoughts. In my heart, I knew Jax wouldn't do that to me.

'I was thinking, maybe Corson teleports away to another part of the realm and that's why you can't get to him.'

'Or maybe Ant lied to me,' I said through my teeth.

Jax held up his hands. 'Just hear me out. I have these magical blocking stones.' He made five crystals appear in his hand. 'When placed around a person or building, anyone inside is unable to teleport, so when you see Corson in the fortress, all you have to do is use them.'

'How do I know they work?'

'I'd offer to place them around myself, but we both know I couldn't teleport from this realm even if I tried.'

'Then place them around me and I'll try them out.'

Jax nodded and began to place the crystals around me. When he had one left to place, I sensed Ant entering the protective layers surrounding my house and garden. I grabbed Jax and teleported us to the garden. Ant was leaning over his dead wife, tears streaming down his face.

I turned to Jax. 'Did you know about this? Were you

trying to deceive me?'

'I'm only trying to help.'

I stared into his eyes, unsure whether to believe him. I'd never been able to read his mind, but Jax had never lied to me before. I trusted him. I turned to Ant. 'What do you think you're doing?'

Ant hesitated before standing up straight and staring into my eyes. 'I'm collecting my wife, who you murdered. She deserves a proper funeral,' he said, his voice full of anger.

Guilt hollowed me out, but when I read his mind, I realised this was a setup. I turned to Jax in disbelief. 'You were going to trap me inside those things?'

Jax ran his hand through his hair. 'Of course not. I want you to get your revenge so you can put all of this behind you.'

'Why?'

Jax looked at me in confusion. 'Isn't that what you want?'

'It is, but you don't believe in revenge.'

'I don't. But you're my best friend. You didn't give up on me when I thought I was beyond saving, so if this is something you need to do, then I want to help you.'

'You're lying.'

'I'm not. I want you to put all this behind you and go back to the Nick I know. The one that loved and cared about his family. About doing the right thing. The Nick that always had my back.'

A tear slid down my face as I thought about everything I'd lost. 'I'm not that person anymore. He died when his family was destroyed.'

'That's not true,' Ant said. 'You might have been

consumed with grief, but you saved my wife's life. You gave us a home, even though you didn't have to, and you cared for what was right. At least until you got that sword. I'm sorry I didn't do a better job of talking you out of it.'

I chuckled. 'You think you could have stopped me?'

Ant shrugged. 'I don't know, but I thought we were friends.'

I tilted my head. 'I thought we were friends too, but friends don't lie and deceive each other.'

Ant raised his voice. 'You killed my wife.'

'You deserved it,' I spat out. It wouldn't have surprised me if he had been in on it all along.

Jax placed his hand on my arm and looked into my eyes. 'You don't mean that. It's the sword talking.'

Maybe he was right. Guilt wrapped itself around me, making it hard to breathe. I'd killed someone's light in anger. I was no better than the demons that had done this to me. 'I ... I didn't mean to,' I said in defeat.

'You killed my wife. Remember when I told you Amare demons shared one heart, one soul. She's my other half. If she doesn't get a proper funeral, I will never see my other half again. I'll be broken.' *Just like you.*

He didn't say the last part, but he might as well have. It was written all over his face. A furious rage that made my skin tingle overwhelmed my guilt. 'You can't have her.'

'What are you going to do? Are you going to kill me too? Let my little girl grow up without her parents?'

He made me so mad. My whole body was shaking. He was taunting me for giving up Cassie. Pretending he was a better father than I would ever be. Hate took over, and before I knew what I was doing, I'd pushed Jax to the ground and stabbed Ant with my sword.

'What's wrong with you, Nick?' Jax shouted. 'He just wanted to bury his wife the Amare way, so she could be reborn and they could be united again.'

My body shook with anger. 'He asked for it. He was taunting me. Telling me I wasn't a good father.'

'He was grieving his wife, but now their daughter will grow up without both her parents because of you. Ant was right – you are beyond saving.' Jax grabbed Ant's and Dalia's bodies and dragged them behind him as he bolted through the garden gate.

'Jax. Come back here.' No reply. If he wasn't listening to me voluntarily. I would make him. I reached inside and summoned him. After all, I was his master, and he had to do my bidding. I would make him realise, make him understand that if he defied me, there would be consequences.

# JAX

# DEFYING THE BOND

I landed with a thump on the hard floor of my living room, still holding on to Ant's and his wife's dead bodies. Cassie came running towards me. 'What happened? Are you okay?'

She stopped in her tracks when she saw the bodies. I doubled over before I could answer. An invisible force tugged at me. Nick was summoning me. I fought it. Dots appeared in my vision, dizziness threatening to overtake me. My breathing became shallow as I kept fighting the force. If I passed out, it would all be over. 'Nick. It's Nick. He's summoning me. I'm not sure I'm strong enough to fight it.' It felt like a rope had been strung around my chest, pulling me away.

Cassie placed a hand on me and disappeared, leaving me

alone with the agony. What had happened to her? Was Nick responsible? Had he somehow got to her? I tried to sit up, but the pain was too much.

A moment later, Cassie was back. She placed my head in her lap. 'I'm right here. We're going to fix you. I tried teleporting you to the witch village, but it didn't work. But Leah's here now. Leaf too. They'll find something to help. Just hold on a little longer.' Cassie undid her necklace – the one I'd given to her for her birthday to help shield her powers. I tried to stop her. The necklace was for her safety.

'It's okay. I'm not sure it'll work, but you need it more than me. She placed the necklace on me and the pain eased a little. I tried to sit up but buckled again as the force of the summoning became stronger.

'It's not working,' Cassie shouted with panic in her voice.

'Just hold on a bit longer. I'm almost done,' Leaf said. 'That should do it.'

The pain eased, but it was still there, like the rope around me had been loosened instead of removed. I sat up and looked around. Both Cassie and Leaf were looking at me with worried eyes.

'How's that?' Leaf asked.

'Better,' I answered in a weak voice. 'What did you do?'

'You're in an invisible barrier. It's dampening the summoning. At least for now.'

I took a deep breath, filling my lungs with much-needed oxygen. I tried to stand up, but Cassie grabbed my arm. 'You need to stay inside.'

'I need to talk to Freya. Nick is out of control.'

'If you leave the barrier, the pull will start again,' Leaf said.

I rubbed my chest. It was still uncomfortable, and the pulling sensation, though now manageable, made it clear I was still being summoned, but at least I wasn't bent over in pain. 'I can't just sit here.'

A stifled laugh came from the kitchen. 'I told you he wouldn't listen,' Leah said. 'Luckily for you, I'm working on a movable barrier.'

I looked up in confusion. Leah was standing over the kitchen counter with several herbs and bottles spread out around her. 'It's like the barrier spell we did on Sky when she visited the hell realm, but with a few changes. I believe it will work, but it'll take me some time to sort out. Until then, stay inside the barrier Leaf created.'

I mumbled a reply. I guessed it could have been worse. At least I had Cassie by my side. I scanned the living room, and my eyes landed on Ant's and his wife's dead bodies. 'Where's Nicole?'

Cassie put a hand on my shoulder. 'Don't worry. She's fine. She's with Sky and Mark.'

'I don't ...' I swallowed, willing the tears to go away. Why hadn't I gone to Nick alone? If I had, Nicole would still have had a father. 'I don't know the funeral rites for Amare demons. They may be stuck and never become whole again in their next life.'

'Shh. We'll figure something out. Don't worry about it,' Cassie said as she rested her head on my shoulder.

Leaf joined us. 'Maybe the witches can help. It may not be the same, but we can release their souls into the universe.

Maybe that will be enough for them to be reunited again.'

We sat there in silence for a while until I became restless. Who knew what Nick may be up to? I looked over at Leah. 'Will it be ready soon?'

She let out a sigh. 'Since when did you become so impatient?'

'Since Nick started killing people he supposedly cared about. What's stopping him from going after me or, worse, coming after Cassie?' A chill went down my spine. Would he really sink that low? I removed the necklace and held it out to Cassie. She refused to take it.

I pushed it towards her. 'I know you're trying to help, but I would feel better if you wore it.' She eventually nodded and let me put it back on.

Leah handed me a bottle. 'Here. Drink this and I'll start calling the elements.'

'Will it work without calling the elements?'

She shrugged. 'I'm not sure.'

'Let's try. We don't have much time,' I said as I finished the drink in one gulp. It tasted awful. 'How long until it takes effect?'

'Hard to tell. Maybe give it a few moments and try to leave the barrier. If the pain reappears, we'll have to do the ceremony and call the elements.'

I kissed Cassie and stood up. Now I was a bit more with it, I could feel the surrounding energy. It amazed me how Leaf had managed to become so good at force fields without anyone to teach her.

I took a step outside it. The rope tightened and the pain came back, but it was manageable. 'It's working,' I said with a smile. 'Right, I'll see you in a bit. I need to talk to Freya.'

'Wai ...' Leah's voice disappeared as I teleported myself to Freya's realm. I changed into a crow and flew as fast as I could to her cottage, hoping I would reach it before I collapsed from the summoning pull.

As I approached, I used my telepathy to call on her. She rushed out of her house as I landed and transformed back into my human form.

She let out a breath. 'I thought you were dying.'

I tried to give her a goofy grin, but the pain stabbed through me. 'I thought you could see the future. Though you really need to do something about this flying. It's not practical when I really need you.'

She let out a sigh. 'I am sorry I was not here the last time you came.'

I shrugged. 'No worries, but I need your help. Nick's out of control. He's not listening to me, and I don't know how to reach him. The sword has completely taken him over.'

She looked at me with sad eyes. 'I was afraid of that. Wanting power pulls you over to darkness. Maybe love will bring him towards the light.'

I rubbed my chest in an attempt to ease the pain. 'I don't think love is going to help. He's too far gone.'

She picked up on it almost instantly. 'Is he summoning you?'

I nodded.

'You are strong to resist. It takes a lot of mental strength.'

'There's too much at stake.'

She moved her hands over my chest, and a glow escaped

them. 'Any better?'

The pain died down. 'Thank you.'

'You are welcome. Leah did all the hard work. I only strengthened the barrier she had already placed on you.' She handed me a glass bottle with a white liquid inside. 'If everything else fails, throw this at him.'

I took the bottle from her hand and examined it. 'What is it?'

'It is a powerful potion that will get rid of all the darkness inside him. It may very well kill him, especially if there is no light left, but because he is part human, there is a chance he can fight it and still live.'

'But he's my master. He owns me. Even if I wanted to, I can't do anything to cause him harm.'

She looked at me with compassion. 'If it comes to it, you will find a way. Let your love guide you.'

# NICK

## Confrontation

I slammed my fist onto the table. Jax wasn't answering my call. How was he able to resist the summoning? It shouldn't be possible. I paced the room as rage built up inside me. He was my best friend. How could he deceive me like this? He had only pretended to be close to me so he could steal the sword. No, that wasn't true. I hadn't had the sword when we became friends.

My gaze landed on the five crystals lying in the hallway. Jax had tried to trap me. Hatred boiled up inside me, and I pulled on the invisible string inside myself to summon Jax again. He was going to pay.

I let out a frustrated sigh when he still didn't respond, sat down on the sofa and rested the sword in my lap. Amber flames played around it. Was Corson really stuck in the realm?

I asked the fire about Corson's whereabouts. It showed me the shadow of someone sitting on the stone throne in the castle. I ground my teeth and picked up the crystals before teleporting to Corson's realm. I searched the castle, hoping to find him there, but it was deserted. Had the fire deceived me? I shook my head. The fire did my bidding. He must have teleported away.

I slowly and quietly made my way to the fortress in the forest. Without having Ant as a guide, I struggled to find it. Eventually I found the glade where I'd first fought Icarus, and as I searched the area, I found the stone circle Ant had created. I took care to keep outside the cloaking shield and placed the five crystals around the fortress at equal distances.

When I returned to the circle of stones, I followed the line and passed through the cloaking shield. The fortress looked the same as before. Quiet. I made my way up the stairs and entered. As I got close to the great hall, the shadows in the corner grew solid and several shadow demons appeared. I unsheathed my sword.

I sliced them in half and moved past them. I was happy the place wasn't abandoned like last time, but why wasn't the fortress better defended than just with shadow demons? The great hall was empty, so I climbed the stairs and emerged onto the roof. The flames on the sword danced in the breeze.

On the opposite side stood a gigantic creature with massive wings. Darkness oozed around him. His skin resembled black rubber wrapped around well-defined bones. Four horns sprouted from his head, and this horn-like consistency extended to the wings. He turned around like he knew I was there, but without any urgency. Like he was the true predator and nothing could touch him.

As I approached, a hollow face with two large round silver eyes stared back at me. 'You've gone to a lot of trouble seeking me out.'

'You're Corson?'

He flashed me a grin, showing off his sharp teeth. 'In the flesh.'

# JAX

# ONE LAST TRY

I arrived back in the living room. My eyes went to the place where I'd teleported back from Nick with Ant and his wife. But there was no sign of them. There wasn't even any blood on the floor from Ant's wound.

'Leaf took them to the witch village so she could perform the funeral ritual on them,' Leah said from the kitchen. 'I've just finished cleaning up.' She put the bucket she'd been using back into a cupboard and walked over to me. 'How are you feeling?'

'Better, thanks to you and Freya. I can't feel Nick's summoning anymore.'

'I'm happy I could help. We were so worried.'

Cassie rushed into the living room and wrapped her arms around me. 'What did she say?'

'Let love guide you.' I gazed into Cassie's eyes. 'And she gave me this.' I held up the glass vial Freya had given me and handed it to Cassie.

She studied the white liquid inside. 'What is it?'

'Looks like a potion to me,' Leah said.

'Yeah, but he doesn't need to drink it. He just needs to come into contact with it, but it's our last resort.'

Leah lifted an eyebrow. 'Why?'

'It destroys the darkness inside. If Nick is completely consumed by it, it will kill him.'

'Ohh ... then I guess time is of the essence. What's the plan?' Leah asked.

I looked at Cassie. 'I think it may be time for you to meet your father.'

She gave me an unsure smile. 'How? I thought you said it wasn't safe and that I can't go to the demon realm until I'm eighteen.'

'It isn't and you can't, but I'm out of ideas.'

'Can we summon him here?' Leah said with a mixture of excitement and worry in her voice.

'That's not actually a bad idea, but it can't be this house. His presence will draw other beings, and I'm not strong enough to deal with both.'

'Maybe we can ask the wolves and witches for help. They can deal with any demons that might turn up, and we can concentrate on Nick,' Cassie said.

'No. This isn't their fight. It'll only put them at risk.'

There was a moment of silence.

'What about our house?' Leah asked.

'What house?'

'She means the house we lived in with Abigail,' Cassie said.

'I think the shield is still in place.'

'You mean the enchantment that kept me from sensing what you were?'

Leah gave me a wide smile. 'Exactly.'

'That could work, but we need to know if the shield is still working.'

'There's only one way to find out. How about you teleport inside?' Leah said.

'What if someone sees?'

Leah rolled her eyes. 'You're thinking too much about this. We won. Hecate can't do anything. You're being overly cautious.'

Cassie squeezed my shoulder. 'Why don't you give it a go?'

'Okay.' I took a deep breath. 'But I'm not teleporting from here. They may be able to track it.'

Leah rolled her eyes with a smirk. 'Ever heard of anyone tracking a teleportation?'

I glared at her. 'No, but I also hadn't heard about a living sword that consumes the soul.'

Leah nodded. 'Point taken.'

'Wait until I come back.' I kissed Cassie and turned into a crow. I could feel both Cassie's and Leah's judging looks as I flew out of the house. Maybe I was being silly and over-cautious, but it made me feel better.

When I was a decent distance away, I teleported to the house Leah and Cassie had grown up in. I wasn't sure what to expect, but when I opened my eyes, I was in Cassie's old bedroom upstairs. It felt weird being there after everything that had transpired. So many memories. I turned back into my human form, lay down on the bed and breathed in the faint smell of Cassie's shampoo. I sent out my energies but didn't pick up on anything. Maybe this would actually work.

I walked from room to room, then heard a door open downstairs. No one was supposed to be here. I tiptoed to the top of the stairs, all my senses on high alert, adrenaline flowing through my body. I was ready to conjure my weapon when I heard laughter.

'I can't believe you teleported us here. That was so amazing,' Leah said.

I relaxed but stayed quiet. I'd told them to stay put. What if they had teleported into an ambush? They needed to be taught a lesson. I jumped down the flight of stairs and flung my arms around them in a surprise hug. They screamed before they realised it was me.

'That's not very nice. I almost shit my pants,' Leah said.

I smirked. 'Be happy I didn't raise my weapon thinking you were an intruder.'

Leah chuckled. 'Your reflexes are too good for that.'

'You sure?' I asked, raising an eyebrow.

Leah flashed me a grin. 'Didn't we just bet our lives on it?'

I guessed she had a point. I turned all serious. 'Why did you teleport here? I thought you were going to wait at the house until I made sure it was safe.'

'I'm sorry,' Cassie said, though she didn't sound sincere.

Leah rolled her eyes. 'We know it's safe. Hecate is gone, and no more sacrifices. Besides, Cassie had me if we ran into anything.' She held up her hand. 'And before you ask, don't worry. We teleported down the road, so nowhere near the house. Now let's see if it works. How about me and Cassie go outside and you use as much energy as you can and we'll see if we can feel it?'

I nodded. After they'd left the house, I mentally sent a message to Cassie asking if they were ready. When she replied, I reached deep inside myself and let the icy feeling brush over me as I transformed into my demon form. I didn't think I'd ever get used to the awful monster inside myself, but knowing Cassie didn't care made it easier. I closed my eyes and let the demon take over before sending out as much energy as I could, hoping it would at least come close to the power Nick expressed.

The door opened and Leah and Cassie walked in. I panicked. My demon part was in charge, and I wasn't sure I had enough control, but before I could push the demon down and turn back, Cassie grabbed my hand, or should I say talons. She planted a kiss on top of my beak. 'I love you. All of you.' She smiled, and a lightness went through me. A second later, I was back in my human form.

'I love you too.'

Leah grimaced. 'I don't think I'll ever get used to it. You look horrendous in that form. But I'm not scared, because I know it's you.'

I let out a breath. 'Doesn't mean I like it.'

'True, but you can't change who you are. And we would never ask you to,' Cassie said.

I smiled. 'So? What's the verdict?'

'Nothing. Couldn't feel a thing.'

'Let's just hope it's the same for Nick.'

'Why do you think he's that much stronger than you?'

'He's a descendant of Surtr. Me, I'm just a demon.'

'Don't be so hard on yourself. Freya said you were a god.'

'Freya says a lot of things that don't make sense.'

'If we are to believe what Sky overheard, you're a descendant of Freya,' Cassie said.

'Don't you think she would have told me, instead of making up a story of how I was abandoned at birth and no one knows who my parents are?'

'No,' Leah said quickly. 'Not if she doesn't think it would do you any good.'

An awkward silence developed. Maybe Leah was right. I still needed to talk to Freya about the god stuff, but in the grand scheme of things it wasn't that important. I'd lived my whole life not knowing. It was more important to stop Nick.

Leah scanned the room. 'So, how do we summon Nick?'

'I have no idea, but maybe you can find a way. Between me being owned by him and Cassie being his daughter, I would have thought you'd have the connection you need to summon him.'

Leah became thoughtful. 'I've got an idea, but I need to talk to Leaf about it.'

'Do you want me to teleport you?'

'No need.' She pulled out a calling stone and went into the kitchen, leaving me and Cassie alone in the living room.

A moment later, Leah came back into the living room. 'Right, I need your blood. It's a fairly simple incantation. It should be harder for Nick to refuse than a normal summoning, but there's no guarantee.'

# NICK

## The Summoning

I raised my sword. 'You've just met your death.'

Corson smirked. 'We'll see about that.'

'You can't escape this time.' I advanced on Corson, sword held high. Whether or not I died killing him, my life would be over. Adrenaline pumped through my body, and the thought of finally being able to avenge my beautiful angel brought me resolution.

Corson snickered. 'Why would I want to escape?'

'Because that's what you did last time.'

He chuckled. 'You think some magical stones will contain me? The mighty keeper of the west?' He narrowed his eyes and stared into my soul. 'I know everything that's going on in my realm. I was only biding my time. It wasn't the right time before, but there's no point in keeping away any longer.'

'Why did you want me dead?'

An evil grin appeared on his face. 'I never wanted you dead.'

'Then why send the demons to kill me?'

'Oh, they were never sent there to kill you. They were there to make sure you chose the path of vengeance so you would bring the sword to me.'

'Why?' Tears burned in my eyes. I wasn't sure if it was from anger or from grief, knowing Lily had been their target all along.

'So that the world can bask in darkness. So I can be free from my chains. Nothing is ever done without reason. Did you not think it strange that a random demon offered to help you?'

I let out a scream. Fire burned through me. Hatred. Rage. He was going to pay.

I transformed into my demon form and lashed out. He moved out of the way with ease, almost like he knew what move I was going to make. I would have to step up my game. Using my fire to my advantage, I filled the space with flames. I wasn't sure how it affected him, but I was immune to it. I danced around him, swinging my sword. Smoke moved around me, and I pretended to struggle. Corson closed in on me. At the last moment, I conjured a large rock behind him as I swung my sword. He retreated, tripped over the rock and fell to the ground.

I had him right where I wanted him. One strike and he would be dead and I would have avenged Lily. I raised my sword and swung, but Corson threw a bolt at me. My aim faltered as I dodged the bolt, causing me to miss my target.

Instead of cutting his head off, I sliced his shoulder. I cursed. A burning sensation grew in my chest, and Corson almost landed a hit. We circled each other. I tried to take him out again, but the pain in my chest made it hard to concentrate; it felt like it was pulling me away. Corson struck, and the sword fell out of my hands. I threw fire at him. I knew it wouldn't kill him, but I needed him distracted. He was advancing on the sword – my sword. I dived for it as he threw another bolt at me. My hand touched its hilt, and I wrapped my fingers around it and let out a scream as the bolt hit my leg.

The stone of my leg shattered, but new molten stone reformed shortly after. The burning in my chest became stronger, like a lasso wrapping itself tightly around me. I buckled, realising I was being summoned.

I tried to stand up and continue the fight, but the pull was too much to bear. I swore under my breath. Whoever was forcing me away against my will was going to pay. I cast one last look at Corson before giving in to the summons and allowing myself to be teleported.

When I appeared, my father stopped working on his sword and looked up at me.

'I almost had him. Why would you summon me now?' I yelled at him.

'The oath has been fulfilled. It's time for you to join my army.'

'No, it hasn't,' I snapped. 'I haven't killed him yet.'

'The oath was never for you to kill him.'

I took a step towards him. Rage burned under my skin. 'We made an oath for me to kill Corson before I joined your army.'

Surtr put his sword down. 'No, we didn't. Killing him would have grave consequences. Did you really think I would allow you to disrupt the balance of the universe? Not to mention if you actually succeeded, you would take his place guarding the seal and be unable to join my army. Or, worse, he would use the sword and consume your soul, tricking the seal into believing the sword is a soul and being able to leave his realm.'

'If that's true, why would you send me to get the sword?'

'To get you to join the army. We need everyone if we are to kill the gods during Ragnarök and bring forth a new beginning.'

'I don't believe you.'

'Then believe in the oath you made.'

He called out Sinmara's name and she appeared in tendrils of smoke, holding the glass orb that contained the flame oath. She held it up to me and I looked into the orb, the day I made the oath replaying on its surface. 'When Corson is hit by the Dauđans, the flame of Nicklause, son of Surtr, shall belong to our army, ready to march when Ragnarök starts. As the flames mix, so shall it be.'

I cursed under my breath. Why hadn't I paid more attention to the wording?

I shoved the orb away, and it fell from Sinmara's hand onto the ground. 'It doesn't matter,' I said as I swung my sword and broke the orb. 'I'm going to finish what I've started. Lily will be avenged.'

'Breaking the orb won't make any difference. The oath still remains,' Surtr said as I teleported away from them and back to Corson. But as I did so, another force pulled me sideways. I couldn't believe Surtr would do this to me.

Bracing myself to fight Surtr so I could have my revenge, I was confused when I landed in a house. I got into a fighting stance and raised my sword. Where was I? This wasn't Surtr's realm. My eyes darted around, trying to decipher where I was, and I met Jax's gaze. This wasn't where I had expected to end up.

'Nick. Stop. This is not you. Look at everything you have to fight for. Our friendship – Cassie. You need to fight the pull.'

He was the one who had stopped me from getting back to Corson? Rage boiled inside me and I saw red. My eyes landed on Cassie. 'I'll see how you react when you lose the person you love.' I threw the sword at her.

The second the sword left my hand, I realised what I'd done, and my heart stopped in my chest.

The sword moved in slow motion as my promise to Lily passed through my mind. 'Promise me you'll keep Cassie safe.' I stood frozen, unable to comprehend what I had just done. I closed my eyes, wishing death upon myself. I'd killed the only part of Lily that still existed. Her parents were right. I didn't deserve her.

The sound of the sword hitting flesh made me open my eyes. I let out a breath. Jax had stepped in the way and the sword had embedded itself in his arm. Cassie bent down to him. She touched the sword but pulled her hand back and shook it, almost like it had burned her. Tears streamed down her face. I stared at her in a haze.

Jax's body started convulsing on the floor, the sword still in his arm, and dark webs grew from it, almost like it was feeding him poison. Cassie let out a shriek, grabbed the sword and pulled it out. It hit the ground with a bang.

Despite the sword not being in Jax anymore, he was still convulsing, and his human form became undone. His skin turned black and his eyes red. I'd only seen his true form once, and that was during Surtr's imprisonment. What had I done?

I met Cassie's gaze. She was furious. 'You are not the Nick Jax always talked about – the one he could always count on to have his back. The sword has taken over you and you don't even know it. You've gone too far. There's no saving you. I'd rather have a dead father than the monster you've become.' She pulled out a vial and threw it at me. It exploded at my feet, smoke billowing up from the ground.

I saw her embrace Jax in her lap, just like I had that awful day when Lily died. Guilt paralysed me. *I never meant for any of this to happen.* I let out a scream of agony as everything turned black.

# JAX

## My Childhood Room

What was happening to me? My left arm and shoulder were on fire, but the rest of me was cold, ice cold, like when my body turned into my demon form. I tried to fight it, but I had no control.

Cassie embraced me and stroked some hair from my face.

'It's burning,' I whispered.

'What can I do?' The panic in Cassie's voice made me realise it was bad. It wasn't just a sword wound; the sword had done something to me.

'Get me to Freya.'

'I don't know how.' Cassie choked up, a tear running down her cheek.

I attempted to smile. 'Think about the waterfall where I proposed and teleport.'

Cassie snuffled. A moment later, the scenery shifted. A waterfall sounded in the background. We had made it to Freya's realm.

The last thing I heard before I passed out was Cassie screaming for help, then everything went black.

I opened my eyes slowly and stared up at the ceiling and its uneven surface, almost like ripples on water. I was in my childhood bedroom at Freya's. Cassie must have reached her somehow.

My arm hurt, and I turned towards it. It was black and my hand had talons. I panicked. Was the whole of me in my demon form? I turned to look at my other arm. It was still normal, still human. I let out a sigh of relief and relaxed back into the bed as Cassie entered the room. I awkwardly tried to move my demon arm, to hide it under the covers, but it wasn't moving like I wanted it to.

'Jax, you're awake. I was so scared.' She walked over and grabbed my normal hand.

I lifted my head and looked into her eyes. 'What happened? How did I end up here, and how long have I been out for?'

Freya came in. 'A few days. You are lucky you are what you are and that Cassie has learned to teleport. Had I not felt the shift when you entered the realm, I might not have been able to get to you in time.'

I leaned back in the bed as my memories flooded back

to me. 'What about Nick?' I couldn't feel his bond anymore.

'Do not worry about that. He is at your house. Unconscious, fighting his own demons. Cassie threw the potion at him before she got you here.'

'Will he die? Is that why I can't feel our bond?'

Freya put her hand on my shoulder. 'It is too early to know. The potion is killing the darkness inside him. Whether he will live or die is up to him and how much goodness still lies in his heart.'

I lifted my arm that remained in my demon form. 'What about this?'

'Your body is still fighting off the poison caused by the darkness in the sword, but you might be able to cover it up with glamour.'

I tilted my head. 'How? I didn't think there was a way to control it.'

'The Fates weaved it into the fabric of the universe so we could appear to humans, and your body unknowingly uses it to portray your human form. But with age and training comes the ability to consciously shape the glamour to do our bidding.'

'Can you teach me?'

She squeezed my shoulder. 'Another time. You need to rest.' She walked out, leaving me alone with Cassie.

'I'm so happy you're okay,' Cassie said as she took a seat on the bed.

'How did you get me here? It's a long way from the waterfalls.'

'I started screaming for help. I thought I was going to lose you. As my voice gave out, Freya turned up and brought us here.' She looked around. 'I've never been in your childhood bedroom before.'

'Well, it isn't much, but it's home.'

She picked up a framed feather from the bedside table. 'Is this your feather?'

The way she asked made me laugh. 'Yeah, the first feather I ever shed as a bird.'

'So it's almost like when humans lose their teeth.' She gave me a wide smile.

I tried to hide the yawn that escaped me without success.

'You should rest. I'll leave you alone.'

I grabbed her hand, stopping her from getting up. 'I rather you got into the bed with me.'

She hesitated before carefully climbing into it and nestling her head on my chest. The smell of spring flowers from her shampoo made me smile. I put my arm around her and fell asleep.

When I woke up, it was dark outside. Cassie was still asleep in my arms. I left her in bed and went downstairs. Freya was sitting in a rocking chair in the living room by the fire with two cups of tea. She handed me one.

'I am sorry about Nick. He has a long fight ahead of him.'

I wasn't sure what to say, so we sat there in silence for a while.

'I would ask you to stay and rest, but I know you will not,' Freya said.

'We'll leave when Cassie wakes up. A few days here means it's been a couple of weeks in the human world.'

She handed me a container filled with ointment. 'Put

this on your wound. It will help it heal. There may always be a scar, a part of your skin that remains in your demon form, but your hand should go back to looking human soon.'

I nodded in relief. 'Thank you.'

'Nonsense. I did what anyone would do for their child. It does not matter how old you are. You will always be my little Jax, and you are always welcome here.'

'About that. Sky said you're my real grandmother.'

Freya gave me a sad smile. 'There is so much we need to talk about. But now is not the time.'

I wanted to ask her all the questions that were lingering in my mind, but I knew it was pointless. She wouldn't say anything more until she was ready, and she obviously wasn't. We watched the flames of the fire in silence for a long time until Cassie came downstairs and Freya teleported us home.

# NICK

## DARKNESS

Black, everything was black. No matter where I turned, there was darkness. I wasn't even sure I had my eyes open, as I couldn't see my hand in front of me. I started walking, my steps echoing in the nothingness. Where was I? Had I died?

'Hello?'

A voice sounded behind me. I stopped and turned around, only to be met by darkness. No one was there. Laughter echoed around me. What was this place?

'Look who it is. It's Nick the dick,' the voices taunted.

I shook my head. No one had said that since I'd left school.

'Nick the dick. Nick the dick,' the voices echoed out of the darkness.

I put my hands over my ears to tune it out, but it continued. The voices died down, only to be followed by another. 'You're pathetic. Weak. No one wants to be your friend.'

'It's not true,' I shouted into the darkness as I thought of Jax.

The darkness changed into my old school. I was walking along the corridor. Owen, my school bully, had said something that put me on edge. Anger and heat coursed through me. The next moment, he was on fire.

'You're pathetic. You can't even control your own powers,' Jax said with an evil smile.

No. This wasn't how it had happened. Jax had stepped out from the shadows and put the fire out and made everyone forget. He'd taken me in and taught me how to control my powers. He'd shown me acceptance, loyalty. The start of an amazing friendship. It was how we'd become brothers – by always having each other's back. But the darkness had twisted it.

My knees buckled and I slumped to the ground, watching the scenes play out in the school hall. 'That's not what happened,' I told the darkness.

A breeze slid along my neck. 'Are you sure?' a voice from the shadows asked. 'He might have said something else, but that was what he really thought.'

'You're wrong. He's my best friend.'

The shadows laughed. 'You couldn't even get him away from your father without assistance. You let him rot there. You deserve what is coming. Even your mother couldn't stand you. You made her sick, and she couldn't wait to leave this world.'

I put my hands over my ears. 'You're wrong. My mother loved me. She told me so every day.'

The darkness laughed. 'Keep telling yourself that. But we all know the truth. No one can love someone like you. Not even Lily. She stayed with you out of pity. And for what? To die because you couldn't save her. Because you were worthless. Pathetic. You're too weak to even avenge her death.'

A tear rolled down my cheek. Maybe the voice was right. I was weak. An image of Lily flashed in my mind. My angel. Her loving voice whispered to me. 'The blue fire shows how strong you are. That you choose your own path, and I love you for it.'

Warmth spread inside me, and I pushed myself up from the ground. 'You're wrong. Lily loved me.'

'But did you love her?'

'Of course I did. With all my soul.'

'Then why did you let her die?'

'It wasn't my fault.'

'But it was. You were weak. But I can make you strong. I can show you how it feels to be respected. To be feared. No one would ever put you down again. And you can finally get the revenge you're yearning for.'

I blocked out the words and concentrated on Lily's voice inside my head. She told me how much I meant to her, how much she loved me. I tried conjuring a blue flame in my hands, but it only sparkled and died. I thought about Jax and what we had been through together. How my mother had taken him in and cared for him, even though he'd said he didn't need it. And he didn't really. He had Freya. But my mother wouldn't take no for an answer.

I remembered the cheerful look on Jax's face when I'd finally learned to control my fire. The way he was there for me in my quest to figure out who my father was. How he had always been by my side when I needed him. I bottled up all the love I felt for people, all the kind gestures. When I couldn't retain it anymore, I visualised it in a ball of light to be released and I threw it towards the voice.

The voice let out a hiss. And a light showed at the far end of the room. I ran towards it.

I entered another room and saw myself staring back at me from all angles. A room of mirrors. A dark shadow slithered into the room and the sword appeared in the mirrors. 'I can give you strength, power, everything you need to deal a lethal blow to Corson and finally get the revenge for Lily that you're yearning for. All you have to do is pick the sword up.'

Excitement rushed through me. I could make Corson pay for killing Lily. Temptation tingled in my fingers, and I lifted my hand to reach for the sword but hesitated. My meeting with Corson played in my mind and his words repeated in my head. *'Oh, they were never sent there to kill you. They were there to make sure you chose the path of vengeance so you would bring the sword to me.'*

I put my hand down, and rage swirled inside me. It was the sword's fault. Everything that had happened was part of some elaborate scheme to bring the sword to Corson. I punched the mirror, and it cracked.

'I thought you wanted revenge.'

'I did, but you made me realise it isn't worth it. I've

sacrificed so much for this revenge, and for what? Lily would hate the person I've become. I lost myself, gave in to my grief and let darkness take over. I should have fought for the light, for the people I love and care about. For Cassie.'

'If you care so much about them, why did you hurt them? Kill them? Abandon them?'

The mirrors around me started showing memories from my life. I saw myself, hatred steaming out of me as I killed Ant's wife without mercy. I looked away but caught sight of another mirror showing me how I'd killed Ant.

I fell to my knees. *I did this. I killed my friend.* A friend who had given up a lot just to help me get my revenge. I started sobbing. 'I didn't mean to.'

The shadow laughed. 'But you did. Anyone that gets close to you dies. You even tried to kill your own daughter, your own flesh and blood.'

The mirrors showed me throwing the sword at Cassie and Jax stepping in the way, causing the sword to penetrate his arm. *'I'd rather have a dead father than the monster you've become.'* Cassie's last words to me.

I crawled into a foetal position. I'd seen enough. I deserved this. Moving my hands to my face, I started sobbing. I had failed Cassie; I had failed at my promise to Lily to keep Cassie safe. I was a horrible person. I wished I could take it all back. I wished I'd never started down the path of vengeance. No vengeance was worth this.

The shadow hovered above me. 'I can make it all go away. Make you forget. All you have to do is give in. Let the darkness consume you.'

I closed my eyes. All this guilt. I couldn't take it

anymore. Just as I was ready to give in, an image of Jax entered my mind. 'This isn't you. The sword has taken you over. You need to fight it.'

I took a deep breath. Jax was right. It wasn't me. I would never intentionally hurt the people I loved. I needed to fight. Getting to my feet, I screamed to the darkness, '*No*. I'm not giving in. I will fight you with all I have. I am not a creature of darkness. I am good.'

The cracks in the mirror became larger and spread to the other mirrors before splitting into fine shards. They broke free from the mirrors and swirled around like a mini tornado.

'You might be able to fight me, but are you strong enough to fight yourself?' The shadow jumped into the tornado, and the shards started knitting themself together, transforming into my demon form.

I stood there mesmerised as I traced the amber cracks in his body with my eyes. Amber, not blue. The being in front of me represented all the horrible things I had done since I'd given up my life to avenge Lily. I knew now that I shouldn't have given in to the rage I'd felt when I lost her. I should have dealt with my grief and been a father Cassie could have been proud of. Instead I'd given her away and then become ... this. This monstrous being filled with darkness and hatred.

No wonder she hated me.

I tried to conjure up my old sword – the one I used before I got my hands on the Daudans. I visualised it, saw it in my mind with all the dents and impurities it had acquired over my lifespan. I expected it to be in my hands just as I had visualised it. But when I opened my eyes, there was nothing.

I'd lost my ability to conjure. My breath caught in my chest as I realised I was completely human and the beast in front of me was my demon half. I didn't stand a chance against him as a human.

I let out a defeated sigh. There was no way I'd be able to beat my own demon. But the alternative was to give up. To let him kill me. But he – *I*– had done some awful things. Things I couldn't even comprehend. I'd never thought I could kill anyone I loved, but that was just what I had done, and in cold blood no less.

No, I couldn't let him win. I couldn't let him take over. Not without a fight. He had almost killed my daughter once, and I sure as hell wasn't just going to give up and give him the chance to do it again.

I circled my demon self. His stone body towered over me and he followed me with his eyes, black as the depths of my despair. I looked around for something I could use as a weapon, but there was nothing, just an empty room.

I let out a blood-curdling scream and charged at him, swinging my arm and hitting him with a straight punch. Pain streamed up my arm as my hand collided with his stomach. He was rock solid, and it felt like I'd just punched a brick wall. It didn't even leave a mark. I hunched over in pain, clutching my broken hand to my chest.

He kicked me and I flew through the air. I landed with a thump and the air left my lungs. He laughed as I tried to get up, a deep rumbling that I felt as much as heard – like the beginning of an earthquake. He stalked towards me and punched me in the face. My head swung back with a crack, and I could feel blood dripping from my nose. Pain exploded all over my face, and my eyes became teary. My head was spinning and desperation churned in my stomach, but there was too much at stake to give in. I shook away my blurry vision and wiped the blood from my face before straightening up. With a racing heart, I took a determined step forward.

We circled each other, and I dodged his advances as I thought of ways to defeat him. The size of him meant I had the advantage of being more agile, but he was stronger. The adrenaline pumped around my body, but fatigue had started to set in and my body was throbbing with pain. I didn't know how many more hits I could take. I needed to think of something. He must have a weakness.

Maybe I could trip him? I backed away, but he slowly stepped towards me. If this was going to work, I needed force on my side. It was now or never. I backed up further, until he was a fair distance away, then started running towards him. As he tried to land a blow, I ducked and kicked his left leg. He stumbled but quickly regained his footing. He swung around and caught me with a cross punch. I crashed to the ground. My head pounded and the world spun around me. Everything was black.

As I lay there on the floor, I heard a sound, like someone whispering. At first I couldn't make out what it said, just mumbles, but it was a soothing voice. It became louder, audible, and I knew it was Lily talking. 'We protect beings that have been touched by darkness. We give them our light to help them fight the hold the darkness has over them.'

My mother's perfume filled my senses, and she appeared before my eyes. She took my hand and kissed it better, something she'd always done since I was a kid. From the kiss, a bright white light engulfed my hand – a warmth spreading from the inside out. I opened and closed my fingers. The pain was gone. The bones were no longer broken. But the light kept growing, slowly covering the whole of me.

My mother hugged me and whispered in my ear, 'I love you. Now show them your light.'

I stood up, and the light transformed into a light-blue armour around me, and all the pain was gone.

My hand was still glowing, and I landed a punch on my demon self. He stumbled back, clearly affected by the impact. With renewed energy and resolve, I attacked the demon again and again, scorching him with my light.

# JAX

# WHAT ABOUT THE DAUDANS

Leah wrapped her arms around me when Cassie and I arrived home. 'I'm so happy you're back. We didn't know if you would make it at first.'

'Only a little setback,' I said as I held up my arm belonging to my demon form.

'It's a shame Halloween has been and gone. It would make a great outfit,' Leah said with a wink.

I looked around the room. 'Where's Nick?'

'He's fine,' Leah said. 'Do you know how heavy a grown man is to lift? I needed Leaf's and the wolves' help to transport him from the house to here.'

I followed Leah into the living room. A bed had been placed by the wall. On it lay Nick in his human form. 'Why

263

did you bring him here? What about the demons?'

'Don't worry. No demons should be able to sense him. I don't think he's radiating any power anymore, at least I can't feel it, but just in case, I had Leaf help me create a barrier around him. I didn't think you wanted him left alone in the house.'

I took a step towards him. 'Thank you. How's he doing?'

Leah shrugged. 'I'm not sure. He hasn't moved since he collapsed after Cassie threw the potion on him a few weeks ago, but he's breathing. Maybe he's in some sort of coma.'

'Maybe. Freya said he's fighting his own darkness. The fact he's still alive must mean there's still light inside him. I'm sorry we left you here with everything for so long.'

'Don't be sorry. I'm happy you're okay. I was so worried until Cassie let me know you were alive.'

'If I'd realised the discrepancy in time, I would have contacted you sooner,' Cassie said. 'I didn't realise it had already been several hours in the human world by the time I got Jax to Freya's house.'

Leah and Cassie left me alone with Nick. I'd thought Cassie would have been eager to see him, but I guess having your father throw a sword at you the first time you meet him isn't really ideal, so I could understand her reluctance.

I conjured a chair next to the bed and sat. A tear fell from my eye as I took Nick's hand. 'I'm sorry it had to come to this, and I'm sorry I wasn't there for you. I didn't realise how much you were hurting, but you need to keep fighting. You can overcome this. There's too much light inside you. Your mother made sure of that. The darkness can't have overtaken it all.'

I watched his eyes move back and forth underneath his eyelids. It looked like he was dreaming. I kissed his forehead and tried to lend him my strength. 'Find the light inside yourself and fight with everything you have. You have a daughter who would like to get to know you, and you've got me. I'm not ready to give up on you. You're my brother. You're not allowed to give up. What would I do without you? The darkness is not you – it's not what you are. Fight. Lily would never have chosen to be with you if your light didn't outshine the darkness inside you. So hold on to that light and fight your way back to us.'

I watched Nick quietly for a while before I went into the kitchen, where Leah and Cassie were sitting.

'Any idea what to do with it?' Cassie asked Leah.

'Not yet.'

'What are you talking about?' I asked and took a seat next to them.

'The sword.'

I hit my forehead with my palm. How could I have forgotten about the sword? 'Where is it now?'

'It's in a protective glass container by the bed, completely shielded until we figure out what to do about it.'

Cassie bit her lip. 'What if Nick wakes up and takes the sword again?'

'Not *if* he wakes up. *When* he wakes up. Nick's strong. I have to believe there's still light inside him and he will wake up despite everything that has happened. The Nick I know would never do anything to hurt the ones he loves.'

Cassie placed her hands on top of mine. 'I hope you get him back. It would be nice to finally meet my dad and not the horrible person who tried to kill me.'

'That was all the sword's doing.'

'All the more reason to get rid of it,' Leah said.

'I think we should destroy it,' Cassie said.

'I agree, but I don't think it can be destroyed. Maybe we should get someone to hide it.'

I ran my hand through my hair. 'If we do that, what's stopping someone from finding it again?'

'Maybe we can give it back to the dwarfs. After all, they created it and hid it before. Maybe they can do it again.'

'Maybe, but I wouldn't want to go there again. They almost didn't let us leave the last time.'

'Didn't the dwarfs say something about the eternal flame being able to destroy it?' Cassie said.

'I think that was before, and it's even more powerful now. Besides, Surtr is the only one that can command the eternal flame. It would kill everyone else.'

'Would it be worth asking him?'

'No.' The memory of being imprisoned by him flashed in my mind again. It was something I didn't want to go through again, especially when I didn't have Nick around to save me.

'Then what can we do? I mean, we don't even know where it came from, so it's not like we can put it back,' Leah said.

'Maybe Sky can direct us to where it was hidden,' Cassie said.

'No point in putting it back. Nick must have killed the guardians that protected it, so it would be pointless, as anyone could just walk back into that realm and take it again.'

'Maybe we can take it to the witch village – have them guard it,' Cassie asked.

Leah raised an eyebrow. 'You don't think that's too much to ask? They're still recovering from everything that happened with Hecate; besides, I wouldn't trust the old High Priestess not to use it to her advantage if she ever wakes up from her coma.'

Cassie sighed. 'We can't just leave it here.'

'We'll think of something,' I reassured her.

A crash echoed from the other room. I rushed into the living room to see if someone had broken in or if something had happened to Nick but stopped when I got there. The sword had shattered into four pieces that were scattered around the room, along with shards of the glass container it had been in. *How the hell did that happen?*

'Everything okay? What happened?' Leah asked behind me.

I pointed towards some shards of the sword. 'The sword. It broke.'

'How is that possible? I thought it couldn't be destroyed.'

I was about to answer her when Cassie made a beeline towards Nick, who was stirring in the bed. 'I think he's waking up.'

# NICK

## GUILT

I dealt the final blow to my demon self, and he collapsed on the floor. The darkness in the room flooded towards the body, like it was sucking up everything around us. I took a step away from it to create some distance and suddenly it exploded and a white light overpowered everything. I raised my hand to shield my eyes, but I must have closed them.

When I opened my eyes again, I could see a white ceiling. I tried to move, but my body didn't cooperate. I knew something was different. The fiery rage that had been below the surface ever since I'd got my powers was gone. But I wasn't sure whether I missed it or was relieved by its absence.

'Nick! You're awake.' Jax's voice rang out, and a second later, he was by my side.

I struggled to sit up, and Jax placed some pillows behind me. 'What happened?' I asked, trying to piece together how I'd ended up in a bed after fighting myself.

'I'm sorry. We trapped you with a potion. There just wasn't any other way to get through to you.' He patted me on my shoulder. 'I'm so happy you're alive.'

I blinked. The memories slowly came back to me. I had tried to kill my own daughter. 'The sword?'

'It exploded into fragments when you woke up.'

I took a relieved breath. 'Good,' I said as I recalled how it had overtaken me, making me into a being I detested. How had I not seen it sooner?

'What happened?' Jax asked.

'I'm not sure. One moment rage filled me, and then there was just darkness. It twisted my memories. But eventually I found the strength to fight it, and when I did, it turned into me – well, the demon version of me – and challenged me to a duel. I won and ended up here.'

'I'm so proud of you. We all are,' Jax said, his voice filled with relief.

'I think I lost my powers. I can't feel them anymore.'

'The potion, it was created to destroy darkness. The only reason you survived is because you're part human,' Jax said.

I looked around. Cassie and her friend were standing a bit further away. She looked so much like Lily. I gave her a sad smile as guilt overwhelmed me. I wanted to turn away, but she deserved more than that.

'I'm so sorry, Cassie.' I knew it wasn't enough. No matter what I did, it would never be enough.

She took a few steps towards me. 'I know it was the sword, the darkness, that made you do those horrible things. But ...' She hesitated and bit her lip. 'You didn't have the sword when you gave me up all those years ago. So why did you do it? Did you not love me?'

My heart shattered. How could she even think that? 'I love you with all my heart, but after your mother died, I was so consumed with what I'd lost that I forgot what was important. I didn't just lose a wife that day, you lost a mother, and I should have realised you were hurting too. But I was a broken mess, and my grief put you in danger. Giving you away was the only thing I could think of to keep you safe.' Tears burned in my eyes as I continued. 'You remind me so much of Lily. You have her kindness, her empathy, and I'm so sorry I wasn't there for you. I should have been. I promised Lily I'd keep you safe, but I couldn't give you the life you deserved. I tried to make it better, but I only made it worse. If I could go back, I would do things differently. I was wrong to let my grief turn into hatred. I don't know how I can ever make it up to you.'

She sat down by the bed. 'I know it wasn't really you. Before, all I could feel was your darkness, but now I see there's still light in your heart.'

I looked at her with tears streaming down my face. 'What I did ... I almost killed you ...'

She reached over and squeezed my hand. I didn't deserve her or Jax. I had tried to kill them, and still they were by my side.

Cassie gave me a sad smile and pulled away. 'When you're up for it, I would very much like to get to know the Nick my mother fell in love with and the Nick Jax always talked about.'

'I don't know if he exists anymore,' I answered.

Jax squeezed my shoulder. 'I'm sure he's in there somewhere. You just need to find him again.'

I woke up early in the morning in the bed located in Jax's living room. What had become of me? Without my magic, I couldn't even go back to my house. It was the only thing I had to remind myself of Lily. Oh, how I'd failed her. Not only had I broken my promise to keep Cassie safe, but I had been the one trying to hurt her. If Jax hadn't been there to stop me, I would have killed her. I would have killed my baby, the one thing my wife had valued more than her own life.

No one deserved that. She would have been horrified to see what I had become without her. I stared at the shards of the sword. It had broken once I had defeated the monster within myself, but was that monster really defeated? If it was, why did I still feel hatred and anger? Although it was mostly directed at myself for giving up the only part I had left of Lily to embark on a path that had brought me nothing but sorrow.

I got out of bed and looked around. I couldn't stay here. The guilt was eating me up inside. I knew Jax would forgive me, but even if Cassie could find it in her heart to forgive me, I wasn't sure I could ever forgive myself. I didn't deserve forgiveness for what I'd done to her.

Cassie would be safe with Jax, I was sure of it. I'd seen him put her life over his own, and if necessary, I knew he would do it again. He was what Cassie needed, not me. She didn't need a father that had given her away and then not hesitated to hurt her. I knew the sword had eaten away at my humanity, but she was my daughter – my flesh and blood. And I had failed her on so many levels.

I decided to go for a walk in the woods to clear my head. Jax had told me werewolves lived there, and as a demon, it wasn't a good idea to walk around in their territory, as they may see me as a threat. But I didn't care anymore.

I detected some wolves walking around nearby. It surprised me they didn't seem bothered by me. But then I remembered I didn't have my powers anymore. So much for the mighty descendant of Surtr. Oh well, at least he couldn't force me to march with him when Ragnarök happened. Not that I really cared.

I strolled over to the cliff. The view was lovely from there, but I couldn't feel any joy.

Peeking over the edge, I made up my mind. Revenge hadn't made me feel better. I had just deceived myself, filling my heart with hatred so that I felt something instead of the emptiness inside. I'd lost my world when Lily died, my purpose in life. I knew I wouldn't be able to be with her. She would have gone somewhere great, maybe Valhalla to wait until her soul was ready to be reborn. Me, there was no hope of that, but anything to numb the ache in my heart would be better than this.

My revenge had made me lose my sense of self. I was just a hollow shell, and the thought of spending time around the people I had wronged was too much to bear. I had caused so much heartache, abandoning Cassie and making Nicole grow up an orphan. There was no forgiveness for that. I deserved to be stuck in a grey, miserable place.

A whiff of my mother's perfume entered my nose. Was she here?

I let out a sigh. 'I'm sorry, Mum.' I didn't want her to see me like this, to see how far I'd fallen. She wouldn't be very proud. She was the light, like my wife, but I'd never managed to be anything but darkness.

Tears ran down my face. I felt bad for leaving Cassie and Jax behind, but the guilt was unbearable. I didn't deserve to live. I looked down over the edge. I was human now. Jumping from the cliff would kill me. That was what I wanted, right? I took a deep breath and pictured Lily's face in my mind. I lifted my foot, ready to take my last step into oblivion, when a voice stopped me.

'Wait. I know what you are planning to do, but it is not right. Think about Jax. He has stood by your side through it all. And think about Cassie. She lost her mother so young. Are you really going to make her lose her father too?'

I turned and saw Freya standing by my side.

'I've hurt so many people. I don't deserve to live.'

'You were heartbroken. People deal with it differently. You gave in to your demonic side and let the hate and anger take over. There are some things you cannot amend, but both Cassie and Jax will forgive you.'

'I broke my promise to Lily,' I answered, tears streaming from my eyes. 'I don't know how to live without Lily. And I caused a little girl to become orphaned.'

'Nick, please do not do this. It will not reunite you with Lily.'

'I know, but it will make me forget.'

'Lily would not want you to forget. She would want you to cherish the life you had together, and she would like you to be here for Cassie.'

'How can you know?' I asked in surprise.

'Because she told me.'

I looked at Freya with sceptical eyes. 'How? She's dead.'

'Yes. I am very aware of that. But I look after the souls that die in battle and bring them to Folkvangr, and what more honourable death could there be than for someone to sacrifice themselves to save their child?'

My heart ached from the knowledge I'd never see Lily smile again, and she would never know how sorry I was for what I'd done. I looked out at the sky and the clouds covering the sun. Maybe ... I hesitated. 'Can you tell her I'm sorry?'

'Of course.' She reached out a hand. 'Let me get you back to the house.'

I dug my heels in. 'I can't go back.'

'Why not? You will be giving up a chance to get to know your daughter.'

'I want to be there for Cassie, but I can't live with what I've done. I'm a monster. I don't deserve to be her father. She's not safe with me around. I'd be doing everyone a favour if I disappeared.'

'Nonsense. You have a lot to make up for, but killing yourself is not the answer.'

'I don't see another way. I'm a liability. If I stay, Cassie will be in danger, and I'd rather she was safe. Everything I tried to do was to keep her safe. She has a good life with Jax; she doesn't need me. Besides, she's immortal. I'm human now.'

Freya became thoughtful. 'There might be a way to change that, but it comes at a cost.'

'What cost?'

'I can make you the guardian of Folkvangr. You would guard the entrance to Folkvangr, but your soul would be trapped and there would be no more rebirths or chances to find the reincarnation of Lily again. So before you choose this path, consider it carefully.'

'If I meet her again in another life, we won't remember the love we shared with each other.'

'That is true, but you can build a new love – but not if you choose this path.'

'Will Cassie and Jax be able to visit me?'

'Yes, but you can never go back to Earth. You will be tied to my realm for eternity.'

'It's worth it. This way I can give Cassie the time she needs and she won't feel forced to forgive me before she's ready. I'd be around to help when she needs it, and it will give me a purpose in life, a chance to atone for everything else I've done.'

'There is no going back once this decision is made.'

'I've made up my mind. I will accept your offer to become the guardian of Folkvangr.'

'Very well. Please take my hand. It may be an uncomfortable ride.'

I took her hand and looked into her eyes, where love and sadness met me. A moment later, the world spun around us. The outside world disappeared until it was only me. The air became thick, and I struggled to breathe as sand fell over me, burying me alive. My lungs were burning, but when I opened my eyes, I realised it wasn't just my lungs. The fire was everywhere. When I thought I couldn't stand the heat anymore, the winds spun me around and forced me into an opening in the ground. I plunged into deep water. The currents were strong, and I was sure they would rip me apart as I struggled to reach the surface to catch my breath.

As I emerged, a calmness entered my senses, and I waded to the shore, where Freya was standing. Only she looked different. My eyes were seeing beyond the illusion of the person she portrayed to the world. She was no longer an elderly lady but a maiden with long blond hair and glowing white wings. The bright white light made it hard to look at her, and I looked away.

'I am so sorry. I forget that happens.'

I gazed at her again and she was back to her short frame and elderly appearance.

'You're an actual goddess?' It wasn't really a question, more of a statement.

'I am indeed,' she said with a smile. 'How are you feeling?'

'Better.' For once, I was at peace with myself. My anger was gone, and my guilt wasn't as crippling.

Freya smiled and started walking. I followed. We reached a stone fence overlooking a vast meadow of grass and wildflowers and continued along it until we got to an archway.

'This will be your guard post. On the other side of the archway lies the field of the dead, also known as Folkvangr.'

'Is Lily there?'

'Yes, but I must warn you, the fields are there to rejuvenate the soul, to make people forget about their past lives and get them ready for their next reincarnation. If you spend too much time inside, you will lose yourself and cease to exist. Here.' She handed me something that looked like a watch, but instead of displaying the time, there was just a white circle. 'When the colour changes, you need to leave Folkvangr behind and stay on this side until it turns back to white.'

My eyes went wide. 'I can go inside and see Lily?'

Freya smiled. 'Of course. She has been waiting for you. Her soul has not forgotten you yet. And I believe it will be a long time before she does. A love like yours is hard to forget.'

I thanked Freya and stepped through the arch. The wind blew, and there under an apple tree sat my angel. I shouted her name. When she saw me, a wide smile appeared on her face and she got up and ran towards me.

I engulfed her in an embrace. Happy tears ran down my face. 'I'm so sorry for everything I've done. Can you ever forgive me?'

She gazed up at me, but there was sadness in her eyes. My heart shattered into several pieces. She wouldn't be able to forgive me.

But then her lips turned back into a smile, and she reached up to touch my face. 'It can be hard to fight the darkness when your light is dimming, but you found your light in the end, and that's what's important. I forgive you, but it is not my forgiveness you need. It's your own. Your light is stronger than you think, and it will always shine through in the end.'

She kissed me and my body felt weightless, like a feather floating in the air. I had my angel back.

# JAX

I got back from my flying trip and entered the living room. The bed Nick had been lying in was empty. What was he doing up this early in the morning?

I went upstairs to greet Cassie. 'Good morning, beautiful.'

She gave me a smile from where she was lying in the bed. 'Good morning. Did you have a nice flight?'

'Yeah, but Nick isn't in his bed.'

She sat up. 'Maybe he went for a walk.'

'Maybe,' I answered. I hadn't seen him during my flight, but I hadn't been looking for him.

'I'm sure he just needed some time alone. He was feeling so guilty yesterday. I'm sure he'll turn up.'

'Maybe you're right. How about some breakfast?'

'Sure.' She held her hand out so I could pull her up, but instead of letting me pull her up, she pulled me into the bed.

'Maybe we should work up an appetite first,' she said with a devious smile.

I kissed her. 'Sounds good to me.'

An hour or so later, we made our way downstairs. Leah was sitting at the kitchen table with several books laid out before her.

'What're you doing? Are you researching or studying?' Cassie asked.

Leah looked up. 'A bit of both. I'm trying to figure out what to do about the shards. I know the sword broke, but what if the shards still hold power? I'm trying to see if there's a way to destroy them for good.'

I looked at all the books spread out on the table. 'Have you had any luck?'

'Not yet.'

'I can ask Freya about it next time I see her.' I looked around the room. 'Have you seen Nick?'

Leah shook her head. 'He was gone when I came downstairs. Why?'

I ran my hand through my hair. 'I haven't seen him since last night, and I thought he would be back by now if he'd gone for a walk. Guess I'll have to see what he's up to.'

I turned inwards, seeking for the bond tying me to Nick, but I couldn't find it. Were we not bonded anymore? Or had something happened? 'I can't sense him.'

'He's human now. Maybe your bond broke when he lost his powers. You couldn't feel him when you were at Freya's either,' Cassie said.

I nodded. It made sense. 'You're probably right. Leah, can you locate him?'

'I can try. Get me a map.'

I conjured a map of the area, and Leah picked up a pendulum. It swung around in circles, and the circles became larger and larger.

'I don't think he's anywhere nearby.'

Where could he be? He didn't have his powers, so he couldn't have teleported anywhere. I looked at Leah. 'Are you sure it's working alright? Maybe I should get a map that hasn't been conjured – maybe the energy is interfering.'

'I don't think it matters.'

Cassie spoke up. 'Maybe I can locate him. He's my father, after all.'

'Okay – give it a try.'

She closed her eyes, and I waited patiently for her to locate him. It felt like ages before she opened her eyes again.

'He's alive, and he's happy.'

I let out a sigh. 'I guess that's something. But we still don't know where he is.'

'I'm sure he's fine. He's a grown man. He can look after himself,' Leah said.

'I hope you're right. I just have a feeling he's up to something.'

One of Freya's cats jumped up on the table.

'Maybe Freya is trying to tell us something,' Cassie said. She felt around the collar of the cat, but there was no note. 'Do you think we should visit her?'

'Can't hurt. But it will take ages walking from a place where teleportation is possible to her cottage, so maybe it's better if I go alone.'

Cassie smiled. 'Hold on. I have just the thing.' She rushed upstairs and came back a moment later holding a bracelet. 'Freya gave me this in case I ever needed to see her.'

The cat let out a meow and nosebutted the bracelet. One of the crystals changed colour.

'Why do you think he did that?' Leah asked.

Cassie shrugged. 'I'm not sure. Freya told me to turn two of the red stones until they glowed to get to her house. Maybe he wants us to go somewhere else? I guess there's only one way to find out.' She grabbed my hand and held her other one out to Leah.

Leah shook her head. 'I think it's better if I stay here in case Nick comes back. I know the house is shielded and the shards of the sword are behind a protective barrier, but it seems dangerous to leave them here with no one looking after them.'

'You're right. We really need to figure out a way to get rid of them. We'll ask Freya when we see her.'

Cassie closed her eyes and the next moment we were in Freya's realm, but not by her cottage. We had landed somewhere else. There was a large forest on one side and a stone wall around a huge grassy field on the other. Looking around, I saw Freya and Nick standing a bit away from us, next to an arch connected to the stone wall.

As we walked up to them, Nick was laughing. I hadn't seen him have a proper good laugh since before Lily had died. It warmed my heart.

'Speak of the devils,' Freya said with a gleam in her eye.

'We were worried about you,' I said to Nick.

He gave me an apologetic smile. 'I'm sorry. It was never my intention to worry you.'

'How come you're here?'

'Freya offered me something I couldn't turn down.'

I was getting suspicious. Why was he so cheerful? Had Freya erased his memories? No, she would not interfere with free will. 'What did she offer?'

'A purpose and more time.' He looked at Cassie. 'So I could have a chance to get to know my daughter. But she also gave me a chance to see Lily again.'

I opened my mouth, but no words came out. How had she been able to do that?

'So you're saying my mother is on the other side of this arch?' Cassie asked as she inspected it.

'Yes, but unfortunately, no living soul can enter.'

'So how can my father spend time with her?'

Freya gave her an empathetic smile. 'I thought it was about time I got someone to watch the souls, so Nick has taken on the responsibility of becoming the guardian of Folkvangr.'

Now things started to make sense. 'And that's how you're spending time with Lily?' Nick nodded. 'Why would you give up your life for this? Once her soul forgets, she will get reborn and you'll be stuck here.'

Nick let out a sigh. 'I didn't do it for Lily. I accepted the position because it'll give me the chance to be around for Cassie and help atone for what I've done. I didn't know I'd be able to see Lily and that she would still have all her memories. Freya was telling me how she used to ask about me and Cassie every time she entered Folkvangr, so she's likely to be around for a long time before she forgets.'

'What happened to the last guardian?' Cassie asked.

'You are looking at her,' Freya answered. 'But times are changing, and I need someone with more time on their hands – someone that can actually guard the place.' She tilted her head towards Nick before looking back at Cassie. 'Know you are always welcome to visit. I know your father was not around growing up, but this is a chance to get to know him when you are ready.'

Cassie played with her necklace, and I could see indecisiveness preying on her mind. After a moment, she turned to Nick. 'I like the thought of getting to know my father, but I have a lot of things I need to process.'

Nick placed a hand on Cassie's shoulder. 'I know it will take time. I will respect any wishes you have, but I will never give up on you again. So if you can find it in your heart to ever forgive me, even if it's in another century, I will be looking forward to that day. The day when I get to know my beautiful daughter.'

Cassie blinked away a tear as she nodded in response, and I put my arm around her.

Freya smiled. 'I hate to cut this reunion short, but we need to talk about the sword. Let me get you back home.' She teleported me and Cassie back to the house.

'Did you find Nick?' Leah asked as she walked into the room. Then she stopped in her tracks. 'You must be Freya. I've heard a lot of things about you.'

'And I you,' Freya replied with a smile.

'How come you're here?'

'We need to discuss the sword.'

'It broke when Nick woke up.'

'Yes, I am aware. I think it happened because Nick was a being created by the eternal flame, so when he defeated himself, the flame within him broke the sword. And though the shards hold no power on their own, there is a possibility the sword can be resurrected by mending the pieces together again, so we must hide them.'

'We can take one to the witch village. I can ask Leaf about it first, but I'm sure they won't mind,' Leah said.

'We can give one to the dwarfs,' Cassie said.

'That is a great idea. I can take the shard to them. I am sure they will be happy to learn the sword is finally destroyed,' Freya said.

'What should we do with the other two shards?' I asked.

'Maybe Nick can hide one in Folkvangr. As for the last shard, maybe it can be hidden on holy ground in the human world. It would make it harder for any demon to get to it.'

'Holy ground? Like a church?' Leah asked with a frown.

'Or a cemetery. Demons cannot enter holy ground without discomfort,' Freya answered.

I scratched my neck. 'Are you sure? We visited the cemetery not that long ago, and even before that, I've never had any issue visiting Nick's mother's grave.'

'Oh, my sweet child. I have told you before, you are so much more than just a demon.'

I tilted my head. 'Care to elaborate?'

Freya grabbed hold of my hands and looked up at me with a sad smile. 'I will tell you everything I know about what happened to your parents. I have carried that guilt for far too long. But first we must hide the shards. Meet me by the cottage once you are done.'

I stared at the spot where Freya had been moments ago. Part of me was angry she'd withheld such important information from me, but the other half of me was excited. Maybe my parents hadn't abandoned me after all.

# ABOUT THE AUTHOR

Cecilia has always been interested in writing and spent many hours writing poems and short stories throughout her teenage years. She has always had an interest in fantasy, mythology and witchcraft.

As she grew up, the writing got put on ice as she followed her true passion – Animal care. She moved from Sweden to England, where she completed her Bsc (hons) degree in veterinary nursing and started working full time at a 24 hour hospital. She later moved to Cambridge with her partner and two dogs, hoping to get a better work- life balance.

It wasn't until the lockdown came knocking on everyone's doors that she picked up her writing and fell in love with it all over again. It started off as one book, but by the time she finished the first draft of her young adult fantasy novel, she knew it would be a series.